J. A. JANCE

VIRGINIA LANIER

CHASSIE WEST

LEE CHARLES KELLEY

Bark M for Murder

AVON BOOKS
An Imprint of HarperCollinsPublishers

D0191106

This book is a collection of fiction. The characters, incidents and dialogue are drawn from the authors' imaginations and are not to be construed as real. Any resemblance to actual events or persons, living or dead, is entirely coincidental.

AVON BOOKS
An Imprint of HarperCollins*Publishers*
10 East 53rd Street
New York, New York 10022-5299

"Red Shirt and Black Jacket" copyright © 2006 by Virginia Lanier
"Nightmare in Nowhere" copyright © 2006 by Chassie West
"The French Poodle Connection" copyright © 2006 by Lee Charles Kelley
"The Case of the London Cabbie" copyright © 2006 by J.A. Jance
ISBN-13: 978-0-06-081537-0
ISBN-10: 0-06-081537-X
www.avonmystery.com

First Avon Books paperback printing: March 2006

Avon Trademark Reg. U.S. Pat. Off. and in Other Countries, Marca Registrada, Hecho en U.S.A.
HarperCollins® is a registered trademark of HarperCollins Publishers Inc.

Printed in the U.S.A.

10 9 8 7 6 5 4 3 2 1

DOGGEDLY ON THE CASE . . .

When her unsuspecting sister becomes the target of a con man, seventy-something Maddie Watkins—the crime-solving "Thank You Note Vigilante"—leashes up her two golden retrievers and sets off on a criminal investigation that will be anything but a walk in the park, in **J.A. JANCE**'s
The Case of the London Cabbie

Following a murder at a local convenience store, dog handler Jo Beth Sidden and her bloodhounds track a pair of cold-blooded killers who fear nothing . . . except canines, in **VIRGINIA LANIER**'s
Red Shirt and Black Jacket

A woman wakes up in a wrecked car teetering above a fast-flowing river—with no memory. She is saved from certain death by a remarkable German shepherd who must help her recover her identity and track down her determined pursuers, in **CHASSIE WEST**'s
Nightmare in Nowhere

Ex-cop turned dog trainer Jack Field gets some unexpected help from Charley, an ill-tempered toy poodle, as he and his fiancée, state medical examiner Dr. Jamie Cutter, attempt to dig up the dirt on the annoying pup's owner—a beautiful bombshell who's surrounded by dead bodies wherever she goes, in **LEE CHARLES KELLEY**'s
The French Poodle Connection

Contents

Red Shirt and Black Jacket

Virginia Lanier

I stepped from the van into a penetrating cold wind. It was an unseasonably chilly day in southeast Georgia. We usually had a few days like this in late January and early February, but not a week before Christmas with carols reverberating in our ears and a Santa in every mall. A northeaster was blowing between 18 to 25 m.p.h.

I had donned my bright Day-Glo orange rescue suit and was fully protected from the cold and wind. I attached the long leads to Caesar's harness, then Mark Anthony's, stepped aside, and watched them bail out of their cages with unrestrained enthusiasm. They are two highly trained man-trailing bloodhounds from my kennel. I tucked items into my zippered pockets and attached a quart water bottle. Jasmine Jones parked her van behind mine.

I watched her unload. We wore identical suits. My hair is a mousy brown. Her black tresses artfully hugged her scalp and complimented her long regal neck. She is African American with skin one shade lighter than milk chocolate. I'm pale, never tan, and look like the girl next door after a bad night.

I hired and trained her in man-trailing, search-and-rescue, and drug searches. She lives beside me in a garage apartment and we are close friends.

Jasmine unloaded Ashley and Miz Melanie and secured them to the van. She smiled and started toward me. I met her halfway.

"For right now we'll leave the backpacks here."

"Right. Aren't you taking your gun?" Her holster was fastened over her rescue suit.

"Never leave home without it." I patted my left breast. "Move yours inside your suit. The dispatcher mentioned shots were fired. We're out in front if we man-trail. I don't want the perps to know we're carrying, might keep us from being used as target practice."

"What do you know so far?" She was placing items in the pockets of her suit.

I glanced across the empty parking lot and saw Sheriff Philip Scroggins emerge from the double door of the Suwannee Swifty convenience store. He spotted us and waved.

"Have you ever met Sheriff Scroggins?" I asked.

"Last June, when the Shop'n Go was hit. You were busy with the seminar."

"Right, I'd forgotten. Brace yourself. Here he comes."

"Oh, dis ol' gal don't have to fret 'bout being bear-hugged," she drawled, parodying southern mush-mouth, "I be duh wrong color for dat!"

I examined her guileless countenance and saw a hint of a smile on her lips.

"It's getting to where I can't take you out in public," I complained. "Behave yourself."

We lifted the sagging yellow crime scene tape, and ducked under.

Sheriff Philip Scroggins was sixty-five, bald, and was almost as wide as he was tall. He was 5'4" and weighed over two hundred pounds. He had been my father's friend and was now mine. His booming voice was always a shock to the senses.

"Jo Beth, darlin', how are you?" he bellowed, grabbing me around my waist and lifting me a foot off the ground.

"Not breathing," I said, grunting. "Put me down . . . please?"

He complied, then grabbed Jasmine.

"Jasmine, my beauty! I'm so glad to see you!" He held her aloft and turned two complete circles before releasing her.

The shocked expression on her face made me start giggling, which I tried to cover with a fake fit of coughing.

He thundered an apology. "Me carrying on like this, while a good woman was murdered in there a little over an hour ago. I'm ashamed of myself."

He contemplated the building and turned back to face us.

"Who died?" I asked.

We were in Collins, the county seat of Gilsford County. It was only 20 miles to Balsa City, my hometown. I know a lot of people here.

"Mrs. Walter Pearson, only fifty-seven years old.

A nice widow-woman with two grown sons." He looked pensive. "Who expects to die during a robbery on Main Street at nine in the morning?" He sighed. "Sergeant Lyons is driving the sons home now. He'll be back shortly."

I didn't know her. "Any witnesses?"

"I think we got lucky on this one, Jo Beth. One of the perps lost his cap inside the store, and I hope we have a credible witness."

My pulse quickened. We had a chance.

"The cap was bagged and not handled by anyone?" I inquired, trying to mask my anxiety.

Some deputies and bystanders will finger a scent item, searching for a name—or worse, pass it around like a collection plate. This contaminated the scent article with other people's scent.

"Rest easy, honey. Lyons was the first officer on the scene. He found the witness and bagged the cap before the ambulance attendants arrived. The scene isn't too contaminated either. The only ones who went inside were me, Lyons, and the ambulance attendants."

Deputy Sergeant Tom Lyons and I were smiling enemies. He hates my smart mouth and feminist ways, and I despise the way he talks about women and mistreats his prisoners.

"Where's the witness?" I was anxious to get started.

"He's sitting in my squad car. Come on over and I'll introduce you."

The three of us walked over to his car. Scroggins opened the door and nodded at me. I leaned down and saw a small black boy who was huddled in the far corner of the backseat. He was wrapped in a blanket and was clutching its folds under his chin. His eyes were showing too much white and his small hands were shaking. He stared at me.

"Hi," I said awkwardly, "I'll be right back."

I straightened, closed the door gently, and glared at Scroggins.

"Where's his mother? He should be taken home!"

"I agree," he said quietly, "but so far he hasn't remembered his last name and I'm certainly not going to let a pile of people line up and try to recognize him. How do I know that one of the perps isn't out there in the crowd standing around watching? Just a look at his face would traumatize the kid, and we'd never get anything.

"He spoke a few words to Lyons when he found him in the store, then he clammed up and started shaking. There were two black perps, and one lost his cap. They both had guns. One fired a shot in the boy's direction when he spotted him peeking around the ice cream case. He's got a right to be shaken up. His name is Malahki, and he's nine years old. I think this calls for a woman's touch so I'll leave you to it."

Sheriff Scroggins squared his shoulders, marched off, and left it to us.

I huddled with Jasmine and spoke softly.

"Which dog do you prefer? I'm going to put two back in their cages. We're going to do this search by the book. No court-appointed attorney is going to question the use of two dogs."

"I'll work Ashley, but why don't I put them back while you question the kid? It'll save time."

Jasmine sensed the way the wind was blowing. "Nope, Malahki is all yours. Cuddle and mother him. After he calms down, get all you can. I'll wait by the vans."

She looked askance at my suggestion.

"I've never cuddled a kid in my life," Jasmine stated succinctly, forcing the words through barely opened lips. "Why me, and not you?"

I used my best mush-mouth drawl.

" 'Cause, honey chile, dis time *you* be the right color!"

I left her to it.

When I walked to the van, I found both braces of bloodhounds with their leads twisted together. As I untangled them I decided to work Caesar. When I commanded Mark Anthony to load up, he sprang into his cage not knowing his day's outing was canceled. The same with Miz Melanie. When they discovered they were being left behind, they would moan and groan.

Bloodhounds love to trail. They enjoy searching for an illusive scent among many, many thousands of others. Every step we humans take, we drop thousands of tiny skin particles, lint, and dust, all impregnated with our unique body odor. No two people smell the same. When a bloodhound is presented with an article that has been worn by one person, it can lock onto the scent and follow.

However, the present strong wind had me worried: The ideal for scent trailing is on a damp windless day with high humidity. The odor drops to the ground and hovers nearby. On days such as these, we could be searching over 20 to 50 feet away from the actual route the perp took. Hell, it could be blown into the next county by now. Who knew?

Our sense of smell is infinitesimal compared to a bloodhound. Many experts claim it can be a million or more times greater. So we humans train them, teach them manners and to follow orders, then let them drag us around. We can only hope that they are following the right scent. We certainly can't tell.

I taught myself from books several years ago, trained the hounds, then other handlers. I mostly used a "brace" of bloodhounds, meaning two. I have strong shoulders, and both of my arms are probably slightly longer than they should be. Controlling two dogs weighing over a hundred pounds apiece is not for the fainthearted, believe me.

Bloodhounds are the only breed of dogs whose testimony is considered in a court of law. Bloodhound owners point with great pride to this long record, on the books for over a hundred years. The upstarts may claim the ability, but they can never match our history in court cases. I know, I know, times are changin', and soon other breeds will be allowed if they can pass the test of having the right criteria.

The rules for bloodhound testimony are very specific. Each owner has to prove his or her mantrailer is registered by the American Kennel Club and has had successful experience in actual mantrailing. The finds have to be documented and proven. The dog also has to be reliable and there must be supporting evidence. Every defense attorney picks at these threads, tries to unravel their evidential worth.

As of this day and as far as I know, the laws of Georgia do not exclude evidence if one handler works two bloodhounds, but the proposed new procedure would be one bloodhound and one human trainer. Seventeen other states now have passed this new provision into law. I know an ACLU lawyer upstate who is working, as I stand here, to get the new law passed. I have no reservations about this one-on-one, especially for beginners, either human or canine. I would also like to note that the aforementioned lawyer lost a previous major case because a good ol' boy did everything right with three bloodhounds and fried his ass in court.

I couldn't take the chance in a murder investigation, so Jasmine and I will work one-on-one: the law might have already passed without my knowledge, but ignorance of the law is no excuse.

"Well, sweet thang, how's tricks? Getting any lately?"

I'd recognize that voice on the dark side of the moon.

"Deputy Sergeant Lyons, I'll make this statement only once." I enunciated each word slowly. "My name is Jo Beth Sidden. You may call me Jo Beth, Ms. Sidden, or hey you, but one more use of my name as slop or sexist drivel, I'll kick your balls into your rib cage."

"Jo Beth, hon— Listen, I'm mortified you're in such a sour mood. Pardon me all to hell and back. You've got a foul mouth just like me. How come you can call me names and I can't rib you a little? Answer me that!"

"Only friends can rib me, and you don't qualify. Also, we have a law that works to protect both you and me. We're equals, remember?"

"When hell freezes over," he said sardonically.

I saw Sheriff Scroggins approaching with Jasmine by his side.

"May the bluebird of happiness shit on your pillow each morning," I whispered.

Lyons opened his mouth to retaliate, then shot a foot in the air when the sheriff's voice boomed a greeting directly behind him.

I laughed and Lyons looked murderous. Even Scroggins could sense the testosterone wafting on the breeze.

"What?" Scroggins barked, looking from me to Lyons.

"We were discussing birds," I explained.

Lyons flushed, but remained silent. I turned to Jasmine.

"What did you get from Malahki?"

"His last name is Fenmore. There were two men; he doesn't remember any facial hair. Both were in jeans. The one who lost the cap had a red shirt, and the other had a black bomber jacket. Both fired one round at the clerk and black jacket shot at the boy. They heard or saw a car drive up. When they went out the door, they turned right. Malahki didn't move from hiding until the customer came in and discovered the clerk's body. He wants to go home."

"You did great," I said. "I don't blame the kid. Did he tell you what he was doing in the store at nine? Shouldn't he have been in school?"

Jasmine hadn't looked my way since she arrived. She was PO'd about having to do the questioning.

"He has a friend with a new computer game. He was killing time till the friend's mother left for work. They were gonna ditch and play games all day. He wants a policeman to take him home and explain why he isn't in school. He's afraid of getting a lickin'."

"Sounds like he's recovered to me," Scroggins commented with a grin. "Tom?"

Lyons reached inside his tunic and handed me the plastic Ziploc with the perp's cap. With my back to the sheriff I pretended to wet my index finger, and drew an imaginary line in the air for a one, meaning I had won the first skirmish. He flushed but remained mute, and left to find an officer to take the kid home. God, I was acting childishly, but it felt so good to pull his macho chain.

Jasmine and I silently unhooked the dogs, held up the sagging tape, and started across the parking lot.

"I'll stay outside," boomed the sheriff. I gave him a backhanded wave, and glanced at Jasmine.

"Thanks. I was right you know."

Her expression softened and she gave me a ghost of a smile.

"Say you're sorry," she demanded.

"I can do that."

"Well?"

We were at the door of the store.

"Later," I said with a grin, holding the door open.

I was the last one in. No sooner than the door closed, both dogs stopped, began an eerie whining, and tried to go through me in their haste to reach the door. Jasmine was struggling to pull Ashley back and Caesar bulled his way between my legs, wrapping his lead around my right leg, with toenails scrabbling on the waxed tile floor.

"Go outside," I yelled to Jasmine over the dogs' frantic baying, straining to grab Caesar's harness and remain upright. But I went down hard, on my tailbone, and saw stars floating in blurred vision. The pain was intense.

"Are you all right?" Jasmine screamed. She was braced against the open door, holding on to Ashley for dear life, who was at the far limit of his lead, pulling backward trying to free himself.

I quickly hit my left shoulder twice, with my left fist. It was a silent command to the dog to get the hell out. My head was throbbing in rhythm with my tailbone and the dogs' howling was an added assault. I didn't feel like yelling. I had Caesar's harness clutched in my right hand and was trying to keep him out of my face. He was squirming on my legs, trying to hide his head in my stomach. He weighs 120 pounds. I had my hands full.

Regaining my feet and choking up on his lead, I pulled him outside. In the open air they both stopped making their terrified sounds and stood hassling for breath. I limped over to the low curb of the sidewalk rubbing my tailbone. I sat down gingerly and Jasmine joined me. We were also panting and trying to regain our breath.

"What happened?" She sounded awed by what she'd seen.

"Blood," I said shortly, gazing out at the people milling around behind the tape. Sheriff Scroggins and Tom were on their way toward us. I'd have to explain again to them, so I was waiting for them to arrive.

Sheriff Scroggins squatted, so we were more or less eye to eye. He looked concerned. Tom remained standing slightly behind the sheriff.

"Blood," I began. "So much blood. I could even smell it, and the dogs got their large muzzles full of the scent. The heat in there just intensified the odor. They went bananas. They smelled death, or maybe they know that so much blood means death. They are very sensitive to human suffering."

While I was speaking I happened to glance at Tom. He was sporting a smirk, making a movement in the air with his finger that signaled he had also chalked up a score. It only took me seconds to remember. He had been by my side more than two years ago when two of my bloodhounds had refused to enter a car where a man had died from his throat being cut. When I had opened the car door, they had leaped back nervously from the blood smell, and bolted. The bastard remembered and let us go in there uninformed.

My ire was so great I felt like I was choking. I had to move.

"The dogs need water," I said in a strangled voice to Jasmine.

She followed after me, trying to keep up with my angry stride.

"What gives?" she asked quietly when we arrived at the van.

"Tom sent us into the store deliberately, knowing the dogs would be spooked. He saw the same thing happen sometime back. Never fear, he'll pay dearly for that rotten trick."

"Good," she agreed.

"Let's put away Ashley and Caesar. They've had it for today. Luckily we held back Mark Anthony and Miz Melanie."

We returned to the front of the store where the sheriff and Lyons were standing.

"Sheriff Scroggins, I'll need four men. Two with me, and two to go with Jasmine."

"Jasmine, start Miz Melanie at the door. We have a fifty-fifty chance she'll pick up black jacket's scent. I'll use red shirt's cap."

Lyons came trotting back across the tarmac with three deputies in tow. One was plump with salt-and-pepper hair. He had to be fifty. I pointed at the two young deputies, and told them to stay with Jasmine.

"You other two come with me," I said, not using Tom's name or rank.

"One drives and the other stays at least ten yards behind us, in case the dogs have to double back. That way you won't contaminate the trail."

I was praying that some scent was left on the ground. The wind was picking up. I put the opened Ziploc under Mark Anthony's nose. He buried his muzzle inside the bag, taking deep sniffs of the cap. I pulled out two pieces of deer jerky and held them under his nose. He gobbled them down.

"Seek, Mark Anthony, seek!"

He bent his head and started working. Nose down, he ranged eight feet or more in a loose figure eight, trying to locate the odor that he was seeking. A bloodhound's long flapping ears are important tools. They are natural funnels that scoop up the scent around him and send it to his nose.

Suddenly, Mark Anthony's tail became a metronome, swinging back in forth with his own personal rhythm. He tugged on the lead, urging me to give him slack. I followed along behind, wanting to believe that he had quickly picked up the scent, but I was doubtful. He had never been fast on the scent.

He hurried around the store and turned right on brown dried grass that crunched with each step. Discarded litter lay scattered among the weeds. The verge was twelve feet wide between the convenience store's south side and the wall of a hardware store. It ran back about forty feet where two large trash Dumpsters sat side by side, facing the alley.

Mark Anthony turned left into the alley. We walked several feet down the road before I glanced back. Miz Melanie appeared and turned *right*, and stopped in front of one of the Dumpsters. Both lids were thrown back and the containers were overflowing with trash.

Miz Melanie stood on her hind legs scratching her front toenails against the metal, trying to climb its vertical surface.

I pulled Mark Anthony off the scent trail and went back to watch. Jasmine shortened the lead by coiling it several times and waved a deputy forward. He started past her to peer in the Dumpster, but she called him back sharply, handing him the lead.

"Place the loop over your wrist and wrap it three times. Don't, under any condition, turn it loose."

She watched carefully as he followed her instructions. She caught the top of the Dumpster and pulled herself up until her body was against the surface, near her pelvis. Balancing there on her left hand, she reached into a pocket with her right and pulled out a baggie. She drew up her right knee and leaned precariously over into the messy contents. I held my breath. If she tumbled in, she would have to be fumigated; the garbage smelled ripe. Her hand came out, carefully holding up a gun, her two covered fingers on the very end of the barrel.

"*Yes!*" I cried, giving her a pumped-fist salute. I hurried over and helped by removing the gun from her lowered hand. She then slid down gracefully. Her two deputies gave a few halfhearted ragged-spaced claps that sounded derisive. She did a graceful curtsy in rebuttal.

It was a cheap knockoff, a Saturday night special. Cradling it in the plastic, I carefully broke open the cylinder. Two rounds were missing. Jasmine and I were grinning with delight. Our fifty-fifty chance just jumped to the max. She had black jacket's scent.

Jasmine retrieved the lead and dropped to her knees, crooning into Miz Melanie's ear while she hugged her neck.

"My big baby is so smart. Good girl, good girl!"

She fumbled in her pocket and produced a generous handful of jerky.

Lyons walked up, acting as if he wanted to snatch the gun from my grasp. It's a good thing he didn't try. I would've probably shot him with it. I walked over to the youngest deputy, who looked as if he just started shaving, and laid it gently in his hands.

"Take this back to Sheriff Scroggins. Tell him to send two units back to follow behind us. You drive for Jasmine, and ask the older deputy to come with me. Lyons will drive behind me."

"Hold it, Pete. Give me the gun." Lyons couldn't hold still for this, his ego was smarting.

The deputy glanced at me.

I gave Lyons a cool smile and verbally pounced.

"Tell him to do as I said or Jasmine and I load the dogs and go home. Now!" I put a nice little snap in my voice.

Lyons reluctantly nodded at Pete. He looked ready to chew nails.

"Remember to stay at least ten yards behind me, where you belong," I ordered. "Have you forgotten we have two murderers to catch?"

I strode away without looking back. I led Mark Anthony to where I pulled him off the scent trail. I patiently let him smell the cap, fed him jerky, and again gave him the command to seek. It took him awhile before he seemed to lock onto the scent.

This gave me time to glance back to make sure that everyone was set to go. The deputy with the salt-and-pepper-colored hair was trudging a few yards behind me, and Lyons was creeping along behind in his wake. The trail had split and Jasmine was leading in the opposite direction with her escort. It was time for a radio check.

When Jasmine and I trail together, we turn to a seldom-used channel and keep the transmissions very short. We use the regular channels to converse with the lawmen. We also choose cutesy names to further confuse. A lot of people in this neck of the woods carefully monitor all channels. Pot growers, DEA, moonshiners, ATF, retirees living in the boonies, hunters—and hunter's wives, who want to make sure the hubby is out there training that blue tick hound that cost an arm and a leg and not off somewhere boozing or floozying.

"Trouble to double. Over."

Jasmine had lowered the pitch of her voice. Over the tinny speaker, it was hard to tell she was female.

"Double here. Be careful. Don't be a hero. Call on contact. Over." I made my voice rough and husky.

"Same back at you. Over and out."

Mark Anthony was having trouble with the trail of scent. He would run sideways from the structure straight across the alley. It was the wind. It had scattered the scent all to hell and gone. This search just might end with a whimper, not a bang. Bad analogy to think *bang*. Success maybe, or roar; never bang. My perp up to this point still had his gun.

When I checked, Salt-and-Pepper was still walking behind me. I motioned him forward and introduced myself. He told me his name was Donald Augustine. He was older than I had guessed. Hearing better diction than I expected, I asked him if he was local.

He hailed from Tallahassee, Florida. His wife had

been born and raised here. After he had put in twenty years on the police force and took retirement with a nothing pension, his wife wanted to move back to her hometown. In six months of idleness and finding that he couldn't live on the small check, and gaining twenty pounds from his altered routine, he became a deputy here two years ago. Told me with a chuckle that he had to hurry up and get killed while on duty because compulsory retirement was fifty-five, which was six months away.

I liked him. He hadn't lost the twenty pounds, but with Sheriff Scroggins in charge he didn't have to worry about his weight for another six months. We talked as Mark Anthony whined in frustration at frequently loosing the scent.

Suddenly the bloodhound tugged forward, impatient with being tethered and wanting to hustle. I waved Deputy Augustine back with a smile and we took off again.

I checked out the houses, small businesses, and alleys we were passing. Gilsford County had 16,000 residents. Collins had 13,000 within the city limits. So the other 3,000 in the county were the people who lived on the edge of Okefenokee Swamp, or in isolated houses scattered among the hundreds of thousands of acres of planted pines. Lots of pine trees and only a few people.

Mark Anthony turned off the alley into small backyards and weedy empty lots. After going through the first yard, the Lyons unit was staying a street over or one behind, trying to keep track of our progress. When the people on the small roads, faces peeking from windows and bodies standing or sitting on porches, became predominately African American, I motioned for Augustine to join me.

"Blacks don't appreciate whites chasing black men through their yards. Have you noticed how quiet the streets have become, and no one is yelling greetings? Stay alert. Unsnap your holster, and if we have to enter a house, you go in with your gun in your hand and stay in *front* of the dog and me. Keep your voice down. Sound does funny things in this kind of wind. Some places we won't be able to hear each other from six feet away—in others, they can hear us for several blocks. The bloodhound's name is Mark Anthony. If something happens to me, grab his lead and don't let go. Running free he would be dead in five minutes. I hold you personally responsible for his safety. I'll return from the grave to get you if he dies."

"Shades of Julius Caesar," he whispered.

"Nope," I returned softly, "that's the name of the other dog I worked with earlier."

"I swear to protect you and your noble beast until death," he vowed, hand on his badge and a smile hovering on his lips.

"Now you're talking!"

We were walking within a six-foot gap between two brick buildings. The wind was screaming around the corners like a banshee wailing of impending death. Here I went again, referring to death. I had to quit relying on ancient history, wives' tales, and southern adages in my thoughts, but what was left? No windows marred the three-storied symmetrical layers of old crumbling bricks.

I felt the clutch of claustrophobia. It was close in

here; and the old bricks have a bad habit of falling down eventually. Could be today, right about now. We were a few feet into the gap. I guessed the lower scent was out of the wind because Mark Anthony picked up speed and I pounded along matching his progress. I couldn't get out of these confining walls fast enough. We left Augustine in the shade.

We burst out into an open alley and Mark Anthony stopped on a dime. I guessed he had lost the scent. I glanced around to scope out the landscape. A tall building was directly in front of us with boarded-up windows and nothing on either side but weeds. Even the parking lot had weeds in the potholes and cracks in the tarmac.

A short brick fence about fifty feet in length was a foot off the easement for the alley, and directly in front of the building's front door. I turned back to see if Augustine had cleared the alley just as Mark Anthony threw back his head and poured forth a loud voracious baying. Red shirt was very near. Mark Anthony was celebrating!

Bloodhounds run mute. Only when they are almost on their target do they unleash that loud mournful bay, so beautiful to a man-trailer's ears.

I was mesmerized with Mark Anthony's vocal announcement of his accomplishment. At the edge of my vision, I saw half a brick pop off into space. It came from the side of the building we had just run past. In that same instant I heard the shot.

"Run!" I screamed to Mark Anthony.

I was jerking him mightily, almost losing my balance. He was slow to react. It took a few seconds for him to process the rarely used command through his large skull and remember its meaning; but it seemed to take eons before he moved the way I was trying to pull him. He was still baying when I dove the last six feet and ended up with him standing over me dripping slobber.

Ignoring the numbing pain in my funny bone where I had rapped my elbow on the low wall, I grabbed him by his harness and jerked his right front leg out from under him, flopping him prone. I lay above him whispering frantically into his ear.

"Hush, hush, low, low, no, no." It was the command for silent trailing and not baying over his joyous victory. I wanted him to lie still and shut the hell up. I was also giving him the signal for silence, by pushing down firmly on his large head with my aching right arm. He finally got my message.

Panting, I lay close to the low barrier, running my memory film of the earlier scan of the building, which now was directly in front of me, a few feet away. I hadn't counted floors and wasn't about to lift my head to do so.

If Red Shirt had fired from the third floor or higher, we were dead meat. His first shot was high and wide. *If* his gun was the same as Black Jacket's, it wouldn't be accurate from that distance. He also had at least four rounds or more, and with enough altitude he could see us easily and pick us off at his leisure. Considering these several factors, I was scared silly but not formulating immediate plans to travel. I hugged my big dog and cogitated.

I heard a noise over the wind and watched aghast as Deputy Augustine bobbed and weaved while awkwardly crouched, gun in hand, trying to cross the gulf of thirty feet. He was moving in slow motion, and graceful he wasn't. Not only was the damn fool gonna die while he was on duty, it was going to be right about now, with me watching.

He slumped in front of me with his face less than a foot away from Mark Anthony's and mine. He hadn't been pierced with a bullet or even shot at; but I was feeling the urge to do that very thing myself, this minute.

"Are you out of your cotton-pickin' mind?" I asked, in greeting.

"Best chance I've had in the past two years, and the sucker wouldn't cooperate," he complained.

His face was the color of chalk, his breathing was labored, and sweat on a day as cold as this one meant fear.

"You may wish to commit suicide, but not here, and not today. Am I getting through to you?"

"Yes'em," he replied, trying to grin.

He was wiping the moisture from his face with a handkerchief.

"And furthermore," I added icily, "I will repeat your conversation verbatim to Sheriff Scroggins. He doesn't need or deserve a loose cannon on his force."

"Don't," he said, grabbing my wrist for emphasis. "She's in a wheelchair with MS. I blabbed to you because I was shook up. I should have kept quiet," he muttered, disgusted with himself. "She needs the widow's pension and the medical coverage. Don't blow me out of the water. I don't fear dying, only that I'll bungle it and need care myself. . . . Please."

I gazed at him appalled. Red Shirt and immediate peril forgotten. I swallowed and tried to sound calm and in control.

"Have you checked out all the *other* possible solutions thoroughly?"

"As best as I can, under the circumstances." He added dryly, "I can't come right out with it, to Social Services. The councilor would remember after the deed was done, so to speak."

"Let me try," I said in earnest. "I'm in a different county, and they'd never connect the two of us. I'll pretend I'm worried about a favorite uncle with similar circumstances. Give me thirty days for research to find a better solution. If I can't find one, you have my word that I'll come to your services and keep silent. But believe this. If you jump the gun before the thirty days are up, I'll be so pissed that you didn't wait for my learned advice, I'll scream your scheme from the roof tops and force them to believe me. Do we have a deal?"

"Give up this golden opportunity?"

He was being sarcastic and cast his eyes upward. He returned his gaze to mine in consternation.

"Did you know that I can see two upper floors and the roof from this position? If *I* can see them and if he's still up there, *he can see us!*"

"No shit, Sherlock." I uttered waspishly. "About the time you were making your suicidal dash, I kinda got distracted. Did you happen to use your radio to call in our location to the dispatcher before taking off on the Death Defying Thirty?"

He looked embarrassed.

"I reported shots fired, but I didn't hold down the

transmitting button during the last half of me describing our present location. Sorry."

"And you turned off your radio?"

I wanted to make certain before I started screaming.

"Sergeant Lyons can't be far away and people must have heard the shot. They'll direct him. Besides, I didn't want the ambulance to get here too fast."

"If asked, the locals will direct him in the wrong direction. Do you see a concerned citizen? Do you hear any sirens, by chance?"

I jerked out my radio and switched it from the private channel where Jasmine could reach me. I was repositioning the channel when I heard the faint wail above the wind.

Ten seconds later, Lyons roared around the corner, screeching to a halt at an angle where he could open his passenger-side door and talk without leaving the protection of the vehicle.

"Dispatcher loused up, sent me two blocks west instead of east, or I'd been here sooner. Is he up there?"

I carefully refrained from looking at Augustine. I was afraid I'd brain him with the radio, which I put back in my pocket turned to Jasmine's channel.

"We think so, unless he went out the back door," I said.

Lyons answered quickly.

"There is no back door. I was in there last month with the fire inspector. Both back doors are nailed shut and boarded up. We have to go get him."

"What do you mean by *we*, pale face?" I retorted.

I tossed a thumb over my shoulder. "He's in there, and my participation in this exercise is over. Deputy Augustine isn't going anywhere. He's staying right here to protect me."

"You're the last one in this county that needs protection!" Lyons yelled.

I smiled when I heard the cavalry arriving. Every law-enforcement car that would run was on its way. Big happening in a small town.

Within minutes, the narrow street was bumper to bumper with yellow-and-tan county vehicles, pale blue for the city police, black government units for the initials DEA and ATF; assorted colors of personal cars for the SWAT team; and a large white boxy ambulance. The Georgia Highway Patrol colors weren't present. They must be out with their unit having coffee. There was even a green-and-yellow truck representing the Georgia Department of Fish and Game. If Red Shirt was still up there, he had multiple choices of targets.

Sheriff Scroggins had duck-waddled from around his vehicle and hunched by my side.

"I know I look damn ridiculous, so quit holding back those snickers. This crouch is hard on an old fat man's knees. What happened?"

"Sheriff, Red Shirt fired one round after Mark Anthony started baying. He panicked. You know how some men fear bloodhounds. I'd say fifty percent still warn their wives and children to stand way back, that the dog is vicious. It's erroneous. You and I know bloodhounds are gentle and don't attack. Some men would rather face a machine gun than a large charging dog."

I continued. "I think I have a good chance to get him out of there with out anyone getting hurt. Will you let me try?"

"You want to try to talk him out?" Scroggins looked doubtful.

"No, I want to threaten that I'll turn the dog loose in the building."

Scroggins laughed. "That'll be the day. He'd lick him to death."

I laughed with him. "We know Mark Anthony is a pussy cat, but the Red Shirt doesn't. Can't hurt."

"Go to it. My knees are killing me. Keep your head down."

He duck-walked back to his foam-cushioned seat in the cruiser.

I made a hand motion for Lyons to toss me his mike.

He glared daggers at me but threw it and flipped on the loud speaker.

"I'm speaking to the man in the red shirt in the boarded-up building."

My voice boomed on the brisk breeze, vibrating in my ears.

"This is the attack-dog handler. I have been ordered to release the dog. This is your one and only chance to come out without getting mauled. If you are on an upper floor, start down immediately. You have less than five minutes to follow my instructions. At the front door, toss out your weapon. Remove your shirt and jacket. Empty your pockets and turn them out so I can see the white. Walk out slowly with your hands on your head. Three steps from the door, lie down spread-eagled on the tarmac. Keep your head down and don't move a muscle. If you do everything right you won't be hurt. I will repeat this message because of the wind."

After I finished, I tossed the mike back to Lyons. My mouth was dry. I drank from my water bottle and offered it to Augustine. He took it and drank. I pulled back my glove and saw that time was almost up. I moved fast to keep from thinking. Did I really want to do this?

I stood, jerked up a comfortable bloodhound from his snooze, and was striding around the barrier before anyone noticed. I began yelling at Mark Anthony.

"Where's your man! Find your man! Find your man!"

I held the cap down by my leg. Mark Anthony raised his head and started his raucous baying while he moved to the far end of his lead, straining mightily to go after his guy.

I ignored the shouts behind me. Maybe, just maybe, they wouldn't try to out-hero me by charging to the rescue. To the uninitiated, Mark Anthony would be deemed a hound from hell. His strident cry was his desire to let the world know where Red Shirt could be found. He was doing everything but jumping up and down and pointing at the door.

I kept a jaundiced eye on the large metal entrance. A mantra wouldn't hurt.

I will not be shot, he's gonna fold, I will not be shot, he's gonna fold. Amen.

A dark gap appeared and widened teasingly slow, and an object sailed on the breeze before landing on the pitted tarmac. It was a gun. A figure appeared in the doorway, then advanced and slowly moved forward. Stripped to the waist with pockets turned out, and his hands locked on his head.

He was saying something but the wind wasn't bringing me the message. Mark Anthony was doing his jiggle dance trying to reach him. I began to haul back on the lead when I could understand the man's message.

"Don't turn him loose! I'm down, I'm down!"

He was indeed down and several feet from the gun.

Figures flew by me, falling on the suspect as if each one wanted to be the one to cuff him. Someone produced leg irons. When they stood him up, I released my tight resistance on the lead and Mark Anthony surged forward to claim his victory. I let him have his moment. He deserved it. He nuzzled and licked the prisoner, whining for joy. He wanted to be hugged and petted, but the man cringed and didn't have a way to touch him, or the desire, I suspected. Mark Anthony did everything but hug him.

Later that evening over a pepperoni-and-cheese pizza, wine for her and beer for me, Jasmine told me about her search.

"Deputy Pete Benifield had his gun drawn as he pounded on the door. I was trying to restrain Miz Melanie on a shortened lead and hold the screen door open, and she was baying her head off. Black Jacket's mother opened the door shouting and praying, and a small child started screaming at her first sight of a huge dog straining to enter. You couldn't hear yourself think. I wasn't expecting a pint of ground black pepper scattered on the front threshold. On the back sill certainly, but not the front. Miz Melanie began sneezing and baying, slipping and sliding . . ." She paused for another sip of wine.

"To make a long story short, she entangled us in her leash, entrapping our legs, and took us all down like bowling pins, with the exception of the little girl. She ran back to tell Black Jacket what was going on. He was hiding under his mama's bed, doing some screaming of his own. His mama had taken his gun, put it in the oven, and turned it on so he wouldn't be tempted to shoot us.

"It took us a long time to pull Black Jacket, his sister, and Miz Melanie out from under the bed. When the sister told Deputy Pete the gun was in a lit oven, he grabbed Bomber Jacket and his mama, and I had the kid and Miz Melanie. We all ran outside and hid behind the house next door.

"The second deputy finally arrived with the fire department. They turned off the propane gas at the tank and were waiting for the oven to cool down when we left. They said it was a miracle that the ammunition hadn't begun exploding, sending rounds and flames all over. You know what mama said when she heard him say it?"

I gave a negative headshake.

"I wasn't born yesterday, young man. I only turned the knob to *warm*, not bake!"

The day before Christmas Eve, I met with Patricia Ann Newton, a recently acquired friend who had more money than Midas. Then that afternoon I met

Deputy Donald Augustine, in the city park. I explained to him that an anonymous donor had added his name to a living trust that would furnish him with ample funds upon his retirement, to enable him to care for his wife comfortably, and it would continue if he died first.

He was embarrassed for having to use his handkerchief to wipe the pine tree pollen away that was making his eyes water. It also bothered mine as I wished him Merry Christmas.

Nightmare in Nowhere

Chassie West

Chapter 1

Wet dog. Definitely essence of wet dog.

A.J. shivered in the cold and groped for her blanket, her dream in which Buster darted through the sprinklers gradually fading away. A frown tugged her brows together as a painful throb at the back of her head nudged her toward wakefulness.

With effort, she opened her eyes, squinting into near darkness, then squeezed them shut again as the pain above the nape of her neck arced around to burrow itself behind her forehead. Bile rose in her throat. Swallowing against it, she counted to ten, exerting mind over matter, in this case the churning in her gut. God, this felt like the granddaddy of all hangovers, but since she rarely drank, that explanation wouldn't hold water.

And she rarely dreamed or, when she did, remembered it afterward. But this one had been so vivid. Not only had she witnessed the beagle's favorite summertime antics, she could smell him, in fact, still could and that was impossible. She had buried Buster in the yard under his favorite red maple years ago. Yet the aroma wafting under her nose was definitely a part of the here and now. She even felt warm doggy breath gusting rhythmically across her face.

Her eyes snapped open, her vision blurred until she willed her surroundings into focus and almost wished she hadn't. She was nose to nose with the biggest damned German shepherd she'd ever seen, at least this close up. She squealed in alarm and was awarded with a slurp across her cheek and chin and a generous lathering of dog drool.

"Get away from me!" A.J. yelped. Struggling to retreat from the unwelcome facial, she discovered there was nowhere to go. This was not her bed, it was a car and she was wedged on the floor between the front and backseats. Furthermore it wasn't even her car. The Miata had no backseat. But she'd sold the Miata, hadn't she? She couldn't remember, couldn't seem to put two coherent thoughts together. Her brain felt as if it had been reduced to pieces of a jigsaw puzzle dumped in a pile, no box, no picture to guide her.

Where am I? she wondered, scrubbing at her face. How did I get here? For that matter, where was here? That she had no idea launched full-blown panic, her stomach, already queasy, roiling even more, her head and heart pounding in synchronicity.

A bolt of lightning zigzagged from cloud to ground as if the gods were cutting the night sky with pinking shears. The dog whimpered, grabbed a jaw full of her jacket and tugged, his massive body half in, half out of the open rear door.

"Stop that!" She nudged his muzzle away and took a deep breath in hopes it would help to clear her head. Didn't work. Thinking straight seemed impossible, but she had to make the effort, had to quell the panic and nausea rising in her throat. This is not the time to get sick, A.J., she scolded herself. Think now, barf later.

First things first: the shepherd. Despite his size, he obviously meant her no harm or she'd have been dog food long since. And he was trying to help, those big teeth now latching on to her collar.

"Okay, okay. I get your point," she said, gasping as limbs that had obviously been in one position too long screamed in protest. Whose car was this anyway? And who had been driving? Confusion overwhelmed her, her disorientation contributing to the chaos in her head. Levering herself from the floor onto the backseat, she looked around. Bad move. The car lurched, the hood tilting down, the rear upward like a rocking chair. She froze until it settled, then eased up slowly, her weight on her hands, to peer out the windshield. A pair of sallow yellow beams illuminated the branch of a tree as it was swept along by a swiftly moving current below her. A stream? Oh, Jesus, a river? She couldn't tell but unless she moved carefully, she would soon find out. The car appeared to be teetering on a ledge a few short feet above the water.

Thunder rumbled in the distance and lightning

speared the darkness followed by big, fat drops of rain. The dog tugged harder, his back legs scrambling for purchase outside the car.

"Let go, boy." Carefully, she pried her collar from his grip. "Out, dog," she said. He reversed until he stood peering in at her, twitching with anxiety. Another bolt of lightning, the thunder nearer this time, sent him scurrying away into the darkness to return a long few seconds later, a soft woof letting her know she was testing his patience.

"Look, hang in with me, okay?" A.J. was appalled at the plea in her voice but in the short time in which he'd disappeared from view, terror at being abandoned had skewered her from top to toe. If she didn't get moving, she'd be down there in the water. With no way to gauge how deep it was, there was also no way to be certain the car might not wind up completely submerged. As few as her options appeared to be, out there on solid ground was by far the better of them.

"Okay, A.J.," she muttered, "let's haul ass." It would be tricky. Leaving this backseat would involve scooting toward safety an inch at a time, waiting after each inch to let the sedan settle before she went any farther.

It turned out to be sheer torture. After each move, the rocking emphasized how unstable the car was. The shepherd pranced, twitched and whined, his attention migrating between her and the lightning. It and the rain were increasing in intensity and volume, the wind lashing at the tall grasses around him.

After an eternity, A.J. reached the edge of the seat

and swiveled so she could suspend her right leg out the door. With her right arm braced along the seat back, she felt something poke her wrist. Behind her she could just make out the corner of something dark and square wedged on the deck between the glass and the headrest. A vicious bolt of lightning, loud enough to make her flinch, revealed a handbag. She didn't recognize it, but in case it was her own, she looped the strap around her wrist, eased her left leg out, and gasped, realizing how high the rear of the car sat above solid ground.

She would have to jump. Now that she was so close to the edge, the sedan was listing toward this side. Terrified that the damned thing was about to fall over, she launched herself as far onto the bank as she could, landing on all fours, her knees taking the brunt of her weight. There was a moment or two of more panic as she felt herself sliding backward, but the dog snared her collar again and braced himself, trembling with strain or perhaps fear of the storm. A.J. felt a couple of fingernails tear as she fought against gravity, but her grip held. Winded, her lungs pumping like bellows, she turned over and sat up.

"Thanks, buddy," she croaked as the dog released her. "I owe you big time." She gave him a couple of pats on the head before turning her attention to what to do next.

Even out here it was too dark to see her surroundings clearly and the rain obscured all but the car and the little illuminated by its headlights. There was no more than a foot or two between the front bumper and the water, but whatever had snared its undercarriage still kept it captive.

A.J. leaned forward, trying to get a better look at the sedan as a whole. A late model Taurus, perhaps blue or black. She could swear she'd never seen it before. How could she have wound up in it? And, again, who had been driving? The front door on the driver's side gaped open. Had the driver fallen out?

Struggling to her feet, she stood up slowly, fighting the return of nausea and a few seconds of vicious vertigo. The world and her stomach settled enough to make her feel that she wouldn't pitch forward on her face, then she peered down into the water. No sign of a soul. As big as the branch was she'd seen being swept downstream, she doubted anyone caught in that current would still be there. She opened the purse and groped around in it, in case it contained a cell phone. Nothing she touched fit the definition of anything close. She had to alert the authorities, just in case. Then she could see about herself. But which way to go? Up, that at least was certain. There had to be a road nearby. The car had to have skidded off it.

"Home, James," she said to her companion, who woofed and scurried up the bank.

It wasn't long before A.J. found herself looking back at the exit from the sedan as a piece of cake compared to getting wherever they were going. The hill outside the car was steep and slippery, making her progress one of two steps backward for every one forward; her shoes, clogs with medium heels, were neither designed nor worn with climbing anything in mind. A yard from asphalt she lost her footing and cartwheeled halfway down again, arms flailing. The purse went flying and disappeared into the night. Face in the muck, she felt two tosses away from throwing in the towel until a multi-legged something skittered across her hand. Scrambling to her feet, she stood still for a moment but saw no sign of the purse. It might well have landed down there in the water.

God, here I am, she thought, no ID, no money, no notion of where I am or where I'm going and feeling worse by the minute. Not to mention scared, she added. She'd never felt so lost, so out of control. Well, tough noogies, A.J. Suck it up. You've got the dog—or more accurately, it had her. He must belong somewhere and wherever that was, she was going with him.

The road turned out to be two lanes, with gullies for shoulders, another rock-embedded bank on its far side and beyond that woods, darker than a coal mine. No signs on the road, at least none visible, just a sharp curve ahead. Beyond that, who knew?

The dog had scrambled up that rise and disappeared into the trees as if he wore night vision goggles.

"Slow down," she yelled. "Please, dog! Heel, dammit!"

He returned. She wasn't sure whether he'd responded to "please," "heel" or "dammit." All that mattered was that he'd come back, and to her surprise and relief, remained at her side with no further encouragement.

From that point time became meaningless, along with direction and distance. There was only the lashing rain, the howl of the wind in her ears, and the weight of her clothes as they became more and more soaked. The smell of the woods clogged her nostrils, the air a musty, moldy miasma. The temperature wrapped her in a frigid embrace, making her teeth chatter. Was this fall or winter? As hard as she tried, she couldn't remember. If this rain changed to snow . . .

Enough, A.J. Gotta keep going. Pushing her discomfort, ailments, and questions to some rear corner of her mind, she thought only of survival, which consisted, for the time being at least, of putting one foot in front of the other, with one hand on the shepherd's head. She couldn't see him, had to trust him to escort her between trees.

After an eternity of slogging and stumbling over roots and other invisible obstructions, the darkness lost some of its opacity, melding into a slate gray, the rain becoming visible. The trees thinned out and they were finally free of the suffocating forest. The dog gave a full-throated bark and raced away into the murk.

"Wait! Where are you going? Heel!"

A.J. trudged faster, blinking as her eyes adjusted. A new aroma perfumed the night. Woodsmoke? The dog reappeared, tongue lolling, tail whipping in overdrive. He pranced a few steps farther, pranced back, clearly urging her to follow. She plodded after him, then stopped, disbelieving, when she made out a pale golden square that seemed to levitate in the gloom. A window! Civilization! Tears of relief blurred her vision and she squeegeed them away with a forefinger. A log cabin took shape, smoke drifting from its chimney. It was a beautiful sight. She prayed someone was home who would let her use a phone.

The dog sounded again, darted up onto the porch and pawed at the door. It opened, a figure silhouetted against the warm glow behind him, tall and male, all A.J. could tell at this distance. As she got closer, she could make out dark hair, lots of it, a long-sleeved shirt and broad shoulders, jeans hugging long legs.

The man spotted her, opened the screen door and stepped out, fists on his hips. A.J. experienced a moment of hesitation, not at all reassured by the vibrations he emitted. This was not a happy camper. Would he turn away, shut her out? Or invite her in and . . . She squelched that thought, only to have fear kick in and bring it to the surface again. She was alone, cold, sick, in no shape to defend herself if she needed to. Jesus, had she gone from a bad situation to a worse one?

Moving to the edge of the porch, the man stood unmoving. His silence screamed in her ears. Finally, he scowled at the shepherd and said, "Well, hell, Duke, what have you dragged home this time?"

Chapter 2

In spite of strains of "Dueling Banjos" twanging faintly in her ears, A.J. bristled. "I am not a 'what,'" she responded crabbily, "I'm a who. And I'm sorry to disturb you, but there's been an accident. I'd appreciate it if I could use a phone to call for help."

The man peered through the gloom at her, his body language registering surprise, as if he hadn't realized she was a female. With her hair plastered to her head by the rain and her bulky coat, slacks, and shoes clotted with mud and grime, she probably resembled an androgynous lump, certainly far from her feminine best, which just might be in her favor.

Or perhaps it was the race thing. He might not be able to make out her features, but her caffe latte complexion made no secret of her African American roots. Since he was still in silhouette, she couldn't be sure, but from the halo of unruly curls framing his head and short ponytail brushing his collar, whatever he was, she doubted he was black. Well, if he was a bigot, he wouldn't be the first she'd had to deal with. Given the straits she was in, a woman alone in the middle of God knows where, a bigot might be the best she'd confront.

"Are you hurt?" he asked, moving to the edge of the porch.

"Just bumps and bruises. I'm more concerned about the driver. He, or she, might have fallen into the water."

"Shit!" He scrubbed a hand through his hair. "Well, you'd better come on in."

It wasn't the warmest welcome she'd ever received, but she'd take it. A.J. followed him into a combination foyer and mudroom, and deposited her coat on a hook. Drawn by the warmth of the massive fireplace to her left, she made a beeline for it, taking in her surroundings as surreptitiously as she could. Aromas assailed her, woodsmoke, lemon oil, and candle wax courtesy of the three fat candles in hurricane lamps on the mantel. What had looked to be a basic one-room cabin from the outside proved that appearances were definitely deceiving.

This was no backwoods shack. Not only were there several rooms, there was more than one level. There was also a permanence about it, as if it was lived in year-round, with all the amenities of home—a fully outfitted kitchen, and a loft above it that overlooked the lower floor. Glancing up at it set off a throbbing at the back of her head and she squeezed her eyes shut against the pain, which oddly enough resulted in something totally unexpected. An image of less than a second's duration flashed behind her eyelids: the interior beyond the French doors up there. She was certain that if she climbed the steps to the loft and opened those doors, she'd find pale green walls, a high-standing double bed with a brass head- and footboard, a folding step stool at one side. In fact everything, even on this lower floor—the worn but comfortable-looking sofa and easy chairs, the mismatched occasional tables—all of it was oddly familiar, as if she'd been here before. She was certain she hadn't been. Had she?

Despite all the homey touches, the only thing she didn't see was a phone. There had to be one somewhere. After she called the local police, she'd find out about getting a cab. How she'd pay for it . . . The question dribbled away. She couldn't seem to hold on to any one thought for very long. What the hell was the matter with her?

The man had disappeared through a door beside the fireplace but the three-second glance she'd gotten of him had stuck, even if not much else seemed to. He reminded her of an ad for Brawny paper towels, the epitome of a woodsman, tall, broad-shouldered, flannel shirt with sleeves rolled back to expose well-muscled forearms, faded jeans hugging a taut backside. Not exactly a handsome face, although she knew women who would kill for those cheekbones.

Reappearing with a pair of beach towels, he tossed one at her, then swiveled toward the dog. But too late. The big shepherd was in midshake, spraying water from his thick coat in all directions. He'd done it outside on the porch but clearly hadn't completed the task to his satisfaction.

"Damn it, Duke! I already mopped once today!" Dropping to one knee, her host swaddled the dog, rubbing him briskly. The shepherd, to A.J.'s surprise, wasn't as big as he'd appeared back at the car. A rip in his right ear gave him a rakish air. He was a smiler, tongue lolling, eyes bright, enjoying the terry cloth massage, until the man started on its front right quarters. The shepherd yipped in pain and added a whine for good measure.

"What's the problem, boy?" Examining the area that had prompted the dog's protest, his owner made soothing sounds, his large hands moving over the shoulder. "Swollen. We'd better let Rory take a look at you soon's we can."

Blotting the rain from her hair, A.J. glanced around, more and more puzzled by her surroundings and a sense that she'd seen them before. Doors flanked a fireplace almost tall enough for her to step into, its surround a rich, red brick. Furniture was spare, worn but serviceable. Books and magazines were everywhere, on the coffee and end tables and crammed in a ceiling-to-floor bookcase behind the sofa. Why did it all feel so familiar?

A granite-topped island with stools separated the kitchen from a dining area. Whoever the man was, he liked his creature comforts. The kitchen appliances looked new, and a microwave was mounted over a gas range. And still, not a phone in sight.

"I'd better call the locals," she said. "If you'll point me to your phone . . ."

"Well, that's a problem," the man said, examining the dog's paws.

"Why?" Then it occurred to her. "Please don't tell me the storm's knocked it out."

"Probably would have if I had one, but I don't."

A.J. got the impression he was almost proud of the fact. Incredulous, she gaped at him. "No phone? Not even a cellular?"

"Not even a cellular. And before you ask," he added pointedly, looking up at her, "that's the way I want it."

Considering how isolated this place seemed to be, she floundered for a rational explanation. "But . . . but what if you had an emergency? What if you needed help or something?"

"I'd handle it." Giving the dog one final pat, he rose to face her with no apology. Except when he was focused on Duke, a scowl was apparently a permanent expression. "I came up here to get away from everything and everybody. 'Everything' includes phones, pagers, and any other means of communication." The scowl became a glare. " 'Everybody' is self-explanatory, and includes drop-in visitors. You look familiar. Who are you, anyway?"

"Call me A.J.," she said, still distracted. "But the driver might be lying out there hurt. I've got to do something. Is there a neighbor close by with a phone?"

"Probably not. The closest cabin is a half mile

from here and as far as I know, it's empty this time of year. I'm Jake Walker. Duke, you've met. And I might as well tell you there's no point in your worrying about the driver. He either managed to walk away under his own steam or he's dead."

Appalled by how heartless he sounded, A.J. wondered what kind of monster she'd stumbled across. "How can you say that? He or she may be hurt, needing help."

Jake shook his head, adamant. "Not a chance, or Duke would be raising hell to go back out there. The fact that he's acting like he's in for the night means that you were the only one around worth the effort."

"Worth the effort?" Outrage intensified A.J.'s headache. "What's that supposed to mean?"

"It means," he said, hand extended for her towel, "that you were the only one he could help. Duke's a retired search-and-rescue dog, although he hasn't caught on to the retired part yet. We're still working on that. If someone else had been injured and immobile, he'd have come rousted me. Since he didn't, that means either the driver wasn't in the vicinity when Duke got there or he was already dead. You, he could help."

A.J. digested the information and felt both relief and more than a smidgen of alarm, but was at a loss for the reason for the latter. "So you're a cop? With a K-9 unit?"

"Well, maybe about the first, but no to the second."

"Maybe?" She backed up a step. "Either you're a cop or you're not."

"I've worn a badge for eighteen years. As for Duke, he's not really mine, something else he hasn't caught on to. I haven't been able to convince him I'm not up for adoption. But I know him well enough to trust his instincts and his training. What exactly happened to you?"

Somewhat mollified, A.J. edged closer to the roaring fire, and tried to rub the goose bumps away. "I don't know. I came to in this car, in the back. I guess it must have skidded off the road and wound up nose down a couple of feet from a creek, or maybe a river, I couldn't tell."

"Simpson's Creek. It's the only water around. Certainly deep enough to drown in, though. Go on."

"The driver's door was open, so I don't know whether he, or she, fell out or what. Considering how fast the current was, if they fell in, they're a goner. But, honestly, Jake, the authorities need to know about the accident, so they can at least search for the body."

Jake gazed at her, eyes blacker than onyx in a deeply tanned complexion. His features were hard, angular, a face for Mount Rushmore. "Anything falling into Simpson's Creek winds up in the same place, up against the bridge a mile or so south. I'll go see if there's any chance the phone in the next cabin's still connected, but not until the lightning has let up some. The trees in this area have bull's eyes painted on them, and I don't intend to be out there if one of those bolts misses. What do you mean, he or she? Don't you know who was driving?"

"No." She hesitated, hating to admit just how muddled she was. It made her feel even more vulnerable. "I can't remember much of anything, who I was with or how I wound up in the car. Where am I, anyway?"

Tossing both towels toward the door through which he'd left, he crossed to her, taking her chin in his hand and peering into her eyes. Startled by his invasion of her personal space, she tried to twist away but he held her fast, the scent of him, a combination of soap and woodsmoke, disconcerting her even further.

"Your pupils don't look right. What are you on?" The question was gruff, abrupt. He grabbed her forearm, pushed up her sleeve.

Angered by his assumption, she yanked her arm from his grasp. "Nothing! I must have hit my head. It hurts like blazes."

"Be still." He probed her scalp with a far more gentle touch than she might have expected, long fingers riffling through her hair yet barely touching her. Despite that, one spot above the nape of her neck exploded with pain when he reached it and she gasped.

"Ow! That hurt!"

Duke trotted over to lean against her leg and whimper in sympathy.

He grunted. "Move, dog. You've got a goose egg back here, lady. Skin's broken. Looks like it's bled a lot, too."

A.J. started. "It has? I didn't feel it."

"Shows what shape you're in." He took a deep

breath, his expression one of exasperation and resignation. "Okay. Looks like I'm stuck with you, too,
for the time being anyway. You need to get out of
those clothes." He fingered the sleeve of her
sweater. "Is this washable?"

She glanced down at the forest green weave and
tried to remember. "I'm not sure." And at that
point, didn't care. She was not one bit comfortable
at the prospect of undressing. "If I stay by the fire,
it'll dry."

Jake snorted. "Yeah, maybe some time tomorrow. By then you'll have pneumonia. Wait right
here." He started toward the door to the right of the
fireplace.

Fighting off panic, A.J. floundered for something
she could say to delay him, her fingertips smoothing the tip of Duke's good ear. He still leaned
against her, bright eyes watching her anxiously.
"You never answered my question. Where is this
place?"

"Nowhere."

Not in the mood for games, she gritted her teeth.
"Well, what's the closest town? For that matter,
what state is this?"

His lips twitched, a trace of humor adding a glint
to his eyes, gone as rapidly as it had appeared.
"Maryland. Western Maryland, to be precise. The
closest town? Adamsville, I guess. But this, believe
it or not, is Nowhere."

It was A.J.'s turn to scowl. "Look, I need to know.
Where am I?"

"You heard me. Nowhere." His lips stretched in

what might have passed for a smile. Or it might have been a grimace. "It started out as Middle Noah, after the man who settled here a century ago, Noah Adams. It's halfway up the mountain, which accounts for the Middle. But there was nothing else around and so hard to get to, folks started calling it Middle of Nowhere and finally just plain Nowhere. Year-around population a couple of dozen, if that. You're shivering. Get those shoes off and put them on the hearth." He strode through the door on the right, nudging it closed behind him.

Oh, this is just ducky, A.J. thought. Not only do I have no idea where I started from, where do I wind up? Nowhere. With a cop who looks like a smile would kill him. There was something else about him that bothered her, something she felt she should know, but couldn't home in on it. At least his dog was friendly. It sat gazing up at her expectantly now, tail swishing a hundred eighty degree arc across the floor.

She stooped, gave him a gentle hug. "Thanks, Duke. You saved my bacon." The tail speeded up a notch, whether due to the hug or the mention of bacon, she wasn't sure.

She eyed the furniture but decided against taking a seat. She was too dirty. Dropping onto the floor beside him, she removed her clogs and winced. They were ruined, the leather soaked, the soles caked with mud and debris. Duke sniffed them and backed away.

"Point taken," she muttered, examining her knee-highs, which weren't in much better shape, her slacks a total loss, a rip in the knee. Giving in to fatigue and the despair stealing over her, she folded her arms around her knees, lowered her head, and closed her eyes. She had to think, figure out what to do, where to go from here. If she could only ignore the insistent throbbing in her head. It wasn't just the pain, which was nuisance enough, she felt muzzy, befuddled, as if something unrelated to the lump was seriously wrong up there. Concussion? Did a concussion make you feel as if you had hominy grits for brains?

"Try these." Jake's voice roused her and she looked up to see him extending a pile of folded items. "They're clean. Sorry. No underwear." He dropped the clothing onto the floor beside her, and walked away.

"Thanks. I really appreciate this." Examining them, she felt some of her anxiety dissipate. These definitely belonged to a woman. The sweater, a thick navy turtleneck with cable stitching on the front, and the five-pocket jeans were both size tens. Under them was a pair of pink socks that looked like they'd fit. A floral scent wafted from everything, as if it had been stored with sachet in the drawer or closet. Duke took a sniff at the socks, wet nose twitching, and sneezed, then suddenly alert, ran to the window beside the sofa and stood looking up at it.

Jake seemed to sense her curiosity about the items. Moving into the kitchen, he filled a kettle and put it on the stove. "Those were my mom's. And instant coffee's all I have."

"Uh—that's fine, thanks." She salivated and swallowed. That was another problem, the taste in her mouth. It wasn't exactly foul, just alien. What could she have eaten that would leave such a weird metallic edge on her tongue? "I hope your mother won't mind my borrowing her things. I'll see that they're returned in the mail, freshly laundered."

"Forget it. Mom died four years ago. We just never got around to disposing of her clothes."

A.J. wondered who "we" was, but couldn't dredge up the energy to ask. He probably would say it wasn't her business anyway.

He reached into an overhead cabinet. "There's a shower through that door on the right. Go easy when you shampoo. It will probably sting like hell, but at least your hair and scalp will be clean. When you're done, I'll put a bandage on it. And if you're hungry, it's canned stew or nothing."

A.J. pushed aside her uneasiness at taking a shower and putting herself in an even more vulnerable position. This was not exactly the seedy motel in *Psycho*, she scolded herself. The man was a cop, for God's sake. Besides, she was filthy. She also wasn't certain how her digestive system would react to food, but she'd try a couple of forkfuls, if only to avoid insulting him. "Stew sounds good. I'll try not to be long." Getting to her feet slowly, she stood, arms extended for balance as the room spun around her.

He squinted at her. "You gonna pass out on me?"

"No." She gritted her teeth, praying that mind over matter really worked. After a few dizzy moments, things settled and she reached down carefully for the clothing. "I'm fine. Through there?"

"Yeah. By the way, what's A.J. stand for?"

She turned to respond, then closed her mouth, stunned. Now that he'd asked, the full impact of her condition whacked her across the face. Because she didn't know. For the life of her, she couldn't remember her name.

Chapter 3

"Is that one of those questions that's off-limits or something? I just asked your name, for Christ's sake, not your age," Jake said, clearly annoyed.

Just as well, A.J. thought, because she wasn't sure about that either, so she said the first thing that came to mind. "Family secret. Maybe I'll tell you later." Mustn't panic, she chanted to herself, mustn't panic. "Back shortly." She hurried from the room, thoroughly rattled.

Easing the door shut behind her, she stood with her back against it, her heart thudding against her rib cage. The chant wasn't working. Panic shrieked in her ears. She could deal with the queasy stomach, the scraped knee, the torn fingernails, even the clash of cymbals behind her eyes and stinging throb above the nape of her neck. The vertigo was disconcerting but she could wait it out. Her name, though, who she was, that was basic stuff. Closing her eyes, she tried to quiet the noise in her head and concentrate.

When Jake had asked the first time, she'd said A.J. with no hesitation. And it felt right. She could remember an ID bracelet, silver, the initials engraved on it. It had been too large; she'd had to have a couple of links removed. But what did the initials stand for? Anna? Amy? Alice? They lacked the comfortable fit that would come with being her real name. And nothing for the J. Was the J. her surname? She came up blank on that as well.

Thoroughly unsettled, A.J. moved away from the door, becoming aware of her surroundings for the first time. No spark of déjà vu this time, just a cozy room with a double bed and dresser out of another era, a blanket chest at the end of the bed. A wall of plank shelving jammed with paperbacks. Doors on either side of the bed, the one directly opposite ajar to reveal the bathroom. She turned to engage the lock of the door behind her. No lock. And no chair to wedge under the knob. The blanket chest wouldn't work either. She could barely shift it. She didn't like this. Surely the bathroom door would have a lock.

It did, but was not in working order. She *really* didn't like this. In spite of her qualms, though, the sight of the thoroughly modern shower stall was more than she could resist. She stripped, wincing at the condition of her clothes. The neck of her sweater in back was icky with blood, the label illegible.

She peered into the mirror, appalled at the image staring back at her. *I look like I'm wearing camou-*

flage, she thought, taking in her features. Dirt streaked her face and circles the size of tote bags sagged under coffee brown eyes. Short, curly black hair was plastered to her head like a skullcap. She was, in other words, a mess.

Stepping into the shower stall, she closed its door. The showerhead had multiple settings so she fiddled with it until the spray was intense and invigorating. Giving herself up to it, she let it pummel her, turning slowly to expose all the sore spots. Clear, hot water cascaded over her, rusty brown water puddled around her feet. Appalled, she thought, please, let that be mostly dirt. She would hate to think she'd bled that much, but perhaps that accounted for the dizziness. Steam rose and before long she was enveloped in it, feeling the chills dissipate. Finally she dialed to a gentler setting, soaped herself and dealt with the shampoo, moving carefully over the area at the back of her head.

She wore a cap full of lather when there was a tap at the bathroom door. She heard it open and froze, her heart revving up to mach speed.

"A.J."

She gasped as the gruff voice echoed against the walls of the small room. Weapon. What could she use as a weapon? Squeezing into a corner of the stall, she held the shampoo at the ready, to give it to him full in the face if she had to. "Yes?"

"I'm leaving a fresh towel on the toilet."

"Oh. Thanks." She didn't move.

"Put your things in the washing machine. The storm's let up a little so I'm going to check on the

Rands' phone down the road. Duke must feel you still need protection because he's on guard duty outside the bedroom door and isn't budging. Stew's in the microwave. And clean up after yourself. Please." The door closed firmly.

A.J. went limp, her legs giving out on her. Shampoo lather drizzled into her eyes, blinding her as she slid down the wall, her bare behind making a squishing noise as it settled on the base of the stall.

"Damn you, Alfred Hitchcock," she muttered. "And clean up after myself? Where does he think I grew up, in a barn?" Well, hell, for all she knew, she might have. But she was glad to know she was not alone. Much more of this and she'd fall in love with that dog.

When the temperature of the water began to cool, she struggled to her feet and rinsed off. Opening the stall door a crack, she saw that a thick white towel waited on the lid of the toilet. Uncertain how soon Jake would return, she dried off hurriedly and slipped into the sweater, jeans, and socks. She felt immensely better, now that she was clean. Smelled better, too.

With the towel draped turban-style around her head, she gathered her soiled outer things and left the bedroom. Duke met her, tail whipping.

"I owe you again," she told him and opened the door on the other side of the fireplace. A vintage Kenmore washer and dryer were tucked into a corner of what was clearly a utility room. As she added detergent, it occurred to her that somehow she'd known this is where she should come, as opposed to the kitchen. Why? The machines might well have been built in under one of the counters. But she had known they were here.

"This is crazy," she told the dryer. "Can't remember my own blasted name, know in my gut I have never seen this cabin before, but am sure where things are located. I swear I've never been in this area. What person in their right mind would come here anyway?"

Which called into question Jake's sanity, or at the very least, his state of mind. Wanted to get away from everybody and everything, huh? He'd done a bang-up job of that. Maybe it had something to do with his being a "maybe" cop. Perhaps he'd had enough of it. Or had he been sent to Coventry?

Inexplicably a frisson of uneasiness zipped up her spine as an image flashed behind her eyes, there and gone so fast that she wondered if she'd imagined it: Jake's face, dark and scowling, chin stubbled with a five o'clock shadow, his hair longer, greasy and unkempt, his clothes dirty and ill-fitting. Along with it a sense of threat, peril. Where had that come from? Was she in danger here? He wasn't the most gracious host, but so far he'd done nothing to warrant genuine concern. Plus he was out in the rain to find a phone and call for help. The least she could do was give him the benefit of the doubt.

She returned to the main room, where she found Duke making a circuit between the window, the front door, and the utility room, his manner agitated enough to make her wonder if he needed to answer a call of nature. Or he might be regretting not having gone with Jake. Thunder rumbled in the distance and he scooted under the coffee table for a second.

"Poor baby," she said, stooping to smooth his muzzle. "My Buster was afraid of storms, too." She wondered what a shrink would make of the fact that she couldn't remember her name but had no problem with a dog's that had died years go. As for Duke, he wiggled out from under the table and disappeared into the utility room.

The full-bore aroma of coffee lured A.J. to the kitchen where a mug, spoon, and a jar of instant sat on the counter. A glass teakettle, steam wafting from it, stood waiting. Not quite ready to trust her stomach yet, she spooned in the coffee, poured and stirred, letting the smell tease her before risking a sip. She swished it around in her mouth, hoping it would get rid of the unpleasant taste on her tongue.

She had to figure this out. Even allowing for the possibility of a concussion, it seemed to her that she might not remember the accident, but she wouldn't have lost something as basic as who she was. She had to find her purse, see if the contents might have survived the storm so she could check her driver's license for her name. And where she lived. Oh, Lord, she couldn't even remember where she lived! Somewhere in Maryland? Pennsylvania?

An address popped into her head: 1422 Main Street. Main Street? Terrific. Practically every town on the map had a Main Street. Think, A.J. Think.

A pale lavender bedroom, a back porch with hanging plants. Another small room, single bed, cement walls. A cell? What could she have done to wind up in jail?

A.J. put the mug down with a thump. She definitely needed help, a therapist or something, she thought. Temporary amnesia as a result of the whack she'd suffered, okay. But to have lost so much of herself, more than just a day or two and the event itself, that wasn't okay. Perhaps the loss of memory predated the accident. Perhaps she really was nuts. Forgetting the coffee, she began to pace, becoming more and more frantic. Duke, perhaps realizing his tail was at risk, watched from the utility room door, his bright eyes never leaving her.

As she made the return trip from the front door to the kitchen for the fourth time, something hit the side of the house with a solid thump and almost simultaneously, a vicious bolt of lightning flared in the windows opposite the fireplace, blinding her. A peal of thunder roared across the sky, followed by a full-throated otherworldly groan, and a series of ear-splitting cracks and pops. Then something hit the front door with such intensity that she felt the floor of the cabin shudder, the vibration racing through the soles of her feet. Panting, she backed toward the utility room, uncertain whether to join Duke and stay there, or get out. Lightning had hit something, whether the cabin or a tree, she wasn't sure.

The lights blinked, then died. The swish-swish of the washer slowed to a stop. Breath hitched in A.J.'s throat, her heart racing. Darkness seemed to swallow her whole.

"Oh, please," she whispered, eyes stretched wide until they adjusted and she could see that it wasn't completely dark after all; the muted yellow glow from the candles in the hurricane lamps on the mantel threw an arc of warm, flickering light a couple of feet into the room. "Thank you, Jake," she croaked. Something brushed her thigh and she looked down to find Duke beside her, growling, the hair on his back bristling. "It's okay, dog," she said, smoothing his head.

A.J.'s thoughts returned to Jake. His concern about lightning strikes had not been an exaggeration. With one of the hurricane lamps in hand, she made her way to the front door, opened the blinds over its small window and peered out, but might as well have been looking into the maw of a black hole. Then a spear of lightning lit the night, illuminating twigs and leaves right up against the glass. No wonder the cabin had been rocked on its foundation. A tree had come down, and its top now blocked the entire front facade.

She should do something. Jake had taken her in. Okay, he hadn't wanted to but had done it anyway. Now he was the one out in the cold, trying to find a phone, and wouldn't be able to get back in his own house.

The limbs at the top of the tree wouldn't be all that thick, she reasoned. If she could get rid of enough of them so that he could squeeze in . . .

She hurried to the kitchen and opened drawers until she found the knives, selected a meat cleaver and rushed back to the door. She opened it and leaped back as a gust of wind almost knocked her off her feet. Limbs that had been pressed against the door sprang into the foyer, thicker than she'd thought they would be. Squinting at them by candlelight, she wondered if her bright idea was feasible. Still, she had to try. She worried that Duke might get out, but he seemed more interested in the window. He stood, front paws on the sill, sniffing at the frame on the right side.

Easing the handle of the hurricane lamp onto a coat hook, A.J. removed her coat from another and slid her arms into the soggy garment. Pulling in a deep breath, she grabbed a limb and hefted the cleaver above her head when she sensed movement behind her. Reacting without thought or intention, her body seeming to move on autopilot, she spun around, her right foot whipping up to land dead center of Jake's chest. It felt as if she had kicked a cement wall, pain ripping up through her knee and thigh. The impact rocked him back a step before he bent over, fists against his chest, face twisted with pain.

"Oh, my God, I'm sorry!" A.J. dropped the cleaver. "I'm so sorry, Jake! Did . . ." She almost hated to ask. "Did I hurt you?"

Duke scurried over, his nail scrabbling for purchase on the smooth floors. He stood, focus switching between the two of them, his doggy expression clearly confused and anxious.

Slowly, Jake straightened, rubbing his chest, eyes hooded as he stared at her. "You sure as hell didn't do me much good, that's for sure. What was that for?"

"I'm really, really sorry, but you scared me!" A.J. slumped against the wall. What had she just done? A karate move? Judo?

Then it occurred to her. "There's a back door? I was about to try to clear a way for nothing?"

Jake picked up the cleaver and took it back to leave it on the counter. "I appreciate the thought, but it wasn't necessary. Neither was the kick, for that matter. What kind of guard dog are you, anyway?" he asked Duke. "She attacked me. I'm the one who's been feeding you, remember?" Ignoring him, Duke returned to the window, and began pawing at the frame.

"So much for loyalty and gratitude." Jake came back and shoved the door closed, rain cascading off his bright orange rain gear.

"You didn't answer my question." A.J. glared at him. "How did you get in?"

"Utility room."

"I didn't see a door in there."

"You weren't supposed to." He removed the hurricane lantern and slipped his coat off gingerly, as if the effort hurt. "It's something my great-granddad dreamed up back in his moonshine days, so I'm told." He gazed down at her. "You were going to hack off those limbs for me?"

"No. For me, so I could get out if I had to," she snapped, annoyed at herself for having been concerned for his welfare, lying about it and at him on general principles. "As for you, like you told me, I figured you could handle it."

His grin was a slash of white in the gloom. "Yeah, I could have. Anyway, thanks for the thought. Nice move, by the way. I'm going to be good and sore tomorrow."

"Honest, I'm really sorry. What more can I say?"

"Nothing that will make my breastbone feel any

better. Forget it. Let me get rid of these wet things and start the generator."

"He's got a generator," she grumbled, remembering her terror when the lights went out. "I should have known."

"Everybody's got a generator. It's in the cellar."

"Don't tell me. You've got a rec room down there, too."

"Nothing that fancy, just a plain old root cellar." He disappeared into the utility room, Duke leaving his post at the window to click along after him.

A.J. was tempted to follow, curious about having missed both access to the outside as well as a door to the cellar. At least she hadn't had a clue about either one, further proof that she'd never been here before.

She waited in the kitchen, sipping her now luke-warm coffee until the lights popped on again. Hallelujah.

Jake reappeared, rubbing another towel over his head and face. "The Rands' phone's been disconnected, so our only option is to go into Adamsville and alert the locals about the accident and your missing driver. We can leave once this squall's over. Thanks to Duke, the pickup smells a little like dog, but it's better than walking."

So he has a truck, A.J. thought. She should have realized there might not be a phone on the property but there had to be some means of transportation. And Jake could leave her in Adamsville. But where would she go from there? 1422 Main Street, Anytown, USA?

Moving to the sink, Jake washed his hands. "How's your head?"

"Better. I could use an aspirin."

"Should be some in the medicine cabinet of the bathroom you used. And new toothbrushes."

"Thank God," A.J. said, dumping the remains of the coffee in the sink. "I can't get this weird taste out of my mouth."

Jake eyed her, head tilted to one side. "What's it like?"

"Slightly metallic, slightly salty. I can't imagine what I could have eaten."

He left the sink and leaned down to examine her, his expression intent. She would have preferred that he wasn't quite so close, but she was backed up against the island.

"Your pupils look better but they're still . . ." He frowned, then straightened. "Does your head hurt in front, too? Like, behind your eyes?"

"Even worse than the back."

"How's your memory? You remember the accident?"

"No."

"How about yesterday morning or the night before?"

As much as she hated to reveal how much she seemed to have lost, she needed his help. The least she could be was truthful. "No," she said, reaching down to scratch behind Duke's ears. The dog leaned against her in ecstasy, his bulk a welcome distraction. "I've got these holes in my memory, big ones, about basic stuff."

"Like your name."

So he knew all along. Heat rose in her face. "Yes, like my name. Birthday? Age? No idea. I remember where I grew up, the street and number, but not the city. And nothing recent at all. I get flashes, tidbits, but everything's disjointed. There wouldn't happen to be a shrink in the neighborhood, would there?" She tried for a smile but the tremble in her lips betrayed her.

Jake backed away, eyes narrowed in thought as he gazed at her, then went to fill a glass of water and hand it to her. "You don't need a shrink, you need flushing out. Drink it down. Your problem is you've been drugged."

A.J. stiffened. "I told you, I don't do drugs." At least she was almost sure she didn't. She was thirsty, though, and emptied the glass.

He refilled it, watched her drain it, absentmindedly massaging the spot where her kick had landed, "What I meant is that someone slipped you a drug, hopefully Rohypnol, or roofies, mixed with—"

"The date-rape drug? Hopefully?" Horrified, she backed away from him. "No. It must have been something else. I mean, I haven't been raped. I'm sure of it."

"I think someone just wanted to put you out of commission for a while. Roofies wipes out your memory for a few hours, and you rarely regain whatever happened during that period. But it usually doesn't do a number on your past and who you are. A new designer drug popped up on the streets for a while that matches what you're describing, plays hell with your memory, which is why it wasn't a big seller. It sort of dropped off the map but it sounds like that's what you've got in your system." His eyes lost focus, his expression one of deep thought. "I wonder . . ."

A.J. considered telling him he could wonder on his own time, but instead asked, "How long does it last? The effects, I mean."

His attention snapped back to her. "It varies from person to person. For some, hours. Others, days. It may depend on body mass and level of activity. That whack you took on the head probably didn't help any either. Time to put something on that open place."

He retrieved a big first aid kit from the utility room, which made A.J. wonder just what else she had missed back there. After enduring the application of the antiseptic and the bandage without a whimper, even though it hurt like the dickens, she downed a couple of aspirins and a bowl of Dinty Moore stew and allowed as how she felt a little better with something solid under her belt.

Duke hovered nearby at first, watching her intently, whether out of concern for her welfare or in hopes of a chunk of beef was a toss-up. Jake watched her every bit as intently as the shepherd, his inky black eyes seeming to burrow straight through her.

She took the empty bowl and glass to the sink and rinsed them out. There was a dishwasher, but if he was anything like her father, he would prefer to load it himself.

Startled, she spun around to Jake. "I remember my dad! He was so proud when we got a dishwasher, insisted that no one else knew how to load it properly!"

"A man after my own heart." He opened a cabinet door and used a measuring cup to scoop kibble from a giant-sized bag of Alpo. Next to the bag was a sizeable Sig Sauer.

Why did she recognize what kind of gun it was? A.J. wondered.

"Any brothers and sisters?" Jake asked, Duke standing by, tail waving at warp speed.

"I-I'm not sure. I wish I could remember my mom."

"Don't push it," Jake said, dumping the kibble into a bowl. He sat it next to the dog's water supply. "Okay, dog, *bon appétit*, no pun intended."

Duke's response was to rush to the window, prop his big front paws on the sill and growl, ears flat to his head. Once again, he pawed and sniffed at the frame.

"What's the problem, boy?" Jake joined him at the window. "What the heck . . . ?" He examined the frame, strode to the utility room, and returned with a monster flashlight. He nudged the shepherd out of the way and focused the beam on the spot Duke had found so interesting. "I don't believe this. A.J., bring me a steak knife. Please," he added, still focused on the frame. "The same drawer where you got the cleaver."

As if she needed a reminder. A.J. selected a knife and handed it to him, saying, "Something hit that wall just before the tree in front came down. Sorry, I forgot to mention it."

"Everything's still standing out there," he said, digging into the frame. Whatever he was after came free and dropped into his hand. "Goddammit!" He held up his find. What was left of a bullet, its point mangled beyond recognition, gleamed in the light.

A.J.'s eyes widened. "That looks like a nine millimeter!!"

"You've had experience with firearms, have you?"

She looked up to find Jake's eyes boring through her. "I . . . I guess I must have. And stop looking at me like that. Seems to me you'd be more concerned about where that came from."

"Oh, I know where it came from," he said, a vein in his temple throbbing. He shoved it in the pocket of his jeans. "It's Newt, that stupid son of a bitch back on Walston Road. I've warned him before about target practice without the least regard for where he sets it up. When he's drunk, he's lethal, just doesn't think. Shot out a window in the Rands' cabin a couple of years ago."

A.J. shook her head. "What kind of idiot would even carry a weapon in the middle of an electrical storm, much less aim one? He'd be a·walking lightning rod. Plus, it was dark. And—" She stopped, as realization dawned. Chill bumps erupted on her arms.

"And what?" Jake asked.

"He just missed me." Her throat seemed to close, reducing her voice to a whisper. "I was pacing the floor when he fired," she said, a sudden burst of rage loosening the hold around her neck, "back and forth past this window like a duck in a damned shooting gallery!"

"And he had to be on my property when he fired." Jake's swarthy complexion darkened with anger. "This came from a handgun, not a rifle, his usual toy. I'm putting a stop to this tonight."

Duke snarled, diverting Jake's attention. The dog was at the front door, circling and pawing at it.

"Something's still got his hackles up. I'd let him out but it might be a bear. This is the way he acted the last time one wandered into the yard." With a guiding hand on the shepherd's collar, Jake led him back to his bowl. "Eat, boy. We've got errands to run. And since it's stopped raining, we might as well see if we can find A.J.'s car—"

"It wasn't mine," she interrupted.

"I didn't mean it literally." He moved the bowl under the dog's muzzle. Duke gazed with longing at the door for a second, then seemed to give up and take comfort in his dinner. "But first," Jake continued, "I'll stop by and return this slug to Doby Newton. He doesn't understand nice so it's time to get nasty. Let me get you settled for the night first. I'll leave pajamas on the bed in there and—"

"Wait!" Spend the night here? Her blood pressure spiked. She couldn't. Even if there'd been a lock on that bedroom door, she'd still be uneasy. "Thanks, Jake, but if you're going into Adamsville, I might as well go with you."

"And stay where?" he asked, head tilted to one side.

"I don't know. A hotel or motel or something."

"Okay, Adamsville does have a motel, but then what? It's not like you can hop a bus in the morning and go home. You don't remember where home is."

That wasn't her only problem. She had no money to pay for a room for the night. "My ID will have my address. I dropped my purse on my way up the hill by the car. It was too dark to find it, but with your flashlight, we should be able to. Please, Jake. I need to know who I am. You want to mix it up with this Newt? Fine, I'll wait in the truck. But, please, let me go with you."

He shrugged his resignation. "If that's what you want. There's a small clinic in Adamsville. This late I'm sure it's closed but you could probably see the doctor on a walk-in basis in the morning, maybe get something to flush that stuff out of your system faster. Make sure he examines that place on your head. Hate to tell you, but you may need stitches."

She winced, but she'd rather look forward to sutures in the morning than the prospect of staying here all night. She wasn't certain whether it was Jake or the cabin itself, but something was wrong here. "I'm a big girl," she said. "I can take stitches."

His lips twitched. "I believe you." He looked down and saw that the bowl was empty. "Since Duke has finished, it's time for him to make a call of nature. I'd better take my rifle and go with him, just in case whatever got him riled up is in the vicinity. Then we can leave."

She started for her coat and soggy shoes. "What about my clothes? They're still in the dryer."

"When you remember your address, let me know and I'll put your things in the mail."

"Let you know how, Mr. No-Phone-For-Me?" Try as she might, she wasn't able to stifle her sarcasm.

He was silent for a second. "Tell the clerk at the

motel that I'll be by to get your address and that it's okay for him to give it to me. How's that?"

She rolled her eyes. Jesus, was he hard-nosed about staying unreachable. "Fine," she snapped. "I'm ready when you are." More than ready, she thought, still unable to shake the conviction that she was in danger, and not necessarily from Jake's idiot neighbor.

Chapter 4

Exiting the cabin from the utility room was a tricky maneuver, entailing A.J. flailing her way from behind a tall bush with foliage as densely packed as a pad of Brillo. Jake's bootlegging ancestor had been a wizard. No one would suspect the bush hid a door.

She settled in the passenger seat of the truck, a model with an extended cab that gave Duke plenty of room to move around behind them. "Geez, it's dark out here," she said.

"No streets, therefore no streetlights," Jake said, getting in. "No need for them anyway; I know this place like the back of my hand. Besides, the porch light is usually on, but it needs replacing. So does a section of the porch roof. That tree did a real number on the front. I'll deal with it tomorrow. Buckle up. This will be a rough ride, but it's the fastest way to Newt's place. Duke, settle."

Evidently this translated to *Sit* in Caninese since

the big shepherd plopped his rear on the backseat and propped his front legs on either side of Jake's headrest, his ears brushing against the roof of the cab. He looked like one happy dog.

A.J. secured her seat belt, suddenly anxious at the prospect of facing the unknown again. Jake's cabin had been a haven for just a couple of hours, but it was the only anchor she had. She almost dreaded leaving it, but she had to go. She needed answers and the only way to find them was to revisit the place where all the confusion had begun.

Jake, it turned out, hadn't exaggerated when he'd warned her about a rough ride. By the time they got to Newt's cabin, she felt as if everything from the waist down had been shaken out of place. After ordering the shepherd to stay put, he left the pickup, torch in one hand, a sizable automatic that appeared from nowhere in the other. But the shack was dark with no sign of life. She waited, barely breathing until he returned a few minutes later.

"Weird," he said, stowing the torch and the automatic under the dash somewhere. "Doesn't look like anyone's been here since summer." After one last look around, he started the engine and pulled away. "It had to be Newt. Nothing else makes sense." He lapsed into silence, clearly puzzled by the state of the cabin.

Once he'd reached the road, he turned right. "I'm guessing that the car probably missed the curve just after the turn onto Simpson's Creek Lane. It's damned near a U and people overshoot it or spin out at least once a season. What kind of car was it again?"

"A late model Taurus, dark color." She shuddered, having returned to its backseat for a second. "Four doors."

"You're sure it wasn't your car?"

"That's the only thing I am sure of. I had a Miata but sold it to Billy."

Jake stole a glance at her. "Billy who?"

"My God." A.J. jerked upright. "Bill Malachi. A—a neighbor! Twenty-something. He wanted a Miata so badly he was always threatening to steal mine. Why would I remember him, of all people?"

"No point in trying to figure it out," Jake said, downshifting as the road began a steep decline. "Memory's a weird thing, files away all sorts of stuff. What's important is that it's slowly coming back. Hold on. Pothole."

The warning came just in time. The nose of the pickup dipped and hit bottom. In spite of her seat belt, A.J. went flying, the crown of her head meeting the roof of the cab as if it was the magnet and she was metal. "Ow!"

Duke too yipped and moved to the other side of the seat.

"Sorry." Jake slowed to a crawl. "There was no way for me to miss it. You okay?"

"Oh, just ducky." She waited for the pain to subside. For a second, she'd actually seen stars.

The ride seemed endless, perhaps because she kept her eyes closed in an attempt to do a mental job on this latest insult to her cranium. She wiggled, trying to get more comfortable before realizing that her underwear was back in Jake's washer instead of on her bottom, meaning that all the wiggling in the world would not solve her discomfort. Thank heaven she'd worn a fairly new pair of panties and one of her better bras. Mom was right; you never knew when you might be in an accident.

She sat up straight, eyes wide open now. "Jake, I remember my mom!"

"Way to go," he said. He reached over as if to pat her thigh, then snatched his hand back.

It barely registered with A.J., still plowing around in her her memory bank. Mom! Dorothy . . . The last name still escaped her, but . . .

"I can almost hear my dad's voice shouting, 'Dotty, the man of the house is home!' And Mom responding, 'Oh, Lord, there's Pete! Quick, Norman! Out the window! And don't forget your pants!!'"

Jake burst into laughter, a surprisingly rich and infectious sound.

"The names of the visitor changed each day," she continued, her excitement building, "always in alphabetical order. It was a running joke between them for years."

A sudden rush of tears startled her and she swallowed around the lump in her throat. "My dad's name was Peter. He and Mom, they're dead, gone within a year of each other. My childhood's back," she said softly. "I lived at 1422 Main Street, a block from my high school in Elm Corners, Virginia."

She could almost see her picture in the yearbook, the list of all the clubs she'd belonged to. But not her last name. As hard as she tried, she couldn't pin down her surname.

Roofies. She shuddered. Who could have slipped it to her? And why? Even if she never remembered the accident or how she'd wound up in that car, if she could recapture the hours before she was drugged . . . She needed a prod, something to kick her memory in the butt. Perhaps the contents of her purse. They had to find it.

"Heads up," Jake said.

A.J. opened her eyes to see that he was turning right where three roads intersected. Here as everywhere else in this neck of the woods, there were no lights, no signs with the names of the road. Suddenly the area on the left of the pickup became one bright, blinding glare, thanks to the spotlight mounted beyond the windshield on his side. The beam swept across a dark emptiness then lowered until she saw a glittering black rush of water between rocky banks no more than a couple of yards from one another.

"This is it?" she asked. It looked nothing like what she'd seen from the car.

Jake must have detected the disbelief in her voice. "Don't let that fool you. Around the next turn, it goes over a waterfall. When I was young and stupid, I jumped from it and damn near drowned, not because it's that deep. It was the speed of the water." He slowed, maneuvering a steep curve that practically looped back on itself. Immediately the sound of the creek escalated. "This is probably where the car skidded off. Keep your eyes open for it."

Duke switched to Jake's side again, suddenly on the alert, and stood up to peer out of his window.

"Is this it, boy?" Jake asked, as he played the big spotlight over the bank. "What the hell were you doing so far from home, anyway?"

Duke gave a soft woof, back legs practically prancing.

"Ah. Here." He pulled over onto what little there was of the shoulder, hit the switch for his emergency blinkers, and got out. Duke wriggled between the seats to follow him.

"Wait for me," A.J. protested, and got out, too, her clogs skittering on loose rocks. She was determined not to fall again. Been there, done that, she reminded herself.

Jake had crossed the road and stood directing the beam of the flashlight toward parallel ruts that angled from the bank to the stream. It was a long way down. "That's probably what stopped the car." His flashlight revealed a boulder at the edge of the rushing water below. "Lots of gouge marks from the undercarriage."

"But no car." Remembered fear slithered the length of A.J.'s spine.

"No car, which means it's downstream somewhere, probably up against the bridge. We'll go there next. Now, your purse. Color?"

"Black."

"Stands to reason," Jake muttered. "Stay put. Duke, come."

A.J. felt a little guilty about leaving the search to them but couldn't bring herself to help. She'd done enough climbing up and down banks for one night. Besides, Jake was the one with the flashlight; she wouldn't even be able to see her feet, much less a black bag.

Jake gave up after several thorough sweeps alongside the creek. Duke spent most of the time investigating several spots he apparently didn't like, considering the amount of growling elicited at each location, and the generous contributions of urine he left.

"Sorry, A.J.," Jake said, scaling the bank with ease. "No luck. If you insist on staying in town, I'll put the motel on a charge card. You can pay me back once you're all squared away. And before you make another snotty remark about my not having a phone, I'll give you a card with my address on it."

A.J. couldn't even toss a mental coin to decide. "I really would prefer the motel, Jake. Besides, it'll get me out of your hair."

She could feel his hard gaze. "There is that. Fine, if that's the way you want it. A lot of help you were," he grumbled at Duke as they climbed back into the truck.

A.J. camouflaged her despair over the purse by going to the shepherd's defense. "He's not a blood-hound. Maybe he's been trained to look for people, not things."

Jake gave the observation a moment of thought as he maneuvered back onto the road. "I hadn't thought of that. Like I told you, he isn't mine. He and his handler were shot in the line of duty. Duke survived, Mack didn't. Mack and I were really tight," Jake continued, his voice flat and without in-flection. "I assume Duke associates me with that crazy Irishman. He kept jumping the fence at home and winding up on my doorstep. So Mack's wife agreed to let him spend some time with me to see how things work out."

"So are they? Working out?"

"More or less, if I can ever convince him to stop coming to the rescue of everybody and everything."

"And dragging them home to you," A.J. finished for him, then decided to keep her mouth shut until they got wherever the hell they were going. Oh, yeah, the bridge.

Silence hung heavy in the cab until, without warning, Jake ended it. "Oh, shit." The pickup shuddered to a tire-squealing halt.

"What's wrong?" A.J. leaned forward. "I don't see anything."

"Exactly. No car and no bridge either." He angled the spotlight straight ahead. "Oh, just dammit!"

The whole of the center section of the old wooden bridge was gone, it and most of its supports strewn about like giant toothpicks, piles of debris swirling around them. The water was higher here, overlapping the banks in places.

Jake got out, slamming the door behind him. Duke scrambled into the front seat and vaulted through the window. With little incentive to be left behind, A.J. hopped out and went around to join Jake and the dog.

"Stay," he snapped at Duke, his expression grim as he walked as far as he could onto what was left of the near end of the bridge. Torch in hand, he knelt to examine the ends of the broken timbers, then the mounds of debris beneath them. Duke whined, prancing with eagerness to follow him, but remained on the roadway for all of two seconds before wandering to the water's edge to sniff around.

"What are you doing?" A.J. asked Jake.

"Trying to see if the water took out the bridge or whether something might have hit it."

"Like the car, you mean?"

"Yeah. I see what might be a tailpipe and a muffler, so I guess that answers the question." He picked his way past splintered boards and massive clumps of trash and tree limbs. "This complicates things, though. Looks like you won't be going anywhere."

A.J. froze for a moment, then trailed him back to the truck. "Excuse me?"

"That bridge is the only way into Adamsville, unless you want to wade to the other side, which I don't advise." He gazed at her across the width of the hood. "Check the speed of that water. It would wash you downstream in a heartbeat."

"But . . . but . . . What's in the other direction? I mean, this road has to go somewhere," A.J. protested.

"It does, to a couple of places too small to be called towns. Definitely no motels. Hey, I don't like this situation any more than you do, but until the creek goes down and I can carry you across, you're stuck in Nowhere with me and Duke."

A.J. managed to control her frustration for a few seconds before she erupted. "Damn it, Jake, this is ridiculous! I can't stay here."

"Got something against Nowhere?" His tone was ash-dry.

"Puh-leeze," she said. "Since I arrived out cold in the backseat of someone else's car, it's obvious coming here was not my idea." Looking around, she threw up her hands. "Nobody in their right mind would, unless they were a hermit or—or running away from something. Which makes me wonder about you." She eyed him, anger fueling suspicion. "Just why *are* you here? Why come with no means of communication with the outside world? Don't want to be bothered with calls? Unplug the phone, or if it's a cellular, turn the damned thing off. At least you'd have it for emergencies. Why aren't you more upset about no way to get back to wherever you come from? For that matter, where do you come from?"

Jake's obsidian eyes bored holes through her. "The bridge gets washed out every few years," he said, ignoring her question. "For me it's just an inconvenience, especially since I hadn't planned on going anywhere. As for lack of a phone, I don't see this as an emergency, at least not for me. For you either, come to that. At least you've got a roof over your head for the time being. Duke, come!" Temper showing, he yanked open his door and climbed behind the wheel. "Duke!"

The shepherd had other things on his agenda, specifically something worth pawing through—a yard-high clump of trash lodged against a foot of the bridge. Mud, leaves, and other unidentifiable matter scattered in all directions as his big paws disappeared lower and lower into the pile.

"Oh, for . . . Duke, come away from there!" Clearly exasperated, Jake got out and strode down the bank toward the dog. "Duke!"

A.J. rounded the front of the pickup, amused in spite of her previous eruption. The dog was now a mess, his thick coat caked with dollops of mud, as was his muzzle as he rooted for his quarry. Suddenly, his tail in hyperdrive, he began to back up, his prize between his teeth. It was long, black, and thin.

"Oh, my God, he's got a snake," A.J. exclaimed, retreating to the far side of the truck again. She did not like snakes, a fact she remembered without having to think about it.

"Which is where I draw the line. Drop it, boy." Jake grabbed the Duke's collar and tugged, in effect, helping the dog break the suction of the mud in which the thing had been buried. His prize dangled from the shepherd's massive jaws, clearly visible now: the filth-encrusted water-logged remnants of the big black purse. A.J. retraced her steps, closing in on Jake. "Is that what I think it is?"

"My apologies, boy," Jake said. "I should have trusted your instincts. Let go." He extended a hand for the bag.

Obediently, Duke backed up onto the bank, his brown eyes gleaming with triumph as he dropped it at Jake's feet.

"Good dog." Jake obliged him with a couple of pats before taking the purse and swishing water on it to clean as much of the exterior as he could. He brought it dripping back up the bank and handed it to her. "Yours?"

She took it, her heart fluttering with anxiety. Its contents had to be past saving. Fingers trembling, she opened the clasp. It wasn't nearly as bad as she'd feared. The top third of the lining was damp but that was all. Everything else appeared dry.

"Come on, dog," Jake said, leading him back to the truck. He dug behind the front seat, found a rag, and began trying to eliminate the grime from

Duke's coat. "At least you can find out who you are," he said to her.

Thank you, God, A.J. thought, returning to the passenger side. Standing in the open door, she began removing what she found, depositing it on the seat, the roof light just bright enough for her to see.

A cosmetics bag, bulging at the seams. Why in the world would she need so much makeup? Keys, one to a Honda. A pack of soggy tissues. A ziplock bag containing something dark and soft that slid into her hand: a wig. A blond wig. She sighed.

There was a penlight on a key ring with a small Swiss Army knife and other assorted stuff but no wallet. Not that it mattered, she thought, as despair crept over her again. The purse couldn't be hers. The blond wig convinced her of that. No way would she have been caught dead in a blond wig.

She turned the purse upside down, just in case she'd missed anything and realized that for an empty purse, it was certainly darned heavy. Inexplicably, the lining dropped from the mouth of the bag and dangled, bulging oddly. A.J. stared at it. "What the hell?"

Jake, watching from the open door on his side, eyed it with disinterest. "Must be a rip in the lining. Easy for things to drop through. Use the knife."

She checked and found that there was indeed a breach held closed by a strip of Velcro. Increasingly unnerved, she began to remove the contents: a wad of greenbacks secured by a thick rubber band, which she dropped as if it was hot to the touch.

"My God," she wheezed, checking a few of the denominations, then flipping through them all.

"These are hundred dollar bills! Where in the world . . . ?"

Jake tossed the cleaning rag back under the seat and rounded the pickup to stand beside her.

A.J. groped into the lining again, her fingers encountering something firm and smooth, a billfold as opposed to a wallet, black leather, several twenty dollar bills peeking from the currency pocket. Far more interested in the window containing the ID, she read the name on the driver's license, examined the photo. It wasn't flattering but how often were they? The name, though—

"Annemarie Johnson?" She repeated it, shaking her head.

"What's wrong?" Jake asked.

"I . . . don't know." She pried the license out. And gasped. Another appeared in the window. Same face, hers. Different name. Anna J. Jamieson.

It was Jake's turn. "What the hell?" He snatched the wallet from her, long fingers wedging the second license free to expose a third. Allie C. Jordan.

A.J. stared at it, a sick feeling in the pit of her stomach. That meant something. Allie C. Jordan. The image of the room with the cement walls flashed behind her eyes again. Was she an escapee, a fugitive from justice?

Jake's gaze locked on her, his dark eyes hard and cold, then at the purse lying on its side, the lining spilling from it like a lolling tongue. He picked it up and something thudded against its bottom. Poking into the lining, Jake suddenly stilled, then removed his hand. In it was a small but lethal-looking pistol, perhaps a Beretta subcompact, she wasn't sure. It looked like a toy against his broad palm.

Closing his hand around it, he glared at her. "Okay, lady, just what the hell's your game?"

She backed away from him. "I don't have a game. I swear, Jake, I'm completely in the dark. I have no idea why that stuff is in the bag. When I saw it in the car, I wasn't even sure it was mine. I grabbed it because it was there with me."

Jake snorted. "Well, does it make sense somebody else would be walking around with three ID's, all with names that match your initials and *your* photo on them? They're yours all right. Which means this pop gun is, too." He checked to see if it was loaded, then jammed the pistol into his pocket. "Just my luck," he grumbled. "I come up here to get away from dealing with the scum of the earth, the dealers, the gang bangers, the just plain stupid, and who winds up on my doorstep? A woman obviously on the wrong side of the law, complete with fake IDs, a bankroll, and a piece."

A.J. opened her mouth to bite his head off but never got the chance. The explosive retort that ripped through the night, along with the solid thunk against the pickup was proof that someone intended to save her the trouble.

Chapter 5

A.J. stopped breathing, which was just as well since almost instantly she found herself face down, nose pressed against the tarmac with Jake's heavy weight assuring that's where she stayed.

She turned her head to one side so she could inhale. "That was a shot!"

"Ya think?" Jake rolled off her just as she realized that the odd rumble in her ears was not a reaction to the blast. It was Duke, rounding the truck. He stood at the front right fender on full alert, staring into the woods behind them, ears scanning for sound. "Down, Duke!" Crablike, Jake scuttled toward the dog. "Come, Duke. Now!"

Duke took off through the trees, disappearing into the darkness.

"Damn it, Duke! Get back here!" A volley of blasts tore through the night, followed by the thud of footsteps and the crackle of dead leaves as the shooter took off running. "Aw, Duke." Jake moaned, then took a deep breath. The shepherd was gone. "Don't move." He said to her.

"Not likely." A.J. folded her arms over her head, her heart banging against her ribs. She was really being tested tonight. She had no memory of how it had begun, and the way things were going there was a good chance she wouldn't live to find out how it would end.

The door above her closed. Sensing movement, she looked to her left to see Jake rolling under the truck. "Have you lost your mind?" she whispered. "What are you doing?"

"We're too visible. No point in making it easy for him." Shortly, the upper half of him disappeared as he got to his knees, then stood. The headlights went out, then the flood on the hood, finally the roof light, plunging the surroundings into impenetrable blackness, the only reminder of where they were the whoosh and gurgle of water rushing into the breach where the bridge once stood.

"Now what?" A.J. croaked, still too frightened to move.

Gravel crunched to her right and suddenly Jake's breath warmed the side of her face. "We've got to get away from here. You'll have to drive."

"Me?" Her voice was a squeak. "Why?"

"Later, A.J. Keep low, go around to the other side and get in. I'll tell you what to do then."

"But—"

"Just *do* it! Please!"

There was something in his voice she hadn't heard before, perhaps a measure of desperation.

Rather than argue, she recited Ready-set-go in her mind, dashed to the driver's side, and climbed in. Jake had beat her to it, closing the passenger door quietly, grunting as he did it.

"Now listen," he said, breathing heavily. "Feel for the ignition. Keep your hand on the key. Got it?"

"Yes. Wait a minute." Her eyes were stretched wide, a waste of effort. He was invisible, a disembodied voice. But something occurred to her that hadn't before. "Jake, were you hit?" She knew it had struck the truck, but had assumed that was the extent of the damage.

"Yeah, I'm hit. Don't worry, I'll live."

"I'm delighted to hear it," she said, determined not to show how terrified she was. The man was hurt, how badly was impossible to tell. "Where did it get you?"

"Right biceps. Rotten luck. If it had been the left, I could drive. Pay attention. When I give you the word, start the engine. As soon as you do, I'll put the gear in reverse for you, since I don't need to see where it is. Put the pedal to the floor. You'll need to back up about a hundred yards before we'll have room enough to make a U-turn. Don't worry, it's a straight shot."

She wished he had worded it differently. "Where's the switch for the headlights?"

"You don't need to know, at least not yet. We—"

"Wait a minute, wait a minute." Her eyes stretched even wider. "You want me to reverse the length of a football field *in the dark*?"

"You want to chance being a target again?" he demanded, his voice grating. "He might hear us leave but at least he won't be able to see us."

A.J. was willing to concede the point, but it didn't make the prospect of backing up at top speed on this excuse for a road any more appealing. It was damned risky. Going down that bank once was her limit. "You're sure you can't drive?" she asked, hoping against hope.

His sigh was answer enough. "If I could, I would, A.J. Are you ready or are we going to sit here until I bleed to death?"

That put things into perspective. She swallowed. "I'm ready. What about Duke?"

He didn't respond immediately. "If he's able, he'll go home," he said softly.

If he wasn't able . . . She dismissed that thought. She hadn't heard him yelp after the volley of shots. "You're right. He'll go home. Let's get this show on the road."

She felt him reach over and twist the steering wheel. "Just checking to make sure the wheels are perfectly straight. Okay, ignition *now.*"

A.J. turned the key. Using his left hand, Jake yanked the gear shift into reverse. "Hit it!" From that point, she might as well have been on a roller coaster, for all the control she felt she had. As instructed, she hit it, flooring the accelerator and cringing as the engine whined in protest. The pickup seemed to fly backward at breakneck speed. She swiveled in the seat to peer out of the rear window, but there was nothing to see. She had to trust that Jake was as good as his word and did indeed know this area like the back of his hand. Regardless, she kept waiting for the next round of bullets. Until this was over, she would never doubt anyone who said their heart was in their throat. Hers had parked there and wasn't moving.

After a distance, Jake palmed her forearm. "Slow down a little. I need to hear the water."

Hear the water? Letting up on the accelerator, A.J. breathed a little easier. "Why?"

Silence filled the cab and for the first time, she caught the scent of blood. God, he hadn't been kidding. Just how bad was it?

"We're close," Jake said. "The current's fast here. It churns instead of singing and bubbling. Okay, the switch for the headlights is on the turn signal. When I give the word, twist it twice toward the windshield. Then turn the wheel clockwise—"

"I know how to make a U-turn." She was relieved to know she'd have the advantage of the headlights, but was annoyed at Jake's thinking she couldn't navigate a three-point turn without help. Hell, she'd had driving lessons from the professionals, passed the obstacle course without nicking one single barrel. She blinked in surprise, trying to place that last piece of information. High school driver's ed?

"Lights," Jake prompted. "Okay, there should be room enough on the shoulder for you to—"

"Oh, shut up," A.J. snapped, and executed a U-turn old Cranshaw would have been proud of. Cranshaw. A walking skeleton, balding, chewed Dentyne by the pack. When had that been? And where?

"Let's try using just parking lights," Jake was saying, his voice faint. "Twist the lever back one go."

It wasn't much, but it was an improvement over driving by Braille, especially once they reached the steep curve where her nightmare had begun. She took it smoothly and evenly, elated to be going forward, and didn't slow until the intersection where the three roads met in a triangular spoke. She turned left without asking, remembering this was the way they had come, but pulled over when she reached a particularly thick grove of trees arching above the tarmac.

"Why are we stopping?" Jake stirred in his seat. His voice was tight, strained.

"I want to see your arm. If that guy's on foot, he's far behind." Leaving the engine idling, she groped for the torch under the dash. Holding it low, she played it over the length of his arm and gasped. The sleeve of his coat was black with blood, his face ashen, his lips drawn tight against his teeth.

She replaced the torch, trying to figure out what to do. After a moment, she put the gear in Park, got out and went around to his side. The rain was back, but lightly, the kind that would be a pure waste of an umbrella. She wiped the mist from her face, opened the passenger door, patted his midsection, and reached for his belt.

A strong hand stopped her, his fingers gripping hers. "Sorry, lady, but we don't know one another well enough for you to cop a feel."

"The man's a comic," she said, slapping his hand away. "We need to stop the bleeding. Lean forward." The buckle resisted, as did the belt but she finally managed to pull it free of the loops. Stomach churning, she moved his arm as gently as she could, trying to ignore his breath whistling from pain. "Sorry, but I've got to do this."

"Then do it." Eyes closed, jaw set, he panted as she fashioned a tourniquet, placing the end of the belt in his left hand.

"Hold it tight, but loosen it every few minutes or it'll cause more problems than it solves. How far to Newt's place?"

He opened his eyes. "About three-quarters of a mile, but why do you want to know?"

"You sure no one's used it?"

"Positive. I'd be able to tell if he'd been there recently. You didn't answer my question."

"We can't go back to your cabin. If this is the same bastard that fired the shot before, he knows where you live and will wait there. It makes more sense to hide out at Newt's. That arm needs tending to. The least I can do is clean it, find something to use as a bandage."

He shook his head. "No way. Newt uses well water the old-fashioned way with a bucket and pulley. I saw the bucket out back. It's rusty, downright nasty. In the second place, Duke may be home. He won't be able to get in. I won't chance that, especially if he's hurt. In the third, I'm beginning to think the shooter's after you, not me."

"Me?" A.J.'s voice was a squeak.

"Who was in the cabin when he tried the first time? You, trotting back and forth in front of the window, according to what you told me. I'd taken the pickup to the Rands' place, so he knew I wasn't there. If he'd been after me, he could have waited for me to come back and picked me off getting out of the truck."

"It was raining like blazes," she reminded him, desperate to make hash of his reasoning. "He probably couldn't see that well."

Jake's response was a snort of derision. "Face it, chickie, I don't care if it was a hurricane, there's no way anybody would mistake you for me. The only person who knows I'm here is Mack's wife, and she hasn't a clue where the cabin is. You're the one with the roofies or whatever in your system, and three different IDs in your purse. The shooting didn't start until after you showed up. And I can't tell you how much it burns my butt that even though you're probably everything I came up here to get away from, it's still my responsibility to save your troublesome neck. Duke's too. So we'll go back to the cabin the same way we left."

A.J. could think of nothing to refute his argument, except for a feeling deep in her soul that she was a law-abiding citizen. Under the circumstances, however, there was no reason for him to believe her. And if they didn't get to shelter soon and stop the bleeding, it wouldn't matter if he believed her or not.

"I guess we'll have to go back without lights," she said finally, her heart sinking at the thought of the washboard road.

"Shouldn't be a problem. Just keep to the ruts."

The silence was heavy, almost sodden, as she drove back, passed Newt's cabin, and let the tires sink

into the gutters that led to Jake's. Again, he was
right; she barely had to steer.

Suddenly, the pickup began to list to the left.
They had a flat, and swore in concert.

She felt his hand grip hers on the steering wheel.
His was clammy, damp with sweat—at least she
hoped it was sweat.

"We're near a clearing," he said. "You can pull
over there. Just as well that we go the rest of the
way on foot. The rain should muffle our approach."
Leaning forward, he peered out. "Here it is."
Again, he was right. The pickup stopped in a niche
that seemed a perfect fit.

"Have you got cat's eyes or something?" she
asked, cutting the ignition. "It's pitch black out
here."

"It is not." He released his seat belt. "But, yes, I
do have good night vision, courtesy of my granddad on my mother's side. Full-blooded Navaho
named Night Walker. That old dude taught me a lot.
Bring the torch and the purse. And don't slam the
door."

She concentrated on this new tidbit rather than
snapping at him. She knew better than to slam the
damned door. She never slammed vehicle doors, especially if she or someone was inside. Driving a VW
Beetle had broken her of that. The increase in air
pressure could play hell on the ears. She was half in,
half out of the pickup when she realized that more of
her memory had just surfaced. Unfortunately, now
was not the time to focus on it. She had to help Jake.

The contents of the purse were strewn all over the
floor. She swooped up everything she could find,

dumped them into the bag, and nudged the door closed. "Oh. The keys. Yours, I mean. To the pickup."

"Got 'em," he said, his voice low. His dark form loomed in front of her. "I'll take the lead. And the torch," he added. "Hold on to the hem of my coat if you have to. Plant your feet carefully and try not to disturb the leaves. We're lucky they're wet. Ready?"

"I guess." I want to go home, a voice wailed in her ears. And by damn, if she survived this night, that's precisely where she was going, just as soon as she remembered where that was.

Chapter 6

Here we go again, A.J. mused grimly, as they left the pickup. At least, she could take comfort in knowing where they were heading this time. But she was concerned about Jake, how much longer he could hold up and hoped he remembered to loosen the tourniquet periodically. No circulation in that arm for an extended period and he might lose the limb altogether. She was just about to give a firm yank on his coattail to remind him when he stopped, causing her to collide with his rear.

"What?" she asked softly. "Are we there?" She had been watching for the soft glow of lights from the windows but saw no change in their surroundings.

"A car." He stepped back to whisper in her ear. "Around two o'clock, about twenty yards away."

A.J. blinked, as if that might dispel the opacity of the night. "You're sure?"

"It's parked on the back way to the Rands' place. I need to check to see if anyone's in it. Stay put. I'll be back."

"No way!" She didn't want to be left behind. He was in no shape to defend himself if he had to. He had stuck the automatic from the purse into his pocket and had his own behind his back, for all the good it did him, since he couldn't reach either one with his left hand. But he had melted into the night as silently as a ghost. "Jake, wait, please!"

She had gone perhaps ten steps when something bumped against her leg. She shrieked, leapt backward, and wound up on her rear end. A warm, wet tongue lathered her face and doggy breath filled her nostrils. "Duke! You're all right!"

The shepherd responded in the affirmative, giving her a good slurp across the chin.

"You lovely dog," she said, her arms around his neck. "If you're up for adoption, I'm putting my name in the hat." She scrambled to her feet and brushed herself off. "Duke, find Jake. We've done this routine before. Find Jake."

He woofed. She followed his lead, surprised to realize that the rain had stopped and the clouds were dissipating. Soon she could make out the shape of something too big to be anything other than the car.

"Where's Jake, boy?" she asked.

"A.J." His voice was hoarse and faint. "Back here."

"Back here" turned out to be the rear of the car where she found him sitting, his back against the bumper.

"Are you okay?" Stooping, she squinted at him.

"Sorry. Duke just gave me his typical welcome and knocked me on my can. Definitely got to do something about his breath. And there's no one around or if they were here, he chased them off." He pulled in a deep breath. "A.J., I don't think I'll be able to make it to the cabin. You'll have to leave me and go alone."

A.J. felt something explode in her midsection. "The hell I will! I'll carry you piggyback, if I have to."

He chuckled. "That'll be a good trick. I'll be okay here. If you'll help me back into the trees, that'll be cover enough. Duke can lead you home."

She stood up and for the first time got a better look at the car, a four-door sedan with something protruding from the rear window on the driver's side: a flag, an American flag extending from a short pole anchored by the closed window. The sight of it set off champagne bubbles in her head.

"This is mine," she managed, her voice little more than a wheeze. "Jake, this is mine, my Honda! What's it doing back here?"

"Well, it's a cinch you didn't leave it," Jake said. "Makes sense, though. There were keys to a Honda in the purse. Use them, A.J. Head west from the three forks. Maybe you can get help in Tyler Abbey."

"The car keys." She didn't have them, hadn't missed them until now. "They're in the truck, on the floor somewhere. I'll have to find my way back and get them." She leaned against the door, an inch from bawling. This was her baby, something solid and familiar. And useless unless she went back into those woods. Then something pinged in her mind, something she should know, a ghost of a memory. It played out behind her eyes, slightly blurred, like a television screen full of snow.

She remembered driving, getting off the Beltway, so that must have been the one around Washington, D.C. She'd stopped somewhere, had run the Honda through a car wash.

"A.J., what the hell are you waiting for? Duke can guide you back to the truck."

"In a minute," she snapped. "I was supposed to meet someone at a restaurant," she said, each thought emerging slowly. It was like pulling teeth. "No, a truck stop somewhere. I was late getting there because I had stopped to fill up and check the oil, but I remembered thinking he could wait. Dad always said take care of your car; it'll take care of you. And it will!"

"Right, with a key." Jake sounded groggy.

She laughed, hysteria creeping up on her. Kneeling in the wet soil, she groped inside the front tire well until her fingers met a hard, round object. Relief and triumph sang through her veins. It took some doing but she finally worked it free.

"A.J., what's the problem?" Jake's voice drifted toward her. He sounded even weaker. "You're wasting time. Help me up."

"I'm coming." The doors were already unlocked, so she opened the passenger door on the rear and Duke jumped in with no prompting. Returning to Jake, she knelt and showed him what she held. "My car, my key."

"One of those magnetic key-tainers," he said, and shook his head. "To think I considered them a car thief's wet dream."

"I took some convincing, too. Let's get you up." She helped him to his feet. "Now hear this: I'm not leaving you in these woods. If the engine gives us away, so be it. Duke's waiting."

Jake gave her a long look, then gave up. "If you're married, I have great sympathy for your husband."

The thought had never occurred to her. It didn't feel right, so she dismissed it and nudged Jake forward. He was wobbly-legged for the first couple of steps, but steadier by the time they reached the front passenger door. A.J. moved the seat back as far as it would go, then held on to his shoulders as he got in. Once settled and restrained by his seat belt, he closed his eyes for a moment, his face shiny with perspiration. "Thanks. That was rough."

She shut the door gently and hurried around to get in. "You'll have to navigate," she warned him. "It's lighter now but not that light."

He nodded. "Straight ahead. Stay in the ruts and you'll do fine."

Famous last words, A.J. mused, and turned the key, her thoughts revving every bit as fast as the engine. She took it slowly, as this too was a washboard road and she could tell that Jake was suffering with every jolt. "You know what?" she said, as much to distract him as to vocalize what was going on in her head. "There's got to be two of them. There's the

Taurus I was in, so somebody had to drive mine. Whoever left the car back there still has the key ring with the remote on it."

"Another reason for you to take off while you can. Let me out at the cabin and keep going."

"Hush, man." Her thoughts were on the purse. Allie C. Jordan. Why had that name twisted her stomach into a granny knot? Not Allie C. Alicia! Slowly a blurred image began to levitate, then recede. She was working as hard as she could to bring it back when Jake cleared his throat.

"I owe you an apology, A.J., so let me get it said, just in case. I don't know what kind of trouble you're in, but I misjudged you. You're okay. You could have left me back there and you didn't. I should have taken my cue from Duke. He likes you and he's a good judge of character."

Duke made a sound somewhere between a bark and a grunt, as if seconding the motion.

A.J. risked a glance at Jake. "Apology accepted. Call me nosy. Why'd you come up here with no way to get in touch with anyone?"

He greeted her question with silence, then sighed. "I've been working undercover for a year and a half, a special assignment. The things I've seen, the people I've had to associate with . . . It was beginning to feel like a slow-acting poison. I had to get away, decide if I could keep doing it, keep watching pure scum take advantage of people, especially kids. That's what pushed me over the edge. Burnout, my ass, it was more like flashover. I needed time and solitude. I get that up here." He chuckled. "At least that was the plan until Duke showed up just as I was leaving home."

"Gotcha," A.J. said, the image of a dirty and disheveled Jake resurfacing again. A photo of him. Where would she have seen it?

Suddenly it was as if the ends of a pair of live wires had been twisted together. She literally saw a spark arc behind her eyes. Alicia. Of course. And Jake. There was definitely a connection but how?

The question dissolved as Duke began a jig and the lights in the window of the cabin suddenly appeared, then the cabin itself, a view of it she hadn't seen before. "We're on the back?"

"Right. Park as close to it as you can so it won't be visible from the front or the sides. Then let Duke out. If anyone's around, he'll alert us."

A.J. was glad he'd thought of that, since she had been dreading having to check around the cabin before they could go in. As soon as she opened the rear passenger door, Duke vaulted out. To her relief, he didn't run off, just stood, tail swishing as he waited for Jake.

"That answers that question." Jake managed a taut smile in response to the dog's goofy grin. "Nobody around." He released his seat belt, swiveled around on his own, breathing heavily, and got out. "Okay, I can make it from here. Take care, A.J. And thanks."

"What part of 'I'm not leaving you' do you not understand, Jake?" She edged the back door closed. "I—am—not—leaving—you. Get over it."

After a moment, he reached over with his good

arm, pulled her to him and hugged her. "Thanks," he whispered.

Disconcerted, A.J. gave him an embarrassed smile. "Can we go now?"

He grinned as if enjoying her discomfiture. "Yes, ma'am. I can use the wall as support until we reach the door. And don't worry, I can make it into the house. If I need a boost, you get to goose me from behind."

"My thrill for the night. Let's go."

All things considered, it wasn't as bad as she feared. Jake took his time. Duke escorted him, running a few feet ahead, then returning to see how far his friend had come. When they reached the bush, she pulled it back for Jake, suffering the scratches silently. It was a big step up from the ground to the interior, but he'd obviously worked it out on the way. With one foot against the ledge, he grabbed the edge of the doorframe and hauled himself up and in. Duke scrambled in after him.

"Shoot." A.J. was giddy with pure relief. "I didn't get to goose you."

"Any time you want, lady," he said, panting. "The first aid kit's in the cabinet beside the dryer. Might as well grab it on your way in."

By the time she got inside, closed the door, and retrieved the kit, Jake, still with his coat on, had collapsed in one of the easy chairs. She left him only long enough to use the bathroom, those glasses of water he'd insisted she drink demanding release.

"Better close the shutters," he said, slowly removing the tourniquet when she returned. "God, it's cold in here."

He's going into shock, she thought, her heart sinking as she secured the heavy louvered shutters over the windows. He needed help, the emergency room kind of help. She tossed a log on the fire, then ran into the bedroom and snatched a blanket from the bed. She covered Jake, leaving the wounded arm exposed. He sat with his eyes closed, his face pale and sweating.

"Jake," she said, rousing him gently. "I'll have to cut your coat sleeve off."

He nodded. "It's okay. Already ruined."

An understatement. It was a bloody mess. Her stomach clenched at the prospect of what was underneath it. Rather than try to find scissors, she went at the fabric with the steak knife he had used to dig the cartridge from the window frame. It was awkward, but it did the job.

"Where's Duke?" he asked, eyes still closed.

She glanced over her shoulder. "Nosing around the front door. Don't move." Steeling herself, she worked her way slowly above his elbow, pulling the fabric free of his skin before slitting through it. "Oh, God."

"That bad?"

His upper arm appeared to have exploded, the muscles flayed and shredded. It appeared to have stopped bleeding but she wasn't sure that was a good sign. This was beyond her capabilities. He needed a professional.

"Where's this Rory of yours?" she asked, with

sudden inspiration. "Does he live on this side of the bridge?"

Jake's brows rose. "In fact, he does. Should have thought of that myself. But you'll have to go get him, A.J. This is it for me. Take a left at the end of the drive–opposite the way we came in. At the three forks, take the road at three on the clock and watch for a big white house, two-story, with a long brick building beside it. That's Rory's place."

God, she hated to abandon him and must have telegraphed it.

He smiled reassuringly. "Just leave some water with me and I'll be fine. Take Duke for protection."

A.J. bit her lip in indecision, but knew it might be Jake's only chance for professional care. She took a two-liter bottle from the refrigerator, checked the fire, and patted her pocket for the car key. "I'd better take the little automatic," she said, carefully working her way into his coat pocket. "Just in case."

"It's not loaded. Hand me the one in my waistband and you take the one in the cabinet by the dog food."

His, she saw, was a twin of the Sig Sauer in the kitchen. With no thought about the process, she checked to see if the one she'd be taking was loaded. It was. It felt good in her hand, comfortable.

"Okay, I'm on my way."

"One last thing." He waved her nearer and she knelt by his chair. "I lied, sort of. I did bring a cell phone."

"What?"

"I forgot to bring the charger. Duke's fault. He distracted me. And the battery died a couple of days ago."

A.J. stared at him, his admission slamming open another door in her memory. Without warning, she was overcome by laughter, bent double, her head on her knees. "I just remembered. My God, I just remembered! My cell phone's in the Honda! It's under the seat! That's where I stash it if I'm on the road and get out to eat or something."

A smile warmed Jake's eyes. "The best news I've heard all night. Rory's number is on the refrigerator. Ask him to come."

She was about to argue that what he really needed was a Medevac helicopter when their run of luck came to an abrupt end. A shot punched a hole in the front door and struck the leg of a stool in front of the island. A second slammed into a kitchen cabinet, shattering glass and dishes.

Jake struggled to sit up. "Again? For God's sake, A.J., who the hell keeps shooting at you?"

Chapter 7

"You know something?" A.J. said, scrambling to get to the light switch. "This is getting really old." Her pulse throbbed, her heart beating so hard she wondered about the possibility of a coronary. It was, she realized, a permanent hitchhiker in her psyche. Her father had died of a heart attack.

"Where's Duke?" Jake's voice held an edge of panic. The dog had been keeping company with the front door ever since they'd returned.

A whimper supplied the answer. The shepherd peered at her from the utility room.

"He's okay." She hit the switch. With the shutters closed, the great room was plunged into a ghostly gloom except for the glow cast by the fireplace and the soft light from a fluorescent fixture above the gas range.

She duck-walked to the door and, trying to ignore the jagged holes in it, popped up, yanked the mini blinds closed over its little window, then scooted out of the foyer. Jake was struggling to get up.

"What are you doing?" she asked.

"I can't just sit here," he responded crankily. "Have you ever fired a gun, A.J.?"

"I'm pretty sure I have, and that'll have to hold you for the time being, so sit down. Whoever's out there isn't going to stop with two shots. Sooner or later, he's gonna try to get in. When he does, with luck I can nail him."

He extended a hand and she took it, surprised when he laced his fingers between hers. "I hate to say it, but I think all the luck is on his side. If he's smart, he'll simply set fire to the cabin and nail us—you, that is—when you try to leave. There's just one chance for you to escape. The only favor I ask is that you take Duke with you."

She squeezed his fingers, hating the note of resignation in his voice. "Stop being a defeatist and talk fast."

"There's a pulldown ladder to the attic in my bedroom. You should be able to climb out the window under the eaves on the back and hop onto the roof of the shed. It's right up against the cabin and no more than a foot and a half drop. Duke's an old hand with ladders so he shouldn't have any problems either."

A.J. sat back on her heels, her thoughts racing. Jake was telling her to leave him here to die. That he was in this pinch was her fault. The pieces of the puzzle, perhaps lubricated by the adrenaline racing through her system, were slowly being manipulated into some semblance of order. There was every possibility she might never regain the whole picture, but she remembered enough to figure out that she'd put her trust in people who clearly hadn't deserved it. And Jake didn't deserve to die because of her error in judgment.

"How many windows are up there?" she asked.

"One on each side, more for ventilation than anything else. Why?"

"I'll give you thirty seconds to work some mind over matter," she said. "I'm not leaving you here. I don't care what it takes to get you to the attic but we're gonna do it."

"A.J.—"

"Don't trifle with me, man," she cut him off, sounding, she realized, for all the world like her mother. "If you stay down here, you're a sitting duck. In the attic, with a view of all sides of the place, we just might be able to pick him off. We're both armed. Doesn't matter if you're shooting left-handed or right as long as you're shooting."

"And if he tries arson?"

"He won't stick around afterward so we'll nail him as he leaves. Then I shove your rear end out the window. Look at it this way: at the least, you'll—no, we'll have died trying."

He groaned. "You're nuts, you know that? And I just figured out who you remind me of, another hardheaded female."

"Later." It could wait. She knew who she reminded him of, too, now. "Let's get you up." She pulled him to his feet, made sure he would stay upright. "How many steps up to your bedroom?"

"Thirteen. Thank God there are railings on both sides." He slid an arm around her shoulders. "Let's go. Bedroom, Duke."

Grinning, the dog raced up to the loft, and stood waiting for them on the landing.

Jake seemed determined to make it unassisted, pulling himself from one tread to the next and listing hard to starboard, counting as he climbed. A.J. trailed a step behind, wishing she could help, but she had to watch the door. He had just ground out "ten" when gunfire punched additional holes in the front door in rapid succession—one-two-three.

"Keep going," A.J. said, kneeling on the stair and firing back, the double-action trigger feeling like an old friend as she echoed the shooter shot for shot so he'd have no illusions about the kind of weapons they had.

"Eleven," Jake wheezed. "You okay?"

"Aside from getting more pissed off by the second and feeling my hair turn gray strand by strand, I'm fine. Keep moving."

"Twelve." Then, after a couple of years, "Thirteen."

A.J. backed up the last three steps, both hands aiming the automatic. Jake hugged the wall on the way to his bedroom, while A.J. hugged the railing that extended the length of the loft, her aim on the front door. They made it inside without the shooter testing the waters again.

"Can't chance a light yet or we'll give ourselves away." Jake, barely visible, had moved to the far corner of the bedroom. He emitted a groan as he reached for the end of the chain and tugged. Squinting, she watched as a square in the ceiling came open and stairs lowered toward the floor. Spring-loaded steps, complete with railings, not a ladder.

"What do you think?" she asked from the doorway where she could keep an eye on downstairs. "Need a boost? How can I help?"

"You're doing it." Jake stood, his body language making it clear that he was steeling himself for round two. "God, I hate asking you to cover for me while I drag my ass up these stairs."

After a second, she said, "Would you feel any better about asking another cop to do it?"

Silence. "You're shittin' me. You're a cop?"

"A rookie, but damned straight, I'm a cop. And I haven't been faking. Returning his fire brought most of it back. Get going, Jake. This guy may be slow on figuring out how he's gonna take us but sooner or later, he's got to make a move. And I'd rather be up there than down here when he does."

"Yes, ma'am. Duke, up."

Needing no encouragement, Duke was in the attic in two seconds flat.

A.J. couldn't afford to watch as Jake climbed the ladder; she had to focus on the lower floor. She knew, however, that the sound of his breathing and grunts of pain would be a part of her nightmares for a long time to come. When she finally heard "I'm here," she wondered if her hair had turned white. It had taken him ages.

"Before you come up, open the drawer of the

nightstand on this side of the bed. There's a small flashlight just inside. Then feel around for a box and bring it. No point in not being able to reload."

Chagrined, A.J. wondered what kind of cop she was not to have thought of that herself. She closed the French doors, jammed a toe against a leg of the bed, but found the flashlight and ammunition and climbed the steps.

Once in the attic with the stairway secured, A.J. promised herself that no matter how much it might cost a month, she would leave a light burning in every room wherever she lived from this night on. She was beginning to feel like a bat. "How're you doing?" she asked.

"All feeling's gone, which I suspect is bad news. Use the flashlight and take a fast look around before we uncover the windows. Not much up here but no sense tripping over what there is."

The beam from the miniature Maglite revealed boxes and trunks in the corners, fortunately only one under the window on the front. She shoved it out of the way. Duke busied himself sniffing at all the new scents, his nails clicking on the hardwood floor.

"How about I watch the front?" A.J. tried to tread carefully. She didn't want him to think she was taking over. "If you're at the back and we have to make a fast exit, you'll be right there."

"Stop trying to be diplomatic," Jake grumbled. "It doesn't suit you. Hand me the light. I'll keep it pointed toward the floor until you've opened the shutters. The windows push out from the bottom."

"No screens?"

"Only on the sides. I never got around to . . . Never mind."

He was right; it didn't matter. The screens were on the inside but wouldn't impede what little vision she had. After cranking open the first window, however, she saw what they would impede. The glass panes protruded at an angle but the opening wasn't that large. She and Duke might be able to squeeze through them. With or without the use of one arm, Jake would never be able to get out. There was too much of him, especially across the shoulders. And he must have known that. Duke followed her from one window to the next, poking his head out as she opened each one, as if testing to see which side of the cabin had the most interesting scents from so high up.

Jake waited until she had finished with the windows before speaking again. "I know you're wondering why I bothered to come up here when you can see now that this is a dead end for me. What got me was finding my granddad. That's where he died, in that chair downstairs, with his crossword puzzle in his lap and his Chesterfields on the table beside him. I want to go out fighting."

She was circling the attic, taking a fast glance out of each window. "Chesterfields?" she echoed, stopping in her tracks.

"Cigarettes. I don't even know if they sell the brand any more. But I didn't want to die down there. At least up here I can help you and Duke out." That said, he rolled awkwardly to his feet and, stooping slightly to avoid hitting the beams over-head, went to the back window and sat down.

"Chesterfields," A.J. said softly, the last piece of the puzzle easing into place. "Fields." She had been set up. Jake, too. But why?

Duke sounded as if he'd found something of in-terest outside, soft, whuffing sounds emanating from his throat, toenails clicking. She scooted across to him, found him with his muzzle stuck out of the front window, tail whipping the air. He gave a yip, began to prance with excitement. It was a sound both familiar and puzzling.

"What's he doing?" Jake asked softly.

A.J. scuttled to him. "Jake, I think whoever's out there is someone he knows. He's acting like he did downstairs, the same way my Buster used to if a friend was at the door. If it was a stranger, he stood still, alert, and waiting to protect and defend. Duke's tail is wagging and he's doing a happy-dog dance. I don't see anything, but obviously he does."

"Maybe Rory, but he always stands out there and bellows for me. Besides, he knows how to get in the side door."

A.J. returned to the dog and slid an arm around his neck. "Who's out there, boy? A friend?"

His response left no doubt. The tail beating against her calf was answer enough.

"Okay, but quiet, Duke." Trying to reconstruct what she knew and how it might dovetail into the night's events, there was only one conclusion that might make sense. "Shhh," she cautioned the dog, and crossed back to Jake.

"I've got a question for you. Do you know a cop

named Fields? Six feet, around one-ninety, black and brown, big ears?"

"Doesn't ring any bells. Why?"

"That's who told me I'd find you here. I came up to look for my cousin—"

"Alicia Jerome."

"You *do* know her!" A.J. plopped onto the floor. "Where is she? We haven't heard from her in a month. Her folks are going crazy with worry."

"She's fine. What's Big Ears got to do with this?" Something, perhaps caution, gave an edge to his voice. "Make it fast, A.J. If it is someone Duke knows, I may know him too. Where did you meet him?"

"At a women's shelter. Running away seems to be Alicia's favorite hobby, but she always phones to let her family know she's okay. And she's never gone more than a week."

"Jesus, that's insane. How old is she, really?"

"That's the problem; she's nineteen but can look thirteen when she wants. This last time she called from Washington, D.C., twice. The first one was typical Alicia, giggly, having a ball, meeting all kinds of new people. Her second call scared Uncle Billy, mostly because she sounded scared. She was at the bus station in D.C., said she only had enough money to get to Richmond and asked if they'd come pick her up. They live in Portsmouth. She was about to tell them what time she'd arrive when Uncle Billy says she gave a little shriek and the phone went dead. You say she's all right? Where is she?"

"In protective custody." Jake groaned and shifted position. "One of those 'new people' she met is part of a group of scumbags who befriends runaways, drugs them so they can't remember squat for a while, gives them false ID's since some of them are underage, and farms them out to johns who prefer them young."

A.J. sagged. "Oh, God."

"Her groomer was the one who caught her on the phone but she managed to get away from him, literally ran into me outside the bus station. I was undercover, but I'd seen her on the streets before and had read her the riot act and walked her to a shelter. I guess that's why she trusted me when she saw me again. I hid her under a blanket on a grate until her groomer gave up looking for her."

"Oh, Jake, thank you." She wanted to hug him but was afraid she might hurt him. "Fields heard me asking about her at the shelter, the third one I'd tried. The purse is hers. He gave it to me. He said someone had told him they'd seen her with you and you'd know where she was but wouldn't tell me unless I paid you. He and the other guy—"

"Who?"

"I don't know. Wait a minute. Let me check to see if anything's happening out there."

Duke was still at the front window. She could hear the crackling of wood below and quiet grunts of effort. The barely visible outline of a figure wrestling with the limbs of the tree blocking the door presented a tempting target, but if she missed or did only minor damage, she would have given their location away for nothing.

She returned to Jake and described what was going on out front. "If you pin him in the beam of the flashlight, I can pop him. I came in second in my class on the target range, so I won't miss. I just want to be sure he'll be in no shape to fire back."

"Help me up." On his feet, he followed her to the front window and peered out. "What the hell's he doing, trying to rip the tree apart with his bare hands? No cleaver?"

A.J. let that pass, since from all appearances, that's what the figure appeared to be doing, and muttering under his breath. Duke wriggled between them, his nose stuck out of the window.

A.J. leaned close and whispered in Jake's ear. "If he's going to keep this up, I can go out the window, get to my cell phone, and call for a police helicopter for him and a medical helicopter for you."

She felt his hand around her forearm holding her fast. "Too risky," he whispered back. "We don't know where the second guy is."

"Maybe he drove the Taurus and fell in the creek. I could swear there's only been one shooter. Or maybe the other man isn't armed."

Duke squirmed his way out from between them and faded into the darkness.

"What makes you so sure this Fields was a cop?" Jake asked.

"He said he was. I didn't get cop vibes from the other guy, which I thought was curious. And they never mentioned that you were a cop, only that you had this place where you 'broke in fresh meat.' They even had pictures of you and this place. Inside, I mean, the great room, your bedroom."

"Pictures? That's impossible. The only person who's ever been here . . . No. Couldn't be."

"Couldn't be who?"

Jake eased an arm around her waist and pulled her closer. "This cop with the big ears. Does he have a scar on one of his lobes?"

"Yeah, he did."

He sighed so deeply it seemed to last for a full fifteen seconds. "His name isn't Fields, it's Fielding. I brought him up here a good ten years ago. He loved the place, took Polaroids inside and out. He's the only cop who's ever been here. But I can't see how he figures in all this."

"He's the one who told me that even if Alicia wasn't here, you would know where she'd gone. I invaded my savings to pay you for the information—"

"Shhh!" Jake leaned closer to the window. "He's talking to someone. Listen."

"—gotta get help, man." The voice was hoarse, faint. "Forget the lighter, I'm dyin' here. I can't hold out much longer. Get Jake."

"That's Fielding, all right," Jake whispered.

"And tell him what?" a second voice demanded quietly. "That we just happened to be in the neighborhood? He knows everything by now. He's gotta go down, her too. The place is as tight as Fort Knox so I'll let the fire do the job."

"You'll need help, Hub. We can set it together."

A.J. clapped a hand over her mouth in astonishment. "One of them's pinned under the tree! Why didn't I see him when I opened the door?"

"Porch light's out, remember? And he's pretty far back. That's Fielding under there. The other dude's his brother-in-law, Hub Marsden, a real scumbag. Shhh."

"This would have been easier if you hadn't come to." The man standing dropped on all fours, tearing limbs off and tossing them behind. "And this is what I get for letting you talk me into quitting smoking. Otherwise I'd have my own lighter. Now shut up. The county cops will probably be here any minute, and I don't plan to be around when they arrive. Which pocket? The right?"

"You can't just leave me." Desperation added a note of pleading to Fielding's voice. "Haven't I always looked out for you, covered for you? What's Sandra going to say if you come back without me?"

Jake's hand tightened around her arm. "You're going to have to kill Marsden, A.J. Fielding may be a rogue cop but he's still a cop and I can't sit up here and watch Marsden shoot him."

A.J. reflected that Jake had an annoying habit of being right. Marsden had no choice but to kill Fielding. There was no way he could get the tree off him and no way we could afford to leave him alive either. Behind them, she heard Duke scratching, then a muted thump but was too distracted by what she'd have to do to wonder what Duke was up to. She had never fired at anything other than an outline on a target. This time the outline would be real.

Jake got to his knees. "Looks like he's on his belly trying to get to Fielding's pocket. That'll make it easy. I'll point the flashlight between his shoulder blades. Don't think about it, A.J., just aim and fire. On three. Take the position."

A.J. could swear she was having an out of body experience, watching from somewhere else as she, too, rose to her knees, braced her hands on the windowsill, and aimed downward.

"One. Two." A.J. inhaled, calmed her mind and spirit. Just as Jake started to say "three," all hell broke loose below them. Out of the lake of darkness at the right corner of the house, something hurdled toward the man on his belly and landed squarely on his back. When it began to snarl and his quarry began to yell, A.J. realized what was happening. The retort of a weapon blasted through the night.

"Duke! Oh, my God, oh, my God," she said, falling away from the window. A second later and she would have shot the shepherd. Instead, apparently Marsden had. "Gotta get down there," she panted and made a quick decision. The folding stairs were slow to unfold. She'd make better time using the same route Duke had.

"Go! I'll do what I can. Freeze, Marsden!" Jake bellowed. "You're in my sights!"

A.J. was already half out of the window, head first, her arms long enough to support her on the roof of the shed while she pried her bottom half out. She rolled to the edge, lowered herself to the ground, then took off running.

"Move and I'll take your head off!" Jake yelled as she rounded the corner.

The scene hadn't changed appreciably. If the dog had been hit, he showed no signs of it. Duke was still firmly attached to Marsden's back, his jaws full of Marsden's coat and shirt collars, tugging for all he was worth and inadvertently throttling him in the processs. A.J. felt no sympathy for him, her primary concern, the location of his firearm. Jake was apparently reading her mind again, the focused beam of the Mini-Maglite scanning the area around Marsden's body. She didn't see the gun and wasn't sure what to do next. She had no cuffs. But she'd used a belt once tonight. She'd use one again.

She knelt beside him and jammed Jake's Sig Sauer against his ear. "Hands behind your back, Marsden. Under the dog, if necessary. Move, Duke. Off," she added, hoping he understood the commands, since she wasn't sure what he'd been trained to hear. Marsden stopped gurgling, and she straddled him, settling her weight on his buttocks.

He screamed. "Get off, get off! I'm hit!"

A.J. knew genuine pain when she heard it. "Where?"

"My—my privates! Call an ambulance!"

A chuckle from the depths of the tree diverted her, but only for a second. The chuckle escalated, became howls of laughter. "You're such a loser, Hub. Wait till Sandy hears that her little brother shot his own wee-wee off! Good! You were going to plug me to shut me up and leave me here to rot."

"So now you'll rot behind bars," Jake yelled down. "All things considered, it's probably a better deal. A.J., I'm coming down. Watch them, Duke."

It took Jake awhile, with A.J. feeling more anxiety about his trying to make his way down two flights of stairs and past the Brillo bush unassisted than about either of the two men on the ground. She kept herself busy until he finally arrived, relieving Marsden of his belt and fashioning an awkward knot around his wrists. She rolled him over far enough to retrieve his weapon, which was wedged under his midsection.

"Are you hurt?" she asked Fielding. He was so completely buried under the tree that all A.J. could see of him was a patch or two of his light-colored shirt.

It was a moment before he responded. "I can't feel anything from the waist down," he said softly. "Guess I'm paying for my sins. What's that noise?"

It was Jake, breathing so hard he could be heard as soon as he opened the side door. He staggered around the corner and made it as far as the porch before he sat down, seeming to fold in on himself. Duke pranced over to him, clearly proud of his part in the night's activities.

"Good boy, good boy," Jake managed. He was in really bad shape. "I'll cover them, A.J. Better get your cell phone and make those calls fast. Please. Time for this nightmare to end."

Chapter 8

Ten days later, A.J. opened the passenger door of her Honda and watched, her heart in her throat, as Jake walked slowly from the main entrance of the Washington Hospital Center. He seemed thinner, his hair indecently long, in fact, much like in the photo she had seen of him. He wore a sling, the bulky bandage barely visible under his coat. An incredibly wide grin lit his face, but A.J. had no illusions that it had anything to do with her.

Duke bounded across the seat from the back and was out and running before she could stop him.

Horrified, she pelted after him. "Duke, stop! Heel! Duke, no!"

Jake turned sideways to protect the arm, and braced himself for eighty pounds of dog. Duke planted his paws on Jake's shoulders and gave him the equivalent of the best facial money could buy, after which Jake, his rich laughter booming across the parking lot, yanked his shirttail free to wipe off the slurp. Duke escorted him to the car, his tail wagging with such ferocity that his whole hind end wagged with it.

"Hi," Jake said, with a warm smile for her. "Thanks for picking me up and bringing my buddy here. You look good."

"Thanks." Startled at the compliment, A.J. stepped back so he could get in. "So do you. How's the arm?" Not standing on protocol, Duke jumped in first.

"Good. Lost some muscle but no nerve damage, and no more infection. I was lucky."

"I'm so glad, Jake. What's the final word on Fielding and Marsden?" she asked, wondering why she cared. "Nobody will tell me anything. Is Fielding paralyzed?"

"Nah, it was only temporary. Busted pelvis but he'll heal. And Marsden missed hurting anything important. They'll be perfectly healthy inmates. God, it is good to be outdoors. Can we just ride around, maybe head for Rock Creek Park or somewhere? I want to put off being inside four walls for a little while."

"Why not?" A.J. pulled the seat belt around so he could reach it. After closing the door for him, she got in. "Duke, settle. And Rock Creek Park is where?"

"I forgot. You're not from around here. I must be crazy, but I missed you. Where are you from? Where do you work?"

Starting the engine, she smiled. "Elm Corners, Virginia, my hometown. Which way?"

The traffic she encountered between northeast

Washington and the park convinced A.J. she'd made a wise decision in sticking to familiar territory. People in D.C. drove as if they were hell-bent on either suicide or homicide.

Jake directed her through the park to a spot where picnic tables and benches sat under trees still shedding their leaves. They cleared off debris and sat down, letting Duke romp and sniff to his heart's content.

"Did they let you see your cousin?" Jake shifted his shoulders, trying to get comfortable.

"Yes, finally. She's fine, told me to tell you 'hi.' She's waiting for a trial date, is chomping at the bit to testify. I think she's run away for the last time. Now, give. What was the point of them sending me to you?"

He scratched his jaw and leaned back, bracing his weight against the picnic table. "Somebody with a badge was swiping the driver's licenses of traffic fatalities and passing them off to someone to alter and sell to whoever needed one. A kid I put on a bus to go back to her parents was carrying a couple of ID's, and I recognized the name on one as a woman who had died after a hit and run a month before. Out of gratitude, the kid ran it down for me, the groomers, the days of not remembering who she was, the parties and services she provided. I started nosing around and Fielding saw me the night I dragged your cousin to a shelter. Marsden had been working on her, but hadn't had an opportunity to slip anything in her food or drink. They couldn't be sure what she'd told me, which is why Marsden was after her at the bus station."

"That silly twit." A.J. watched absently as Duke poked through a pile of leaves.

"She's got guts. Anyway, after you showed up looking for her, they figured they could use you to find out what I knew."

"I was supposed to wear a wire," A.J. said, getting mad all over again. "Only they showed up at the truck stop where I was to meet them with this rinky-dink tape recorder. They said they'd follow me, mark the bills I'd pay you with, and once you'd told me where Alicia was, they'd come in and arrest you. That's when I got suspicious."

"Why?"

"One, they'd be out of their jurisdiction and two, Marsden just didn't smell like a cop. When I asked to see his badge, I figure that's when they slipped that crap to me. It was smooth; Marsden knocked over his drink and splashed it all over me. I went to the Ladies' room to clean up, trying to figure a way to tell them I'd changed my mind. All I took was a couple of sips of my coffee when I got back. The next I know, I'm waking up in that car. Where had they gone?"

"Marsden was following Fielding, who was driving your car. Marsden took the curve too fast and ran off the road. And you were right, he slipped getting out and wound up in the creek, got a fast trip downstream. Fielding took off after him in the Honda. Marsden got lucky and grabbed on to a stanchion under the bridge, but it took Fielding a while to fish him out. By the time they drove back to the Taurus, you were gone. There went their plan to come visiting and kill me, dump your body—"

"So they were going to kill me, too," she said, pulling her coat closed against a sudden chill.

"You got it. Whenever we were found, Fielding would make sure I got credit for the prostitution and false ID scheme. But you, like your cousin, have guts. You turned out to be my guardian angel. I would not have survived the night without you."

A.J. shrugged. "I think that cuts both ways, so we're even. It's Duke you should thank. Looks like he's going to be yours, by the way."

Hearing his name, Duke abandoned the pile of leaves and trotted over to sit and listen.

"Which means I'll have to get used to him bringing home the halt and the lame," Jake said, with a groan for effect.

"I've repaid him for saving me, bought him a rawhide bone the size of Texas, but you owe him double. I've figured out why he kept showing up at your place."

"Why?"

"You were in such a funk that you needed rescuing. He was just doing his job."

Jake considered it for a moment. "You're right. I do owe him double. I'll keep him. Could I interest you in a bowl of beef stew?"

"You mean," A.J. said, "since I have two good hands and opening a can would be a problem for you? You really know how to make a woman feel needed." Typical Jake, she thought. But she'd take it. "Sure. You're on."

He looked genuinely pleased. "One last thing and we can go. Your name. What is it?"

A.J. couldn't contain her smile. "And here I

thought you were being sly, slipping in that bit about my being your guardian angel. That's it. Angel. Angel No-Middle-Name Jericho."

Jake's groan was genuine this time. "God almighty. I've been living a rerun of *Touched by an Angel*. Come on, Duke. It's time to go back to Nowhere."

The French Poodle Connection

Lee Charles Kelley

Chapter 1

The Dog Who Dug Bullets

I was explaining the flaws in the alpha theory to Cady Clark, tall, early twenties, with a face made to be stared at—lush, ripe lips, big emerald eyes with supple lashes, a strong nose, and high cheekbones, lightly freckled, all framed by a loose tumble of strawberry curls. There was also a crescent scar just beneath her left eyelid, which in no way marred her beauty but enhanced it; its dark, sere shape, jagged and violent-looking, made a stunning contrast to the bone china clarity of her skin. She wore faded Levi's and a sun yellow V-neck sweater, smelled of citrus and oak moss, and had that long-limbed yet ample roundness you can't get at the gym—it either comes with your DNA or it doesn't.

Not that I paid much attention to all this, mind you. I'm a one-woman guy; just ask Jamie. Besides, I was only sitting in the sagging armchair in the shabby living room of Cady Clark's rundown, one-bedroom "modern" to teach her how to get her cinnamon toy poodle, Charley, to stop biting.

Or so I thought.

Cady had been told by her vet and a previous trainer that Charley had "alpha tendencies," which he didn't (no dog does).

"Then why is he biting me?"

"Because he's feeling insecure and defensive," I said and noticed that she and Charley were looking over my shoulder.

I was seated facing away from the kitchen and heard quiet footsteps coming up behind me. Before I could turn to look I felt cold gunmetal being pressed against the back of my neck.

"Don't move," a man's rough voice said. "This is a gun."

I believed him.

Charley barked from the safety of his mama's lap.

As for me, my mouth dried up and my heart invented a new form of calisthenics.

"Earl!" said Cady, eyes wide. "What are you doing here?"

"The question is," the rough voice countered, "what is *he* doing here?"

Charley jumped out of Cady's lap and began racing around the room, barking in a red blur of frantic circles.

"Listen, Earl," I mumbled, "is the gun really necess—?"

"Shut up! Put your hands on top of your head."

I did as I was instructed.

Cady stood up. "He's just a dog trainer, for god's sakes! Charley's been biting and—"

"No, he's not. He's that famous detective—Jack Field. Don't you know who he is?"

Cady sat down. I gave her an eyebrow shrug. "I retired from the NYPD a few years back, though I still dabble."

Earl began frisking me with his free hand. "Well, you picked the wrong day to dabble around here, bud."

I said to Cady, "Maybe you should introduce me to—"

"I'm her husband," said Earl, still behind me.

"*Ex*-husband," she spat at him.

Charley, tired of doing donuts, jumped back up in mama's lap and continued his vocal protestations from there.

"Where'd you get the gun?" Cady asked sharply.

"What do you mean where'd I get it?" Earl asked, his fingers still tickling my wardrobe.

"Don't tell me—your idiot cousin Bruno."

"Don't knock Bruno. He just made us fifty grand so you can have your operation. It was supposed to be a surprise."

"I don't like surprises. Especially like this."

"But I did it for you, babe," he said as he finished his search. I'd been waiting for the gun to move away from my neck for a fraction of a second. It hadn't.

Cady shook her head. "I don't want your money, Earl."

Charley was still barking in a loud, shrill voice.

"But baby, you don't have health insurance, and—Jesus!" The gun wavered nervously at my neck. "I swear to God, I'm going to shoot that damn dog if you don't shut him up!"

Cady's face flushed; her scar was swallowed up in red. She snapped a "No, bad dog!" at Charley then tried to grab him by the snout, but he bit her. She shrieked. He squirmed out of her grasp, jumped to the floor, and kept barking.

I stifled an impulse to praise Charley; it probably would have quieted him (and taught Cady a lesson), but I wanted the distraction. I held my breath and waited for the gun to stop wavering and actually move away from me. I thought if I could disarm Earl before he got a shot off at the dog I could control the situation, but I didn't get the chance. The damn poodle suddenly stopped barking and lay down on the hooked rug, panting, with a happy grin on his face.

"Finally," Earl said, with a sigh of relief. Then to me, "Okay, detective, on your feet."

I stood up, with my hands still on top of my head. Cady and Charley stood up too. The dog started barking again. Cady took a step toward us then thought better of it.

"What are you going to do?" she said, wringing her hands.

"What do you think?" said Earl, moving the gun down to my rib cage. "Take him out the back way to the garage, lay down a tarp, and put a bullet in his brainpan."

"Earl!" Another flush of red. "Don't *kill* him!"

"Too late. He knows who I am. Now let's walk, Field, you and me, very slowly."

I said, "Killing me's not such a good idea, Earl."

"Shut up! I don't know how the hell you found out about the job me and Bruno just pulled in Bangor, but I already killed the bank guard. What's one more body?"

So that's what was going on. I'd unwittingly stepped into a situation. "Still, there has to be a better way."

"Sure, better for you. Shut up that damn dog!"

"Charley!" Cady scolded. "Quiet!"

Rrrr-rrrr-rrrruff!

Cady glanced behind me and said, "Earl, watch out!"

The gun swerved from my ribs, to my right.

I gave a hard, downward chop with my forearm. The weapon went off—*blam!*—making my spine itch and my blood freeze; then in what felt like slow motion, a tuft of white stuffing plumed out of the chair, I jabbed my elbow back hard into Earl's solar plexus, whirled on my right heel; facing him now and finally getting a look at his pallid, gray, lizardlike face and a whiff of his stale cigarette breath, I gave him a stinging uppercut to the chin. The gun flew out of his hand, toward where Cady stood. He caved in on himself and crumpled to the floor, out cold.

I looked behind me. Cady had been bluffing; there was no one there. I stood trembling, trying to breathe and work some feeling back into my knucklebones. Then I looked down to see that Charley had hold of my pants leg and was entertaining himself with his own game of tug. The violence was still in my system so it was a struggle not to kick him hard with my other foot. He's just a harmless little doggie, I told myself, feeling damp points on my back and neck. Then, still hobbled by my ankle attachment—*rrrr-rrrr*—I took a few steps toward the phone, which sat on a side table next to the sofa.

"What are you going to do?" asked Cady.

"Call the cops. And thanks for distracting him," I said, then saw something in her face. "Oh, no, Cady. Don't do it."

She got to the gun before I could. It was a Colt .45 automatic. Her hands were steady as she aimed it at me.

"Now, come on," I said, somewhat tiredly.

"No. Put your hands in the air."

I put them up. "I thought you were on my side."

"I am. Just shut up. I have to think."

Charley was still at it—*rrrr-rrrr*—and Earl was starting to moan, meaning he'd be coming to in a little while.

To ease the tension I sat down, with Charley nibbling my jeans, and said, in a light tone, "And another thing, it's biologically impossible for a dog to want to dominate others. His brain simply isn't capable of forming the requisite—"

"Shut up!" Hard lines unprettied her face. "Just let me *think*!" She waved the gun crazily at me.

I shut up and let her think.

Charley gave one last tug on my jeans and let go. He sat back on his haunches, all worn out and smiling again. In some ways I shared the feeling, or wanted to.

Cady thought hard. "What if I let you go?"

I liked that idea and said as much.

"Okay." She let out a breath; her face got pretty again. "But you have to promise not to call the police or go after Earl until he has a chance to get away."

"Like a head start?"

"Yes."

I made a casual toss of the hand. "Well, of course, that goes without saying."

Her eyes narrowed to slits. "You're lying. You'd call the cops first chance you got."

I hung my head and shrugged. "You're probably right."

She let out a breath. "Okay. Where are your keys?"

"My keys?"

"Your car keys. Where are they? Toss them over."

I got them out and tossed them over.

"Okay, get up."

"Don't do this, Cady. It'll make you an accessory after the . . ." I let my words trail off. There was no sense in pointing out what her legal imperatives were until my biological imperatives—like staying alive—were taken care of.

"Okay," she waved the gun. "Unplug that table lamp."

"Why?"

"Just do it."

I did.

She told me to pull the cord out. I argued; she aimed the gun; I pulled it out. She told me to tie Earl's hands behind his back, saying, "Make it tight but not too tight." I argued; she aimed the gun; I tied Earl's hands behind him.

When I was done, I stood up.

"Now, get your coat," she said.

"You're just going to leave him here like this?"

"For the time being. Now, get your coat."

I got my coat.

Charley jumped up on the armchair, sniffed the bullet hole, and began barking and digging at it with his front paws.

"Charley, leave it," Cady said, but he kept digging. "You're an expert," she turned to me. "Why's he doing that?"

I'd seen abusive or insensitive trainers use a shake-can to scare a defenseless puppy, most of whom will cautiously sniff the offending object once the trainer is out of range. So the way I figured it, the gunshot had frightened Charley, which is why he'd been playing tug with my pants—to relieve his nervous tension. Now that he felt more secure, he was checking out the bullet hole by digging and barking at it.

Anyway, that was my *theory*, but I just said: "I have no idea."

"Well, you're a dog trainer. Make him stop."

"Sure."

I clapped my hands and praised Charley in a high, silly voice. He leapt down, came over, and jumped up to my shin.

"Huh," she said. "What'd you just do?"

"I interrupted him with a neutral sound distraction and then praised him, using a high, silly voice."

"And that's all it takes to get him to stop him barking?"

"Yeah, in a situation like this, anyway. And it works better than shouting 'No!' in *any* situation."

"Couldn't you have just told me that over the *phone*?"

I shrugged. "People don't usually believe it until they see it in action."

She shook her head in disbelief, praised the dog, then said, "Come to mama, Charley."

He ran over to her. She picked him up with her free hand, grabbed her coat, then .45ed me toward the door.

We went out to my car. Cady had me get in the passenger side, made me crawl over to the driver's seat while she got in, still holding the gun. She tossed the keys and I backed out of the driveway, making a mental note about the make, model, and plate number of what I assumed was Earl's car, a battered tan Toyota that hadn't been parked out front when I'd arrived. The car had a Maine license plate and I was able to memorize the first three characters—H67.

I drove out of town, with Cady holding the dog in her lap and the gun on me. "Turn here," she would say, or "slow down," until we got past the Belfast city limits and onto Lincolnville Road. She sat slightly sideways, with her knees and the gun pointed in my direction—and damnit, she still looked astonishing, even over the barrel of an automatic. Charley was curled up in her lap now, fast asleep and happy.

"Are you really a detective?" she said after a while.

"Yeah, my fiancée is the State Medical Examiner. I'm her consultant in criminology. So, now you know that I'm a law enforcement officer, and you know that you can't get away with this, so why are you risking jail time for this guy Earl?"

"You wouldn't understand."

"Try me."

She shook her head. Her hair fell pretty across her eyes and she brushed it back with the steel of the gun. "Let's just say I owe him."

"Owe him, how?"

She shook her head again but didn't answer me. "Anyway," she said, "it's not like I'm going to actually *do* anything to you. I just needed to give Earl a chance to get away."

"Still," I said, "you're committing a felony."

She shook her head, smiled. "You won't file a complaint against me. And even if you did, I'd get off anyway."

I chewed my lower lip. She was probably right.

After a while she said, "I'm a paralegal so I know what a criminologist does."

"A paralegal? That takes a bit of study."

"Well, I'm not dumb. Of course, all I ever really wanted to be was an actress but . . ." She touched her scar.

"You could have it removed."

She shook her head sadly. "Still, with my face scarred like this, maybe I could do some edgy, independent films, you know, like Sundance-type stuff?"

"Uh-huh. So why are you stuck here in Maine instead of living in New York or Los Angeles?"

"It takes money." She stared out the window then looked back at me. "So, you analyze the criminal mind, huh?" I said I did. "Well," she snorted, "don't waste your time on *Earl's*. He hasn't got one. It's his cousin, Joe Bruno." She squinted at me. "You never heard of him? He's an evil bastard but Earl worships him. He'd do anything for Bruno."

"No, the only Joe Bruno I know of is a republican state senator from New York. I suppose some people think *he's* an evil bastard, but they're democrats, mostly."

She scowled. "Sure, make jokes. Meanwhile Earl's ruining my life again, just like he always has." She looked at me. "If you're a detective then how come you didn't have a gun?"

I laughed. "I told you I'm retired. There's not much call for most dog trainers to carry a gun around with them."

"I wish you'd had one; you coulda shot Earl for me." She sighed. "I shouldn't say that. He actually saved my ass once, the dumb sonovabitch." It was an epithet, but the tone in her voice made it sound like a line from a love song.

"Care to elaborate?"

She looked out at the road. "Not really."

Time passed; she sighed and elaborated: Earl's father ran off when Earl was ten and his older cousin, Joe Bruno, took Earl under his wing. She described Bruno as a low-life scumbag who taught Earl how to shoplift, break into stores, hot-wire a car, shoot a gun, and a lot of other useless stuff.

"Bruno was one of those types where if there was a right way or a wrong way to do things, he'd go the wrong way just for the hell of it."

"Sounds like he might have sociopathic tendencies."

"I don't know what you'd call it. Anyway, he'd been in jail a few times for petty stuff and he decided it would be to his advantage to have an underage accomplice like Earl to take the rap for any future crimes or shenanigans."

"And Earl went for it?"

"Are you kidding? He did it all the time. In fact, he *loved* doing it. It was only a matter of time, though, before some overzealous judge decided enough was enough and put him in jail instead of another juvie hall. He was seventeen."

There was something off-key about the way her grammar veered from criminal slang to legalese and back again.

We came to the village of Dog Island Corner; a church, a gas station/general store. I slowed to twenty-five, went through the intersection, then picked up speed again.

Cady checked her watch. Charley snuffled, shifted around a bit, then went back to sleep.

I looked at her knowing that such sheer beauty as hers has its own gravity. I think she knew this too and had used it to pull Earl into her orbit the same way Bruno used Earl's youthful need for a father figure to get him to always take the rap for his crimes. The thought galled me. Don't get me wrong; I'm not crazy about dumb crooks who threaten to put a bullet in my brainpan, but if Cady's bio on Earl was true, then his whole raison d'être, crookwise, was based on honor and loyalty, two things I admire in anyone, even a moron.

I let out a harsh breath then said, "The next thing you'll tell me is that Earl only robbed the bank in order to pay for your eye surgery, or your cancer treatment or—"

Defiantly: "And what if one of those things is true?"

I laughed bitterly. "If it *is*, don't tell me about it while I'm driving. My tears might cloud the road."

"Bastard! Why are you such a hard-ass all of a sudden?"

"Hey, I'm sorry, but when people start pointing guns and threatening to kill me, I tend to lose my natural vivacity."

"Your natural *what*?"

"Never mind. It just means I start feeling anti-social."

Silence held the car for a while then she said, "I don't know why you're mad at *me*. I certainly never asked Earl to rob that bank."

"Maybe not. But we both know he did it for you."

"That's true." She spoke the words so sadly that I almost had some sympathy for her. Almost.

By now we'd gone about five miles past Dog Island Corner. She checked her watch and told me to pull over to the irrigation ditch, leave the keys in the ignition, and get out. I did, and stood in the dead leaves by the side of the road.

She crawled over to the driver's seat. "I'm not a bad person," she said through the window. "I distracted Earl earlier when he had the gun on you, remember?"

"Yeah, I think you did that to protect Charley, not me."

"No, I didn't. I knew Earl wouldn'ta shot Charley. He *loves* dogs."

"Huh, no kidding . . ." I was starting to like this punk Earl, lizard face and all.

"Yeah, the dumb sonovabitch," she said. "He just got out of jail a few weeks ago and he has to do this. I only hope that—"

I took the bait. "What?"

"That him and Bruno don't kill each other over it."

"Why? I thought Earl idolized Bruno."

She didn't say anything; she just shook her head again.

Then she and Charley took off, with the little dog barking at me, his voice smearing the distance, and I was left alone at eleven-thirty on a bright October morning to hoof it back to Dog Island Corner to try to find a pay phone.

"I'll tell you one thing," I said to a blue jay who seemed to be listening, "I'm screening all my prospective clients a lot more closely from now on."

"Yeah, right," he seemed to say, but it was mostly just derisive chirping.

*   *   *

I made the 911 call at the general store, gave them the make and partial plate number of Earl's car, and my location, and in short order I was picked up by Jamie's ex-uncle-in-law, Rockland County Sheriff Horace Flynn, a big-boned, big-bellied, salt-and-pepper mustached tough guy with a soft spot for Jamie. He drove me back to Cady's place in hopes that she'd driven my car back there. She had.

We also found a couple of Belfast and Bangor P.D. cars parked out front. Earl's car was still out front too, but Cady and Earl were long gone.

The cops were doing the usual cop things: searching the house, yard, and garage, dusting for prints, extracting the bullet that had wounded the armchair so ballistics could see if it matched the one that had killed the bank guard, etc.

My keys were on the dinette table next to a note that read: "Sorry Jack, thanks for your help with Charley."

I gave my statement, once to a Belfast detective, and then again to a state police investigator, who showed up while I was finishing my first go-through.

When I was finally done I drove back to the kennel with Cady Clark's voice in my head: "That dumb sonovabitch," she'd said, as if reciting the words to a love song.

Jamie's cell phone woke me around one A.M.

"Honey," I said, nudging her.

She mumbled something vaguely disagreeable in her sleep.

I reached across her to the nightstand, fumbled the phone out of her handbag, and held it next to her ear so she could hear it ring. She groaned and turned over.

I watched her for a moment as she slept, with her face scrunched in slumber like a little kid's. Even so, talk about long-limbed and gorgeous, Cady Clark had nothing on Jamie.

"I'll call him tomorrow," she mumbled in her sleep.

I chuckled, gently. "You'll call who?"

"Okay, I will," she softly agreed, nodding slightly.

I laughed outright, opened the phone, and said, "I'm sorry, Dr. Cutter is currently napping. Can I help you?"

"Jack?" It was Flynn's voice.

"Oh, hi, Sheriff. What's up?"

"There's been a shooting. Is Jamie there?"

"Yeah, but it'll take me a while to wake her up. Do you want to hang on a minute? Or twelve?"

"No. Just tell her we've got two bodies waiting for her at the Pine Woods Motel in Wiscasset."

"Okay. Who got shot?"

"Looks like Joe Bruno and Earl Brown shot each other."

"No kidding. Were Cady Clark and her dog with them?"

"Mattera fact, yeah. She's okay but that damn dog won't shut up. Anyway, it looks like these two tied her to a chair with duct tape before they had their little shoot-out."

"Huh. Okay, Sheriff. We'll be there in about an hour."

He gave me the location—about a mile south of Wiscasset on U.S. 1—then said, "You shouldn't have any trouble finding it. You'll see a lot of police vehicles out front."

He was right. The motel was set back from the highway, with individual cabins spersed among the pines the motel was named for. There were about a dozen official cars all told, parked along the highway or in the dirt in front of the motel office, and even between the cabins. Most of the cars were State Police cruisers along with Wiscasset and Bangor PD cars; some were unmarked black FBI vehicles, distinguished by federal plates. There were also a couple of sheriff's Jeeps.

A few curious motel guests and cynical reporters (who'd brought along their own coffee) were camped out behind the yellow tape, which allowed the cops to run around unhindered. The reporters were busy snapping pictures or capturing video images of the "death cabin." The motel guests just gawked.

Jamie and I waded through the activity and up to the porch of the death cabin, where we spoke to Greg Sinclair—a plainclothes state police detective, a few inches shorter than Jamie (she's 5'11"), with a thatch of straw hair and a doughy face. I'd worked a case with him before. He was smart and had a wise-ass sense of humor, both of which reminded me of me. While they palavered I stood there and inhaled the fresh, wild scent of a Maine pine forest on an autumn night.

Sinclair poked his head inside the cabin and said to the four-man forensic team, "Let's give the ME the room, guys."

They gathered their gear and left; Jamie went in.

Sinclair asked if I'd mind coming inside too, to take a gander at the scene. "It looks pretty open and shut," he said, as we followed Jamie inside, "but we might be missing something you could pick up with your famous eagle eye."

"It's two A.M.," I grumped, "I need coffee not flattery."

"Sorry," he said. "I'll see if I can get you some."

"Eh, that's okay."

The cabin had plain pine boards for both walls and floor, though the floorboards had at least been varnished—albeit with just one coat, and that not recent. There were two full-size beds, fully made, with no headboards. A tired nightstand sat between them, with an old lamp and rotary phone sitting on it. There was a hazy mirror on the opposite wall, and a low bureau with a twenty-year-old TV chained to it. There was a simple wooden chair, with a padded cushion that might have matched the drapes at one point. Strips of duct tape were stuck to the legs and arms. To the left was a doorless closet with nothing hanging in it, and to the right was a bathroom with a hook-and-eye "lock." On the far side of the beds were two small windows. One gave a view—I supposed—of the pines. The other held an antique air conditioner. On the floor beneath it was a space heater, with a partially corroded chrome face.

Jamie knelt next to Joe Bruno's body, which sat

slumped next to the front window, his weight holding the flowered drapes apart. His legs were spread out on the wooden floor, his back against the wall, his chin on his right shoulder. He had a .32 Smith & Wesson revolver in his right hand and a bullet hole in his chest. A red rivulet ran down his shirt to the pine floorboards. He was shortish, black-haired, toad-faced, with a dark complexion and beady eyes, still open. His black, glazed eyes had that weird expression the dead have of almost looking at you, but not quite. I shivered, once.

I looked over at Earl's frail body, which was facing Bruno's. At least his eyes were closed so they weren't giving me the creeps. He was slumped against the foot of the far bed, both arms flung at his side, a Colt .45 automatic still in his bony right hand. He had a perfectly round red hole right between, and slightly above, his eyes. There were stippling marks around the wound.

I asked, "So, how'd it happen?"

"Our witness was tied to the chair with duct tape when the motel manager found her. She said these two had a dispute over how to split the money from the bank robbery. They pulled their guns and shot each other simultaneously."

"Simultaneously?"

Jamie glanced up with a teasing look in her brown eyes and said, "It means they shot each other at the same time."

I laughed. "I know what it means, honey, I just think it's quite a coincidence." I turned to Sinclair. "How many shots were fired?"

"Just two, she says. The motel manager and a

couple guests confirmed that. But the squatty one"—he gave a nod to Bruno—"has a through-and-through, probably from a .45. The other guy"— he looked over at Earl—"was shot between the eyes with a smaller caliber. Which fits with what Bruno's packing. The bullet's probably still inside that one's skull."

"You mean his brainpan," I said, looking at Earl.

"His brainpan?"

"Just quoting something he said about me earlier. Did you find it?"

"Find what?"

"The through-and-through."

"Nope. Our witness said the window might've been open."

"It 'might' have been open?" I shook my head. "Mind if I check out the memorabilia?" He gave me a questioning look and I said, "I can't remember the last time I saw a Colt .45 automatic and a Smith & Wesson revolver used in a crime."

"True enough," he said then reached inside his jacket and handed me a pair of Pliofilm gloves. After I'd put them on I knelt down and took the Colt from Earl's hand. I ejected the clip and counted the cartridges. Three rounds were spent. I put the clip back, handed the gun to Sinclair, who put it in an evidence bag. Then I checked the chambers in Bruno's .32. Unlike Earl's gun, only two of its bullets had been fired.

While I was examining the hardware, Sinclair was giving me details about the bank robbery: It happened shortly after ten. An armored car made their usual weekly delivery around nine-thirty. Witnesses say two men came in wearing masks and held up the place. There was a driver, waiting out front in a blue sedan. We haven't got the make or license number yet."

"Probably stolen," I offered.

"Yeah, but there's a security tape from the ATM. The Feebs have it," he said, referring to the FBI. "Meanwhile, the robbers got away with over two hundred thousand dollars."

"Wow. Which one of them shot the guard?"

"He was shot once with a .32," he nodded at Bruno, "so it was probably the little guy. Unless they switched guns."

"Huh," I said. "This Bruno's thrifty with his ammo." I scratched the back of my neck. "Where's Cady Clark?"

"Outside, sitting in my cruiser."

"Has she got the dog with her?"

"Yeah. He's kinda loud for such a little guy."

"I know," I chuckled. "What'd you get from her?"

He scratched *his* neck. "That's hard to say."

"Why?"

"She's so—I don't know—just looking at her makes it hard for a guy to think clearly."

"I know what you mean," I said and felt Jamie suddenly glancing up at me. I didn't acknowledge that I knew she was watching me, waiting for my reply, I just said, "That's how I feel whenever I look at Jamie."

"Nice save, Jack," she said, then went back to checking the liver temp, pulling a meat thermometer from a hole she'd made in the dead man's side. "He's been dead about two or three hours," she said. "And who exactly *is* this woman?"

"Cady Clark?" I shrugged. "A new client."

"And two of her boyfriends just happened to rob a bank today while you were at her house for a dog training session?"

"One is her ex-husband. The other she doesn't care for much. And, yeah, quite a coincidence, huh?"

"I thought you didn't believe in coincidences."

"Not usually, but they happen sometimes."

She shook her head, not in disagreement but disbelief. "Well, it seems to me they're starting to proliferate in this case." She sighed. "I'd just finished the preliminary on Robert Parrish earlier, and now there are two more bodies."

I said, "Robert Parrish?"

She nodded. "The bank guard."

Sinclair said, "He's a retired Bangor cop. Got a wife, three grown kids, seven grandkids."

"Ah, that's rough," I said. "Let's talk to Cady Clark."

"I already gave my statement," she said, standing outside Sinclair's cruiser, holding Charley in her arms. The skin under her eye had been redecorated: there was a new cut on her cheek, about half an inch in length, just at the bottom edge of her scar. "The detective even made me write it all down."

"Pretend I can't read," I told her.

She looked at Sinclair then at me. "Fine," she huffed.

She said she'd come home and found Earl still tied up. She'd untied him, given him back the .45, and told him to leave. He said he couldn't go until Bruno and the getaway driver showed up.

"The split was prearranged to happen at your house?"

"Yeah, it was Earl's idea, not mine. I didn't know—"

"Okay, go on."

She glared at me, stroked Charley, and went on: They got a call from the driver, whom she didn't know. He was paranoid and wanted to meet them at the motel.

"Uh-huh. And how did you happen to come along?"

"Once again," she sighed, tiredly, "that was Earl's idea. Plus, I was worried about what Bruno might do."

"Yeah? So how'd you get tied up?"

"The driver was already here. He freaked when he saw me, even though I didn't know him."

"What was his name?"

"I don't know. I told you I'd never met him before. Anyway, to calm him down Bruno duct-taped me to the chair. I wasn't happy about the idea." She touched her cheek. "That's how I got this," she said, meaning the cut.

"Who gave it to you?"

"Bruno. Earl wasn't too happy about it either. Him and Bruno had a big argument over it, they pulled out their guns, shot each other, and then the driver—"

"Don't tell me. He ran off with the money."

"That's right."

"And you were tied up with duct tape this whole time?"

"Of course. I heard his car start, then I started screaming and the motel manager came in to free me."

"I guess you were right to be worried earlier about those two killing each other. Let's go back inside the cabin."

"Why?"

"I want you to show me exactly how everything happened."

"Do I have to?" She looked at Sinclair. "He's not a real cop, right? He just dabbles, so he says."

He shrugged. "I think it's a good idea. Besides, you'll want to stay on Jack's good side. He hasn't pressed charges yet for how you kidnapped him at gunpoint this morning."

"But I *had* to do that," she told him. "You don't know what Earl's like when he's mad." She turned to me; her eyes were soft, pleading. "If I go back inside and tell you how it happened, you won't press charges?"

I drew my gaze away from hers and said to Sinclair, "I guess it could be argued that she saved my life this morning."

He shrugged and nodded.

Cady shifted Charley in her arms, squeezed my left hand with her right, and thanked me profusely.

"Yeah, don't get extravagant," I advised.

She huffed. "There you go again, Mr. Hard-ass."

"That's me. Let's go back inside the cabin."

We went back inside the cabin. Jamie looked up at Cady then gave me an eyebrow shrug to indicate that the girl really *was* a looker. I hadn't paid much attention to this fact while we'd been out in the dark, but now her fair hair and skin seemed to gather what little light there was in the room and focus it on her green eyes until they were all you could see.

I found myself staring at her, not listening.

She was pointing to the chair where she'd been held prisoner, then to the two bodies. I came to myself again and realized that her story sounded even more implausible now that we were inside the cabin. I was about to point this out to her when she suddenly stopped talking, pulled out her cell phone, and opened it.

"Hello?" Pause. "Oh, hi, Amanda. Hang on a sec." She cupped her hand over the phone. "It's my sister, Amanda. She heard something on the news. I need to tell her I'm okay."

"Funny," I said, "I didn't hear it ring."

"It's on vibrate." She held it up for me see.

I couldn't determine anything by looking at it, but I don't know much about cell phones. Dumbly, I said, "Okay."

"Can I go into the bathroom and talk to her a minute?"

"The bathroom?"

She glared and handed me the dog. "I want to talk to her in private. Besides, I have to pee. I can do both, can't I?'

"Yeah, go ahead," I said, holding on to the poodle.

"Thanks. Take care of Charley," she said, then

went into the bathroom, talking on the cell phone with her sister.

I said to Sinclair, "This reminds me of a story."

He smiled. "From your days in New York?"

"No, it's a story about a tribe of Indians and the local weather forecast."

I told him the one about the new Indian chief whose tribe asks him if it's going to be a cold winter. He doesn't know but tells the tribe to collect lots of firewood, just in case, then goes into town the next day and calls the weather service to get the official forecast. They tell him that it really *is* going to be a cold winter. This goes on for several weeks, the tribe collecting firewood, the weather service predicting a colder and colder winter, until one day the chief asks them how they know what the winter will be like.

"Oh, we use a number of scientific indicators," they say. "Though, to be honest, the real tip-off is that the local Indians are collecting firewood like crazy."

Sinclair laughed. "Well, I don't know if present-day Indians still go around collecting firewood, but what's it mean?"

"Some do, I would imagine. It beats paying for it at the general store. And it means that you have to be careful where you get your information from."

"Meaning what, exactly? That our witness is lying?"

"Well, for one thing, she told you the gunfight happened over an argument about how to split the money. Now she's saying it was over Bruno wanting to tie her up. So she's either got a faulty memory or else, yeah, she's lying."

"You think she might've done the shooting?"

"It's a possibility. I noticed some stippling marks around Earl's wound, but Bruno's jacket is clean."

"So they were shot from different distances?"

"Maybe. Forensics will tell us more once they determine the trajectory of the bullets. Another thing, the bullets don't add up. Bruno shot the guard once and Earl once. That fits because there are two bullets missing from his revolver. Earl shot Cady's armchair this morning, but he only shot Bruno once, too. So why are *three* bullets missing from *his* gun?"

"Maybe it wasn't fully loaded?"

"I don't think so. You don't go out to rob a bank with a half-loaded gun."

"We could check the girl's hands for GSR. We already did it with the two victims, though, and they tested positive."

That put a bit of a crimp in my theory. I looked over at the bathroom door. I could hear the water running.

"Meanwhile," I said, "this guy Bruno seems to be the ringleader, which means he'd most likely be the one to handle the cash until the split takes place, not the driver."

"You think *she* might've been the driver?"

"I doubt it. You'll want to check her alibi to be sure. But her story about why she ended up here and what went down is just screwy. Who was the first officer here tonight?"

"Mike Delgado."

"Can I talk to him?"

He made an apologetic face. "He wasn't feeling well. He threw up in the bushes outside and had to go home."

"What is he, a rookie?"

"No. He used to be on the Bangor PD. In fact, he and Robert Parrish were partners at one time."

I sighed. "Okay," I said, "that's one too many."

"One too many what?"

Jamie, who had finished with Bruno's body for the time being, said, "He means it's one coincidence too many."

"Exactly," I said. I looked at the bathroom door again, stood up, put Charley on the bed, and said, "Cady?"

There was no reply. I went to the door and knocked on it. Still no reply, just the sound of water running.

"Cady, you in there?"

Sinclair stood up and said, "Ah, hell. What'd she do, go through the window on us?"

"It sure seems like it," I said as I took out my driver's license and flipped the hook up and went in. The faucet was running, the window was wide open, and the green-and-white striped curtain was fluttering prettily in the October breeze.

I heard Charley barking and turned back to the bedroom. He was on the bed, barking and digging at the bedcovers.

Sinclair got on the radio and told dispatch what had happened, giving them a description of Bruno's car.

"Wait," I said. "Where'd you get the description?"

"The girl gave it to us," he said, then shook his head in disgust. "Probably a phony, huh?"

"Yeah," I said, going to the bed. "Like practically everything else she told us. The thing is, I was starting to get suspicious about her story when her cell phone rang."

Jamie stood up, dusted her knees, pulled off her gloves, and said, "Then why'd you let her go into the bathroom alone?"

"Because she let me hold her dog; it didn't occur to me—"

"—that she'd go without him."

Sinclair went outside to let the rest of the crew know about Cady's disappearance.

Jamie said, "She sure played you, Jack."

"That she did. I wonder how she knew I was on to her."

"Probably because you have a terrible poker face."

"That so?" I said defensively. "Then how come I always beat Otis Barnes and his cronies at our Thursday night games?"

Her eyes twinkled. "Because none of them are pretty young women. She used her looks to throw you off guard."

"What can I say? When you're right, you're right."

Sinclair came back in. "We've got everyone out combing the area for her."

"Good," I said. "And you'd better have someone find Delgado and bring him back in too."

He nodded sadly. "I hope he's not in on this."

Charley was still digging at the covers. I pulled

them back to reveal a nice round bullet hole in the mattress.

"Huh," said Sinclair, scratching his neck. "Why the hell would someone shoot the bed?"

I puzzled it out a bit and said, "My guess would be that if she shot these two but wanted it to look like they'd shot each other, then after Earl was dead, she'd want to hold his hand around the gun, fire it into the bed, which would—"

"—leave gunshot residue on his hands. Smart." He thought it over. "Why not do that with Bruno's gun as well?"

"She might not have had time; she might not have thought she needed to. Not if Bruno shot the bank guard earlier."

"This is an awful lot of speculation," Jamie said as she put her Pliofilm gloves into an evidence bag and sealed it.

"True enough," I replied.

She put on another pair of gloves and knelt next to Earl's body. She put two fingers to his neck for a moment, then looked up at Sinclair. "Um, detective? Did anybody actually check to make sure these two were both dead or was that just more speculation?"

"No, I checked them myself," Sinclair said. "Why?"

"Because this one's still got a pulse."

Chapter 2

Give My Umbrella to the Rain Dogs

Earl was rushed to Rockland Memorial and put on life support. He was in a coma, though he still had some good brain function. The doctors gave him a fifty-fifty chance.

"If he makes it," Sinclair said after we got the report, "maybe we can get him to finger Cady Clark for the killing."

"Earl?" I scoffed. "I wouldn't count on it."

Ballistics proved that the two men were, indeed, shot from different distances, so there was no way they could have shot each other. As for how Cady tied herself up with duct tape, that was still a mystery.

Since the shootings were connected to a bank robbery, we had the FBI's manpower available to track down every possible lead. They interviewed anyone who knew either the victims or the suspects: friends, family, business associates, but after two days of intensive investigation, Cady Clark got away clean, probably thanks to help from Mike Delgado.

The evidence suggested he'd been waiting in his State Police cruiser on a dirt road behind the motel. We knew this from the footprints Cady had left between the bathroom window and a set of tire tracks on the dirt road, where the prints disappeared. The tire tracks matched Delgado's radials. His cruiser was found in the Portland Airport parking lot.

Delgado had once been a good police officer while he was on the Bangor force, but left due to a conflict with his partner, Robert Parrish, who'd been sleeping with Delgado's wife. Delgado found out about it, fists were thrown, both were written up, Parrish took medical retirement (due to a heart condition), and Delgado quit the force.

Delgado was an ex-marine trained to work with explosives, and had raced stock cars and done stunt driving. He lived in a cabin in the woods and considered himself a modern-day mountain-man with a badge who believed "God and Family First, Law and Order Second," and reportedly had twin tattoos—one on either bicep—to prove it.

The FBI did a dump on Cady's home phone, which showed an interesting (to me) cluster of calls to a Dr. Robert Atkinson, OB-Gyn, of Belfast. She'd called his office dozens of times and had even called him at home several others. I had to wonder if something personal, not medical, had been going on. Meanwhile, Cady had made no calls to any ophthalmologists, internists, or cancer specialists.

She'd also taken out a life insurance policy on Earl a few days before the bank robbery. The beneficiary was someone named Amanda Hitchcock (Cady's sister Amanda?) and the policy was good for half a million dollars. The FBI immediately began trying to track down this Amanda Hitchcock.

The third day after the murders was sunny yet cold and I had a training session with a couple of pit bulls named Fuji and Nessie—good doggies with sweet dispositions (like most pit bulls) but with spotty recalls, which means they didn't always come when called. Luckily, they loved to jump up, which can increase the reliability of almost any dog's recall. Within twenty minutes of getting them to chase me around and jump on me, their recalls had improved by almost 50 percent.

When I got back to the kennel, Frankie my black-and-white English field setter, and Hooch, my dog de Bordeaux, jumped around the office, but not on me (they're only allowed to do that on command); they were very happy to see me. Then D'Linda, Mrs. Murtaugh's assistant groomer, told me that a woman had come by earlier to pick up Charley.

"Cady Clark's poodle? You didn't *let* her, did you?"

"Yeah. She said she was the owner's sister, Amanda."

"D'Linda!" I yelled; Frankie thumped his tail nervously against the front counter.

"Don't yell at me, Jack. She had proof."

"Sorry, Frankie. What kind of proof?"

"An affidavit. Plus, she had a cop with her."

"A cop? What was his name?"

"I don't know. He was a state trooper."

"He didn't tell you his name?"

"No."

"Did you see his name tag?"

"I don't know. I don't think he was wearing one."

"Jesus, D'Linda. Was he in a state police car?"

"No. He came in *her* car."

"Oh, this is just great." I resisted an impulse to shout at her again. "What did this woman look like?"

She gave me a description that could have been Cady Clark except she had brown eyes and brown hair, and dark skin.

"How dark?"

"I don't know. Like she's part Asian or something."

"Did she have a scar on her left cheek?"

"No. She had perfect skin. And I'm not a total idiot," she said, handing me a slip of paper and a legal document. "Here's the affidavit. Plus, I made her leave her address and phone number."

I took the slip of paper to the phone and dialed it. I got a recording saying the number I had reached was no longer in service. D'Linda hovered while I made the call.

When I hung up she said, "Can I go back to work now? I was in the middle of doing Susie Q."

"No, get out; you're fired," I wanted to say, but grumped and told her that she could go back and finish work on the Maltese but that she was never to do anything like this ever again.

"Okay, I get it."

"I don't think you do." I picked up the phone to call Sinclair and told her, "That woman may be the only lead we have to solving a couple of homicides."

"How was I supposed to know that?"

"D'Linda, just go finish Susie Q, okay? I'm sorry I yelled at you."

"Okay. Jeez Louise."

I told Sinclair what had happened with the dog and the sister. He said he'd have someone look into the address, and that he'd come out himself to pick up the affidavit and show Delgado's picture to D'Linda, to find out if he was the cop Cady's sister Amanda had brought to the kennel with her.

He arrived an hour later, showed D'Linda a photo of Mike Delgado, gray hair, balding, and a face that was going pouchy, but she said she couldn't tell if it was the same man or not.

"It *looks* like him, but I'm just not sure."

Then he showed her a Polaroid of Cady Clark that he'd taken at the motel. She said that the woman who'd come to pick up Charley looked similar to the one in the Polaroid, but that it definitely wasn't the same one.

"She had dark hair and eyes," she said. "And no scar."

He thanked D'Linda and she went back to work brushing Saki, a black-and-white akita.

I gave Sinclair the affidavit and pointed out that the name and signature were those of Amanda Hitchcock, which might be Cady's sister Amanda.

He said the state police and the FBI's search hadn't found anyone named Amanda Hitchcock yet. "But we'll keep on it, obviously. And what's the disappointed face for, Jack? Did you like the yappy little dog that much?"

"Who? Sir Barksalot? Not really."

"Don't let him kid you," D'Linda said from the grooming room, now brushing out Saki's undercoat. "It takes him about two seconds to fall in love with *any* dog."

"That's beside the point," I snapped at her.

"What interests me about this girl," I told Jamie while she stood in pajamas, brushing her teeth that night, "is how there's always a bit of truth spersed among her lies."

"Spersed?" She rinsed, spit in the sink, and said, "There's no such word, Jack."

"I know. It's my own back-derivation of *inter*-spersed. It means scattered."

"Maybe so, but it makes you sound like an idiot." She dried her mouth on the sleeve of my terry cloth robe, which was hanging on the back of the bathroom door.

"Honey, could you do that on a towel, next time?"

"Yeah, whatever."

"Anyway," I said, putting the cap back on the tube of toothpaste, "she tells me this sad background story about Earl, for what purpose I can't quite figure, when she could've kept quiet about it or made up a complete fabrication. Some pathological liars are like that, I guess. They can't tell the whole truth about anything, but they can't shut up about things either. And they can't help giving themselves away a little by mixing the truth in with the lies."

She pushed past me through the door to the bedroom. "Why do I get the feeling that you kind of like her?"

"Cady? She's a cold-blooded, sociopathic killer. At least I think she is. And I have a bad feeling that what happened at the motel wasn't her first murder."

"Really? But . . ." She got under the covers and Frankie, who was lying next to the pillows, moved to the foot of the bed. (Hooch has to sleep in the kennel; he snores.) Jamie patted the mattress for me to come join her "I still think you sort of like her, even if she is a serial killer."

"I just find her intriguing, psychologically speaking," I said, getting in next to her. "And she's not a serial killer, honey. There's a huge difference between the psychopathology of a serial killer and that of a sociopath."

"What is it?"

"You really want to talk about this before bed?"

"Why not?" she asked.

"It'll give you bad dreams."

"Not if I'm sleeping next to you it won't."

"Okay." I explained that a sociopath lacks empathy for others and has no conscience. They'll usually only kill someone if that person stands in the way of a goal they have. They don't have a compulsive *need* to do it.

"A serial killer, on the other hand, knows that what they're doing is wrong; they just don't care, they *have* to kill in order to satisfy their sickness. They're usually the victims of childhood abuse or suffer some kind of neurological damage during a development phase. They can't feel sexual pleasure unless it's strongly associated with extreme violence against others. For them killing is intensely pleasurable. For a sociopath it's more of an annoyance than anything."

She shuddered and clutched me tight.

"I told you you'd get bad dreams."

"I'll be okay. So I guess if Cady Clark is a sociopath, then someone must've gotten in her way at some point."

"Right." I turned off the lamp. "And although she supposedly needs some kind of surgery—for cancer or an eye operation—the only phone calls she made to any doctors in the last six months were to an obstetrician."

"So?"

"So? Dozens of phone calls, even to his home?"

"Ohhh."

"Yeah, 'oh'. You have to read the little clues that are spersed among the mundane data."

"There you go again, Jack. The word is *inter*—"

"I know. That time it was just to annoy you. Besides, interspersed means 'scattered among,' but you never hear anyone say 'the clues were interspersed the mundane details.'"

"Maybe so, but spersed is not a word."

"Well, it *should* be. Anyway, I've got an appointment tomorrow afternoon to talk to Dr. Atkinson to see if he and Cady Clark were having an affair or something."

"Good idea." She yawned and put her head on my shoulder, then laughed softly. "I wish I could be there to see you in the stirrups. One word of advice, though, honey . . ."

I shook my head. "What's that?"

"Make sure he warms up the speculum before he uses it."

"Oh, that's cute."

"Though I can't imagine where he'd *put* it!"

"Yeah, that's *very* cute," I said, but she was laughing too hard to hear me, so I kissed her till she shut up (though a few of her giggles got spersed amongst my kisses).

Frankie just grunted and thumped his tail. Then—when things got more enthusiastic—he jumped off the bed and curled up by the door.

It poured buckets the next day, which made life at the kennel work-intensive. I spent two hours mudding around with the dogs in the play yard, a fenced-in area downhill from the kennel building, roughly the size of the infield at Fenway Park. I always give them two hour-long play sessions: one in the morning and one in the afternoon. When it rains you have to hose them down afterward then dry them off with a towel. Mrs. Murtaugh wasn't much help since her hip always acts up when it rains. And D'Linda had an emergency involving a sister-in-law's car that was stuck in the mud somewhere.

Jamie called around three and said she wanted to go over some things with me at the morgue, so I drove up to Augusta before making the trip to Dr. Atkinson's office in Belfast.

I came into the autopsy room just as she was speaking into a microphone: "The blood also showed elevated levels of creatine kinase MB—oh, hi, honey." She switched off the recorder. "I didn't know you were here."

"Yeah," I said, "Keith let me in."

She laughed. "You mean Kenneth?"

"Okay, Kenneth. You know, Dr. Unger."

"Udall," she said, laughing some more. (I can never keep the names of her friends or co-workers straight.)

I said, "So what was that you were just saying?"

"Hmm? Oh. The blood work on the bank guard came back. He wasn't killed by a bullet. He had a heart attack."

"Really? How can you be sure?"

"First of all, it's what I do," she said. "Secondly, the bullet caused very little damage. It didn't hit any major arteries or internal organs. Secondly, there are certain substances in the bloodstream that prove definitively that the victim was having a cardiac event at the time of death."

"Okay," I took a seat on a metal stool. "What are they?"

"Troponin, a protein found in the heart muscles."

"Oh, yeah. I remember that from my first year at Harvard Medical School." (I'd dropped out after my mother committed suicide during my second

year.) I said, "Troponin shows up in the blood because during a heart attack it leaks out of the heart
cells and into the bloodstream."

"That's right, Jack. Very good. Then there's creatine kinase MB, which is an isoenzyme that—"

"Okay," I put my hands up. "I believe you. Still,
couldn't the robbery have caused the heart attack?"

"Well, I suppose it could be *argued* that's what
happened, but I'm a medical examiner, not a DA."

"I guess it doesn't matter much, since Joe Bruno's
the one who shot him and he's dead." I paused. "It
makes you think about this guy, Earl, though. He
was ready to protect his cousin by confessing to a
crime he didn't commit."

"Yeah, you almost have to admire someone like
that."

"Yeah," I shook my head, "almost. So, how's he
doing?"

"Earl? He's stable but guarded. Oh, and forensics found some skin cells under Joe Bruno's fingernails, along with pyroxylin, which is a form of
nitrocellulose."

"Nitrocellulose? Isn't that guncotton?"

"Sort of," she smiled. "I'm surprised you know
that."

I shrugged. "If I recall, I got an A in my organic
chemistry classes in college. Plus, I was a cop for fifteen years so anything that explodes, I remember."

"Good point. And from what *I* understand, you
got an A in all your college courses." Then she explained the difference between pyroxylin, or *tetra-
nitrate*, which is what's called collodion (and is

safe), and *hexa*nitrate, which is guncotton (and explodes easily).

"Collodion sounds familiar; what's it used for?"

"Making photographic emulsions. It also has surgical applications as an adhesive to close small wounds and hold surgical dressings. In an emergency situation it can even be used in place of surgical gloves."

"Hmmm. So maybe that's how it got under his fingernails? He was using it to hide his fingerprints?"

"It's unlikely. There would have been a lot more of it then just the one little speck we found."

"Okay." I stood up. "I'm going to the gynecologist's. I know there's another use for this collodion stuff, but I just can't put my finger on what it is right now." I yawned.

"You look tired."

"I'll be all right. I've just had a long day."

"Too tired to come to yoga class with me later?"

"No, I love going to your yoga class; it energizes and relaxes me. It just depends on how things go with Atkinson."

"Okay. And when you see him, remember what I said."

"I know. Have him warm up the speculum. Hah-hah."

He was a shortish, slender, ugly, crook-toothed man with thinning brown hair and a sparse red beard. He said good night to a thickset office nurse and invited me into his private digs in the back. There were no stirrups or specula visible.

He nodded me to a chair as he hung up his

smock. Then he sat behind his desk, and said, "So, how can I help you?"

I settled in. "I'm looking for information about a young woman named Cady Clark. I think she may have been a patient of yours?"

He gave a shake of the head with a tired smile attached. "I can't discuss my patients with you. But even if I could—" He stopped himself. "Cady Clark. That name sounds familiar."

"So she *was* a patient."

He shook his head. "No, I think I recognize the name from something I heard recently on the news."

I nodded and told him about the bank robbery and the motel shooting.

"Oh. That's terrible." His face got busy with thought. "But why would you think she was one of my patients?"

I told him about the phone records.

The barest shadow of a glint formed in his eyes. He'd just realized or decided something. His face got busy again, made a stab at inscrutable, and finally settled on mild puzzlement. "All right," he said finally, "so she may have called here. I still don't remember the name."

"Really? Even though she made dozens of phone calls to your office, even to your home?"

He cogitated. "Sorry."

"Uh-huh." I reached in my jacket for a copy of the Polaroid Sinclair had taken of Cady at the motel. I tossed it onto the desk. "Maybe this will refresh your memory."

He picked up the photo and his face changed to

what seemed like genuine surprise. "Yes. I know her."

"So, she was a patient?"

"Yes." He looked up. "Her name is Amanda Hitchcock."

"Huh. What can you tell me about her?"

His face changed again. He said, "Not much. Of course, I can't divulge the medical reasons for her office visits, and other than that . . ." He stopped and looked at the photo again. "So she's wanted in a homicide investigation?"

I said she was, then added that she'd apparently been using her sister's name when she'd seen him as a patient.

"I see. Would knowing something about her medical history help your investigation?"

"It might." I paused then gave him a level stare. "Did the two of you have a private or personal thing going?"

He met my stare. "No," he said and stood up.

"Then why the phone calls to your home?"

"Some patients are very . . . needy. Look, I've had a long day and could use a cup of coffee. Would you like some?"

I looked over at the window. Thick drops splattered against the glass then merged and turned to flat waves, pulled downward by gravity. I felt pulled down by gravity myself.

"Sure," I said, with a yawn. "I take mine black."

"Fine. And I take mine with a splash of Irish whiskey."

"I like your way better. Especially on a rainy night."

He smiled again, went to a filing cabinet, got out a folder, opened it, placed it on the desk, and said, "The coffee machine's in the other room." Then he left me alone.

I looked at the file, as he'd wanted me to, and found that Amanda Hitchcock had had three appointments with the good doctor: one for a pregnancy exam, one for an abortion, and a final one for a tubal ligation. All three took place within three month's time.

I had just settled back in my chair when Atkinson returned with our high-octane coffee. He handed me my cup, sat down at the desk, and looked at me.

He seemed to be waiting for me to take a sip, so I did.

"Nice," I said, feeling relaxed by the whiskey.

"Yes, it is nice."

He sipped from his cup, which had a logo on it that said, "First, Do No Harm." I liked that. I took another sip of coffee. The second one made me feel a little sleepy.

Sleepy? I'd had a hard day, but not hard enough to want to curl up and take a nap right there in the man's office.

I looked down at my cup, then up at Atkinson.

"Is anything the matter?" he asked.

"I think you put too mush wh'skey in my drink."

"No," he said, as if from far away, "I simply gave you a mild sedative to help you relax."

The cup slipped from my hand as I tried to stand up. "But I don' wanna relax." I sat back down—or my body did.

"Here's the thing," he said sadly. "I did have an

affair with Amanda. I couldn't help myself. You've seen what she looks like. And a man like me?" His eyes filled with desperation. "I mean, I lost my mind! I love my wife and I was going crazy over this situation with Amanda, but she's a—a very difficult girl." His hands trembled as he took a sip of coffee. "She had such sexual control over me that I—I couldn't think straight, I couldn't work, I couldn't do anything but wait to see her or—or hear from her every day."

I nodded dumbly.

"This went on for—I don't know—about three weeks, maybe more, maybe less. It was like an addiction." Another sip from trembling hands. "Then one night she tells me she needs money for eye surgery. Apparently when she injured her cheek and got that scar she also detached the retina."

I struggled to keep my eyes and ears open.

"I'm not a rich man, Mr. Field! I have a small practice in a small town in a rural state. I explained this to her and she became furious. She threatened to tell my wife about us. She even threatened to *kill* Susanne if I didn't—"

A door opened behind me and I got a whiff of citrus and oak moss. Cady Clark came around where I sat, parked one lovely hip on the edge of the desk, and stared at me. She was wearing her usual Levi's and V-neck sweater, this one a royal blue, and she looked both beautiful and dangerous. Over her shoulder she said, "That's enough, Robert."

The doctor nodded and put his head in his hands.

"Did you give him enough to kill him?" she

asked, without emotion and without taking her eyes off me.

"No," he sighed. "Just to knock him out. I'm a doctor, remember? You'll have to do the rest yourself."

"Then why is he still awake?" Her mouth was petulant, like a spoiled child's.

Atkinson lifted his head. "He has too much strength of mind, I guess. More than *I* do, anyway."

"Don' sell you'se'f short, doc," I said. "You went to med'cal school, right?"

"Yes." He looked me square in the eye.

"That takes some kin' willpow'r."

"That's true." A tear of hope sprang up in his eye.

Cady's face flushed red with anger. "Stop it!" she commanded. "You two stop talking to each other!"

"Sorry," said Atkinson. Then he stood up tiredly, turned around, and did something we couldn't see.

Cady kept her eyes on me but said to him, "*Now* what are you doing?"

"You want him to pass out quicker, don't you?"

"Good," she said, smiling and in control. "That's good."

"So," I muttered into my chest. "Gonna kill me too?"

"Too? Who says I ever killed *any*one, Jack?"

"You kil't Bruno. You *tried* kill Earl."

She shushed me. "That was a matter of necessity."

Atkinson came up behind her; his face set now. "Yes," he said. "And so is this." Before she could turn, he wrapped his left arm around her neck and held a sterile gauze pad to her nose with his right. She struggled, then her head went limp, her eyes turned up, showing the whites, and her legs no longer held. The good doctor let her fall gently to the floor. "You've become a liability, sweetheart," he told her inert form sadly.

"So?" I said.

He drew his gaze upward. "What?"

"You said she's a li'bility, but you're d'ctor, right?"

"Yeah, so?" His eyes were dead, his face flat.

"So, don' you have li'bility insur'nce?"

"That's funny," he said tonelessly.

I thought it was. I *must* have. I started to laugh. But somewhere in the middle of laughing I fell asleep.

I woke up to the smell of gasoline and vulcanized rubber, and the sound of tires rolling swiftly on pavement. I opened my eyes but could see only darkness. I was lying on my side and felt myself being bounced around inside an enclosed space. I was still a little groggy so it took me a moment to realize I was in the trunk of a moving car. The rain was pelting against the roof in hard, staccato bursts, like machine gun fire. It took awhile longer to figure out that I was bound hand and foot with what felt like dental floss (probably surgical sutures) and that my arms were twisted painfully behind my back. I also felt a burning pain coming from my forehead. I'd probably hit it on Atkinson's desk as I fell.

I thought of what Cady had said when she'd wanted me to tie up Earl—"tight but not too tight"—and hoped Atkinson had followed the same dictum with me. I tested the flex in my wrist bindings and felt enough give to try a little yoga maneuver. I moved around, found I had a bit of space to do so, and got the impression that I was in the trunk of a luxury car. Then, with a lot of grunting and straining and a little tearing of my shoulder ligaments, I got my hands under my feet, then in front of me. My wrists were searing with pain from where the ligatures dug into my flesh, but at least I now had my hands where I could do things with them.

I didn't know what kind of plans Atkinson had for the rest of my evening, but was disinclined to cooperate with them, whatever they were, so I felt around for something to cut the sutures with. There had to be some sort of sharp edge inside the trunk—a broken weld, a cracked section of the steel reinforcing that hadn't been riveted tight enough, the edge of the spare tire holder. I couldn't find anything.

I thought of my keys, but it's easier to rub your wrists against something solid than it is to try to rub a set of keys against the bindings while your wrists are tied. But thinking of the keys made me think of the lock, which I hadn't felt around for yet. I did and my fingers found a good spot where the casing was attached to the back part of the lid. It wasn't much, just a sharp lip of metal, but I began pulling the sutures against it over and over, grunting and sweating.

The car kept moving and I was periodically thrown one way or another as the driver occasionally took a curve too fast. Each time it happened I added another bruise to my collection but immediately got back to work on my wrist binding.

I finally freed my hands and as soon as I did the car stopped, just stopped dead. I was worried that they'd somehow found out that I'd gotten free and were going to come back and retie me, or worse. Over the rain, which sounded pleasant now that we were no longer moving, I heard some doors open and shut, footsteps, muffled voices arguing, then doors again, another car started, there was a pause, and we started moving again, fast.

Then faster.

Then faster and faster and faster.

We were really flying when the car swerved hard as hell to the left, slamming me against the right wall. There was a wet *skrish* of tires slipping on rainy concrete. I buttressed my arms and legs on all sides of the trunk. Then came the impact of the crash, which shook me like a penny in a shake can, despite my bracing. Then, when that was over, there was a moment of utter nothingness. Things went into slow motion; with no sensation except the whine of the engine, the slow, dull spatter of rain on the roof of the trunk, and a sickly feeling of being in an elevator that's falling a bit too fast. Then gradually came the sound of swiftly moving water, a lot of water. The sound got nearer and nearer as we fell farther.

We hit the river, which bounced me hard against the roof of the trunk, popped it open, and threw me again, sideways, head first against a sharp edge of the metal molding.

It was dark where we were—out in the middle of the river—but nowhere near as dark as it had been inside the trunk. Above me I saw the outline of a bridge, with a steel railing smashed and twisted outward. I felt warm blood coursing down my forehead mixed with the cold sting of rain on my face and hands. The smells of gasoline and rubber were mixed with the sudden, musky fish/algae smell of river water.

The car was rocking and bobbing. We were sinking, but we were also being carried along by the current. I grabbed the back edge of the trunk to push myself over the side and into the river when the explosion came—a sharp, hard, sick-making concussion, every cell in your body being stunned repeatedly by multiple G-force waves, thrusting you in all directions at once. Then came the smell of gasoline flames mixed with the stench of burning flesh (not mine, thankfully), and more heat than I'd ever known. The impact threw me high into the air and the searing blaze of the explosion was instantly replaced by freezing cold as I was plunged deep, deep underwater and was caught in the river's current.

I tried swimming but my ankles were still bound with the sutures and my arms were dead, too numb to move. I flailed around for a while, trying to find the surface, to get some air into my lungs, but I was frozen, paralyzed, helpless.

I let the current carry me and I fell asleep again.

The next thing I remember was the trooper's face—framed by his dark, shiny rain hood—as he leaned

over me dripping water on my face and saying
something I couldn't make out.

"What?" I said. "Ears . . . ringing . . ."

He repeated whatever it was he'd said, louder.

I still couldn't hear him and said so.

Finally he screamed, "Are you all right, sir?"

I nodded, looked around. I was on my back
among some rocks and gravel at a bend in the river,
a couple hundred yards downstream from the
bridge, where black figures now strode purpose-
fully, arms waving, between the flares and flashing
colored lights of parked cruisers. On the river, near
the half-submerged wreck, a police boat hovered,
its spotlight stabbing vainly at the dark gloss of
moving water.

"C-c-cold," I said to the trooper. "Head h-h-
hurts."

"I've got someone bringing down a blanket and
some hot coffee," he screamed. "Just hang in, sir."

"Ok-k-kay. C-c-call Dr. Cutter."

"Who?" he yelled, his lips bent to my ear.

"State Medic-cal Examin-n-ner," I explained.

"She's probably on her way, sir," he shouted. "We
think there are a couple bodies out there in the car."

"Serves them right. They can't drive worth sh-sh-
sh . . ."

"What do you want me to tell Dr. Cutter?"

"Tell her it's Jack. I'm Jack. My name is Jack."

"Okay, Jack; you got it. Anything else?"

"Yeah. Tell her I want my mommy."

"Say again? You want your *money*?"

I didn't repeat it; I'd run low on vivacity. Besides,

just having uttered the words was comfort enough. I knew that Jamie would come soon and take care of me. So I smiled, closed my eyes, and went back to sleep again.

I spent three days at Eastern Maine Medical Center in Bangor due to a mild concussion and a not-so-mild case of hypothermia. No bones were broken, unless you count a tiny radiating skull fracture where I'd banged my head hard, twice. The injury caused some minor intracranial bleeding, so I was stuck in bed until the doctors could see if it stopped on its own (with the help of steroids) or if they had to operate.

While I was undergoing CT scans, the murder case went on without me. So did life at the kennel, though my foster son, Leon, a black teenager from Harlem, and my kennel manager Farrell Woods, a reformed pot dealer, took care of things.

Jamie came when she could, which was several times a day and for long hours at night, when she also brought Frankie and Hooch. They're licensed therapy dogs so they're used to hospital visits and were happy to see me, though they wanted to jump up onto the bed. Jamie, between holding my hand and acting worried, told me what she and the state police were able to figure out about the case.

The car was a Cadillac Eldorado, registered to Robert Atkinson. Only one body was found, a young woman's. She was in the passenger seat and had been badly burned in the explosion. Still, Jamie was able to determine that she was in her early twenties, with the same basic body type as Cady Clark, and that she'd had an abortion and a tubal ligation.

A suicide message was found on the computer in Atkinson's office. It read: "Jack Field knows the truth, now we all have to die." The incident was tagged as a murder/suicide, with me added on as an attempted murder.

"If the message wasn't signed," I told Jamie, "it may not be authentic. What time did the crash take place?"

"Around one in the morning."

"Wow. And I got to his office about five. That's eight hours. I'm lucky it took so long for him to get his courage up or the stuff he put in my coffee wouldn't have worn off."

"I know. You barely made it out alive as it is."

The police found that the guardrail on the bridge had been tampered with, enabling the car to easily break through.

They kept looking for Atkinson's body, which they assumed had been carried down the Belfast River and out to sea. (The river's real name is the Passagassawakeag, but I always refer to it as the Belfast—I think you can figure out why.)

The FBI discovered that a New Jersey girl named Cady Clark had disappeared in New York City five years earlier, when she was seventeen, and had never been heard from again. Her Social Security number was now being used by the Cady Clark in our case. Some New Jersey State Police troopers showed the girl's parents a photograph of our "Cady," and they said they'd never seen her before.

Our Cady's skin cells, the ones that were found under Joe Bruno's fingernails, were too degraded to provide a useful DNA sample to see if it matched the DNA of the charred corpse from the car. (That was another problem, getting viable DNA from a charred corpse.) So they took a sample of the epithelials (sloughed-off skin cells) from the duct tape in the motel room, then extracted a molar from the victim in the car to get mitochondrial DNA, or mtDNA, from the dental pulp. MtDNA is inherited directly from the mother. It can't be used to prove an exact match between two samples, only that the two samples came from the same maternal line, but it was *some*thing.

The FBI lab was doing the tests, but they had a serious backlog and there were no other labs available that work with mtDNA, so we had to wait awhile for the results. Still, as things stood, all the evidence seemed to point to it being the phony Cady Clark's body that was found in the wreck.

The FBI got tons of fingerprints from her house, her car, her office, etc., but she wasn't in the system. She'd worked as a paralegal, or so she'd told me. That turned out to be one of the few true things she *did* tell me. And oddly enough, the law office where she worked was right across the street from the bank that was robbed; just another in a long string of coincidences.

The feds interviewed her co-workers, neighbors, employees at the places she shopped, had her dry cleaning done, etc., and though none of these people had ever met her sister Amanda, more than a few of them had heard her talk about the woman, and not in the most glowing terms.

There were no records of anyone named Amanda Hitchcock living anywhere in Maine or surrounding areas.

I learned all this between visits to radiology during my first two days recuperating. Meanwhile the press had decided that I was either a hero or a chump. Personally, I didn't feel like much of a hero: a survivor, sure, but not a hero. I *did* feel like a chump though and—as I fell asleep my last night in the hospital—I decided that if I had to do it over, I wouldn't have gone to Dr. Atkinson's office alone. That had been a freshman move. Really dumb.

A hospital is mostly silent at night. And dark. You might hear the faint, steady beep of a heart monitor from another room, or some muffled footsteps passing down the hall, or the soft murmur of voices and a few strains of "light" music from an FM radio at the nurse's station. That's all. So when I woke up suddenly from a deep sleep, my last night at EMMC, I knew something was wrong.

The hairs on my arms and the back of my neck tingled as I listened carefully for any sound that was out of place.

Nothing happened; no sounds were made. I noticed I was holding my breath and started breathing again through my nose, very soft and slow. I tried to play back in my mind the sounds that had awakened me.

The door to my room had been left ajar, and I had a dim recollection of a startled female voice crying out from somewhere down the hall, and then the soft, distant thump of a body falling. Now, nothing.

Then, I heard the squeak of a leather shoe in the hall. I could just faintly hear it coming slowly toward my room.

Squeak . . . silence . . . *squeak* . . . silence . . .

Coming closer and closer.

I slid out of bed, put some pillows under the blanket to make it look like I was still sleeping, then looked around in the dim light for a weapon. The only thing I could find was a shiny bedpan, sitting needlessly on the chair by my bed. I picked it up, holding it by the narrow end, tiptoed to the bathroom, and waited.

The squeaking sound got to my door then stopped.

The door creaked open, there was a pause, then it closed with a soft click. The squeaking shoe started up again, this time within inches of where I stood.

I held my breath as a dark figure slowly passed my line of sight. He was about my height (I'm 6'1"). He was wearing a state police uniform, and had a gun drawn, holding it like cops do, with both hands. It looked to be a small caliber revolver.

He stopped just a few steps past the bathroom door, aimed the gun, and shot at the bed, three times. In the middle of his third shot I sprung through the door and, using both hands, hit him as hard as I could across the back of his head.

He groaned, sagged, the gun flew out of his hand; he went down. I stepped forward—in bare feet, wearing nothing but my boxer briefs and a hospital gown—and tried to hit him again, but he twisted away then tackled me awkwardly at the knees.

I made another swing, but it glanced harmlessly off his shoulder. He was strong, built like an old football player, and used his weight advantage to tip me over, banging my head against the wall.

We both stood up slowly, breathing hard, our heads bleeding, neither one sure yet what to do with the other.

As I stood there I caught a good glimpse of his face in the dim light. He had gray balding hair and a grim face, sallow and going pouchy. I was looking at Mike Delgado.

Before he could try for the gun, which had skittered under the bed, we heard the sound of faltering footsteps and anxious voices coming from the hall, and, in the distance, the wail of approaching sirens.

"Count yourself lucky this time, Field," he panted.

"I count myself lucky *all* the time, Mike," I said, but the words floated, as if coming through layers of cotton.

I teetered, swayed.

Delgado smiled an evil smile and ran past me to the door as I passed out. Good, I remember thinking as I hit the floor, at least he left his gun behind; that's evidence.

After Delgado got away, and I was revived by a night nurse (not the one he'd sapped), they put an armed guard on my door. The next day brought more trips to radiology, more CT scans, more worried visits from Jamie. After a full day of this, I was finally pronounced fit for civilian life. I left for home with a clean bill of health, an armed FBI agent on my property, and a large scab on my forehead that gradually turned into a small white scar that I eventually grew fond and a little proud of. Michael Delgado was still at large.

I made cold curried chicken for dinner that night (with golden raisins, apples, and cashews), along with Cajun red beans and rice, and homemade French onion soup. What can I tell you; I had cravings that didn't necessarily go together, at least not ordinarily. (In my defense, I'd been whacked on the head numerous times in the previous three or four days.)

Jamie and I drank a cold, dry viognier that went well with the curry and the beans and rice, yet didn't clash with the cognac in the soup. Leon drank Pepsi.

"So, what's your next move?" Jamie asked.

"I guess I'll call Kelso and see if he can track down Delgado with his computer." Lou Kelso is a friend from my days on the NYPD. He was a prosecutor for the Manhattan DA's office and is now a private investigator, though he doesn't need the money. He recently won a lawsuit against the estate of a former client—a very *rich* client—so he's on easy street.

"Good," she said. "Maybe he can come up with something the cops and the FBI can't that'll stop

Delgado once and for all. It's nice, though, that the FBI is keeping an eye on you and the house. Oh, I forgot to mention; Dr. Atkinson's corpse was found floating off Eggemoggin Reach this afternoon."

"Um," Leon said, "it's dinner? No morgue talk, please?"

"Sorry," said Jamie, sipping her soup.

"Are they sure it's Atkinson?" I asked.

"Pretty sure," she said. "God, this soup is delicious. And who would've thought these three dishes would go together? Anyway, I'll know more after I perform the autopsy tomorrow. The body is pretty badly decomposed."

Leon said, "Jamie!"

"Sorry."

I said, "I make it with Bermuda onions."

"Well, it's really good."

"Thanks. You want some more?"

We engaged in culinary conversation until Leon and Magee (his wheaten mix) had gone back to his quarters in the guest cottage, a converted carriage house between my Victorian two-story and the kennel, which was once a dairy barn.

When dinner was over I called Kelso and gave him the story. After he'd asked about my current health and my prospects for it continuing, he made an interesting comment:

"How sure are you that this client of yours is really the fried corpse they found in the car?"

"Former client," I said.

"Fine, 'former client.' Maybe it was her sister."

"You could be right. If she really *has* a sister."

"In the meantime, I'll keep hacking into any database I can to locate Delgado, and also try to find out what the connection is between your former client, whoever she is, and the real Cady Clark."

The next day Earl came out of his coma and one of the first things he wanted to do was talk to me.

So I went to Rockland Memorial in Glen Cove, where a nurse with a crisp manner told me he'd suffered some brain damage and short-term memory loss because of the shooting. The bullet had damaged his corpus callosum, which divides the right and left hemispheres of the brain.

She had me sign a visitor's log at the nurse's station, then took me to a room where Earl was wrapped in cheap hospital sheets, handcuffed to the bed, and had a morphine drip in his arm and a breathing tube jammed up his nose. Though he wasn't very tall, his bony feet stuck out of the sheets at the bottom of the bed.

Earl didn't say anything to the nurse as she brought me in; he just nodded.

She cleared what was left of breakfast off the meal tray, pulled it back to the wall, and left. I found a chair next to the bed, pulled it out, sat down, holding a file folder in one hand, and said, "So, what's on your mind?"

"I guess I should apologize for the crack I made about putting a bullet in your brainpan," he said, his lips and tongue straining to form each word, like an idiot or a stroke victim.

I nodded. "You mean since Cady put a bullet in *your* brainpan you feel bad about threatening to do that to *me*?"

"Screw that," he said. "Cady didn't shoot me."

"Really? You remember how it happened? I thought you—"

"No, I don't remember, but I know she wouldn'ta done it."

"Uh-huh."

"Anyway, I just wanted you to know she had nothin' to do with the robbery or whatever happened at the motel."

"Ballistics tells a different story about the motel."

He shrugged and his eyes withdrew. "Then they got it wrong," he said. "And the bank job was all Delgado. He was the wheel man and the one who held the dough after."

That fit. I said, "So Cady never mentioned the bank? That it was right across the street from where she worked?" He shook his head. "Really? Because we got her phone records from work and know she called you at least a dozen times before the robbery. You're saying she never dropped a casual mention of the exact time the armored car showed up each week, or that the bank guard had a heart condition, or that she needed money for her eye operation?"

He thought it over. "It don't matter what she said to me, she wasn't in on it. She didn't even know about it."

"Right. Then why did she schedule a dog training session with me at the exact time she knew you'd be arriving, fresh from the bank, with money for her surgery?"

"She didn't know I was comin'," he said, then struggled to take a breath. "That was just a, a, a accident."

"I don't think so, Earl. Maybe she thought I'd have a gun with me and that I might use it on you, I don't know. But I *do* know it wasn't an accident. She wanted you dead, just like she did at the motel in Wiscasset."

His eyes struggled to hold mine. "That ain't true."

"Really? But which makes more sense, that Cady shot both of you or that you shot your cousin, who you look up to?"

"I don't care what you say."

"Okay, then," I said, taking the life insurance policy out of the folder and handing it to him. "Explain this."

"What is it?"

I told him what it was and when it had been made out.

He looked it over briefly, muttering, "This can't be real, this is a forgery," and shaking his head.

But as he handed the document back to me a brief sputter of heartrending emotions sparked and died in his sad, lizardlike eyes, and I could tell that he finally knew the truth.

I wanted to say, "What did you think, you moron? That a girl like that was really going to fall for a reptile like you?" but held my tongue. I'm not saying I felt sorry for him, but he certainly looked pathetic.

"What diff'r'nce does all this make if she's dead?"

"True." He kind of had me there. "But we need to find Cady's sister, Amanda, Earl. And we need to find Mike Delgado. Do you know how to find them?

He shook his head sadly. "But if anyone's the kind of scheming bitch you think Cady is, it'd be Amanda, not her."

"Good. That's good, Earl. What do you know about her?"

"Amanda? Nothin'. Just what Cady told me. She's been ruining Cady's life ever since they was kids."

I doubted that. I wondered what Amanda Hitchcock was *really* like and if Cady hadn't been the one ruining *her* life. Or maybe Kelso was right. Maybe Amanda had been the one to die in the explosion in the river and Cady Clark—or whatever her real name was—was still out there, planning trouble for more innocent victims—or half-innocent victims like Earl and Amanda Hitchcock.

I put the insurance policy in the folder. "Anyway, thanks for the conversation. I've got dogs to get back to."

"You're wrong about her, Mr. Field," he said, but the brimming look in his eyes told a different story.

That afternoon I was scraping the dried residue of Hooch's drool off the kitchen floor with a putty knife (that stuff is impossible to get rid of), when Kelso called.

He'd found out a few things:

A few months after the real Cady Clark disappeared, a former Belfast PD detective was hired by the missing girl's family to find her whereabouts. His name was Mike Delgado.

"What? Why would a New Jersey family contact Delgado?"

"They wouldn't. He contacted *them*. He spent a few months looking into it, then they never heard from him again.

"But get this," he said, "there was another teenager, this one was from Queens, who went missing around the same time. Her name was Janet Slemboski. Both girls were enrolled in an acting school in New York. They had an acting class together, plus a tap class, and a theatrical makeup class."

"You think this Janet Slemboski could be the real identity of the girl in our case?"

"I do. I glommed an 8-by-10 from the school and she looks similar to the girl in the Polaroid you faxed me. The thing is, a girl's face can change quite a bit from the time she's sixteen to when she's twenty-two. Plus, a lot of these girls are like doppelgängers of each other. But get this: the real Cady Clark had just won a two-year scholarship—with a bit part on a soap opera attached—the day before she disappeared."

"Sounds like you could be on to something. If Slembaski felt the scholarship and soap part should have been hers, she might've *made* Cady Clark disappear, right?"

"It's a good possibility."

"Sounds like she's our guy."

"Yeah," he said, "except for one thing: as far as I can tell Janet Slemboski doesn't have a sister."

I thought it over. "That's moot since no one around here except D'Linda has ever *seen* Cady

Clark's supposed sister. Hell, maybe the woman D'Linda saw was actually Janet Slemboski pretending to be Amanda Hitchcock." I stopped. "She could've worn a wig and dark makeup and contact lenses, I guess, but how could she have gotten rid of her scar?"

"You got me. She *did* take a theatrical makeup class."

"A fake scar? Maybe."

"Meanwhile, Slemboski's parents are dead, so we can't ask them if she's your Cady Clark, or get a DNA sample from them. And I'm having trouble finding her dental records."

"Let me know what you *do* find. Nice work as always."

"Yeah, yeah," he said, "I'd bill you for my time but—"

"I know. You're a millionaire now so you don't need it."

"Life's sweet, ain't it?"

"For some people. Not for that family in New Jersey."

The next day, the motor vehicles lab found evidence that the explosion that had taken place after Atkinson's car hit the river was probably caused by an incendiary device. They couldn't verify this to more than a good probability, but it made sense; cars only explode on impact in the movies, not in real life. This also fit Mike Delgado's profile since he'd been a demolitions expert in the military.

Jamie's autopsy on Dr. Atkinson's body showed blunt-force trauma to the skull as the probable cause of death. There was no water in his lungs.

It took over a month for the mitochondrial DNA results to come back from Washington, and when they finally did we were still pretty much in the dark. It could have been Cady's (or Slemboski's) DNA. It could have also been her sister's (if she actually *had* a sister); or it could've come from almost any female relative on her mother's side going back tens of generations.

Still, the district attorney thought it was enough to close the case and that's what he did.

I went for a run with Frankie that night. (Frankie likes jogging, Hooch hates it.) It was mid-November and the air was cold and a light snow was falling. It felt good to run in the snow. It felt bracing and cold and good. When the run was over and we came in the front door my heart was pounding, my blood was rushing, and my skin was flushed. I noticed this as I looked at the full-length mirror in the mudroom, just after I'd kicked off my shoes. The funny thing is, the scar on my forehead wasn't pink. It had turned even whiter than normal, or had *seemed* to, while the skin around it was a rosy red.

Why did that seem backward? Then it hit me: collodion. I raced to the living room and called Kristin Downey, an ex-girlfriend from my graduate school days at Columbia. She'd been a theater major and was now a successful Broadway set and costume designer. I asked her about collodion and was it used in theatrical makeup.

Meanwhile, Frankie had gone into the kitchen to lap up some water. He came back, jowls dripping, just as I got off the phone with Kristin. I ran up the stairs to find Jamie, who was in bed, with a bed's worth of pillows behind her head, reading. Frankie raced in after me, wagging his tail.

"Did you and Frankie have a good run?" she said.

"Yes, it was great. And I just realized something."

"What?"

"Look at my forehead."

"Okay . . ."

"What color is my little scar?"

"It looks white to me, but that's probably because—"

"—the rest of my face is red from exertion, right?"

"Yeah? So?"

"So Cady Clark, or Janet Slemboski, is still alive."

"But, Jack, the DNA . . ."

"Yeah, mitochondrial DNA. You know what that means: it's a maternal relative but it may not actually be her."

I sat on the bed and explained my thinking on the eight-hour lapse from the time Atkinson had drugged Cady and me to the time the car went over the bridge, the fact that driving off a bridge is an unusual way to commit suicide, and the flat-out unreasonableness of the logistics involved for a smallish, slender man like Atkinson to load two inert bodies into the car, one a woman—yes, but a *tall* woman—and the other a healthy male over six feet; he couldn't have done it.

"Not alone, anyway," I said. "And even if he *had*," I went on, "why does he choose driving off a bridge instead of giving himself an overdose of Demerol? Spur-of-the-moment,   maybe   someone would choose that way to die. But not with an eight-hour cooling-off period. Besides, I heard two voices arguing when I was in the trunk that night, just before we went off the bridge. And the state police think the guardrail had been tampered with in *advance* of the crash."

"Okay. But Atkinson could've done that."

"Yeah, but it's not very likely. And how does Atkinson put a bomb in his own car? That's got to be Delgado."

"Okay, but what does all this have to do with the color of your scar?"

I told her that when Cady had lost her temper at Earl, at her house, her whole face had turned red, including the scar.

"That's impossible."

"Yeah, I know that *now*."

"Scar tissue has fewer open capillaries to—"

"Yes, honey. That's what I just realized downstairs. I also realized what that other, arcane use was for collodion that I couldn't put my finger on before. Remember? It's used in theatrical makeup to create stage scars."

"You're saying this woman wore a fake scar?"

I nodded. "It's—I don't know—it's a sympathy card. Think about her psychology: if the one thing you totally lack is empathy for others, and you look around and see that everyone you know, your friends and family, are all capable of feeling sorry for other people, you might a) think that's the best way to get people to relate to you, and b) see it as an exploitable weakness in others."

"And she did that by giving herself a fake scar."

"There may be more to it, but that's part of it, yes. Plus, I think it's also part of what enabled her to impersonate her sister."

"Okay. So what do you think happened that night the car went off the bridge? I mean, if Atkinson wasn't driving—"

"It was Mike Delgado."

"Okay. Explain it."

"I will," I got up, "just as soon as I've had a shower."

"Jack!"

I ignored her, hopped in the shower, and once I'd toweled off, I sat on the edge of the bed again; she put down her book again, and I explained my theory.

Janet Slemboski wanted to be an actress. She went to a school where other, less pretty girls, did better than she. She wanted that scholarship and killed Cady Clark to get it, but after the NYPD started nosing around, looking for the missing girl, Slemboski got worried and flew the coop for Maine, where she took Cady Clark's name and SS number, and started a tense, symbiotic relationship with Amanda Whoever.

"But who's this Amanda, anyway? Is she real?"

"Good question. I think she's a relative of some sort, but I don't really know that for sure. It's all speculation at this point."

"It certainly is."

"Yes, but when you're down on your luck and you need help, where's the first place you turn, friends or family?"

"Family first, I guess."

"Right. So my thinking is: her parents had passed away, she was seventeen; maybe she had family in Maine. So that's how she ended up here, and that's probably where Amanda came in, whether she was a half sister or a cousin or whatever."

"Okay, that sounds reasonable. Go on."

At some point Janet Slemboski met Earl and Bruno, and was probably involved in some of their capers but got bored with Earl's stupidity or just his lizardlike face, met a "nice," gullible doctor, seduced him, and started blackmailing him, thinking he had more money than he actually did.

Meanwhile, Delgado had been snooping around, had probably fallen in love with her, too. Then she set up the bank robbery by manipulating Earl and Bruno into doing it. Delgado was probably in on it too because he still had it in for his former partner. In fact, he probably helped get her the job at the law office, though that's just a wild guess."

"Isn't all of this just a wild guess?"

"Some of it. Then she reads about me in the newspaper or sees me on TV," (I do a bi-weekly dog training segment on the *Saturday Morning Show* at a Portland station), "and decides to hire me to come for a training session at the exact time she figures Earl will be coming back from the robbery, showing off the money he got for her surgery. That way if there's a shoot-out, which she's maybe hoping there *would* be, she's in the clear as far as Earl's demise is concerned, and can still collect the insurance, through this other identity of hers."

"Do you think she really needs eye surgery?"

"Of course not. It's another sympathy card."

"Okay," she sighed, "now get to your visit to the doctor's office and what happened that night."

"My pleasure. Okay, after I called that day, telling him I needed to speak to him, he must have told Janet Slemboski about it, not knowing that the meeting was to be about her. *She* knew, though, and she came running over to pressure him into getting rid of me. She hadn't counted on him giving her the chloroform, though. That's where he finally came through in the clutch. But here's where it gets tricky:

"He's got two bodies in his office and no easy way to dispose of them. Then let's say there's a knock on the door. It's Delgado, who followed Slemboski. He was waiting outside, and when she didn't come out he came inside to find out what's going on because he's jealous and crazy in love with her."

"Aren't *all* the men in this story?"

"Anyway, he sees that Atkinson has two unconscious people in his office, me and Slemboski—and so he kills Atkinson, probably takes him to a shower stall, because there was no blood evidence found at the office—though if the state police had treated it as the primary crime scene, they might've found some—and he does the deed there, using a blunt instrument."

"That would gibe with my autopsy findings."

"Right. Then he comes back to office and finds that Slemboski has come to, either that or he revives her, then they devise the plan to set up the fake murder/suicide, putting me in the trunk for good measure. He goes out to the bridge, tampers with the guardrail, then comes back and plants the bomb under the car. Meanwhile, she somehow gets her cousin to come to the doctor's office and kills her there."

"This would've taken an awful lot of work and planning."

"Yeah, but Delgado was a stunt driver and the whole point was to have a female body in the car that would be mistaken for hers and as you know, it's hard to get good DNA from a charred corpse."

"Yes, but why kill her cousin now and not before?"

"We don't know for sure that Amanda is her cousin."

"But you just *said*—never mind. Go on."

"And she doesn't kill Amanda before this because she was useful. Now her only usefulness is as a body so Slemboski can fake her own death."

"Of course; I get it."

"Right. Then they leave the suicide note on the computer, load up the doctor's car with the two bodies, one in the passenger seat and me in the trunk, and Delgado takes off, with Slemboski following in *her* car."

"Where's the doctor's body at this point?"

"Probably in her car. They probably dumped him off the bridge before pulling the fake suicide stunt.

"Then Delgado drives the car off the bridge, gets out of his seat belt after the car hits the river, ignites the detonating device just as he's swimming ashore, and the car blows up, destroying all the evidence. Except they hadn't counted on my getting free. When he finds out I'm still alive, he comes to the hospital to try and finish the job."

She sat thinking it all over. "It's a pretty wild

story, Jack. Are you sure that's how this whole thing happened?"

"No, but it's the only explanation of all the details that makes any sense."

"But, Jack—how can we know for sure?"

"Easy," I said, snapping my finger at Frankie, who was lying comfortably in my spot. He looked up at me and I pointed to the foot of the bed. "All we have to do is find Janet Slemboski and Mike Delgado and get them to confess."

Frankie moved to his usual spot at the foot of the bed.

Jamie said, "But what if no one ever finds them?"

"Then they get away with it."

"Well, that sucks," she said.

"I know, but you can't solve every murder that comes along, honey. Sometimes you just have to accept that and move on to a case you *can* solve."

"Maybe *you* can do that, but I can't."

I got under the covers and said, "Well, you're going to have to sooner or later. That's just the way it is." I turned off the lamp and lay holding her, listening to her think.

After a while she said, "Maybe we'll get lucky and find them."

"Well, maybe," I yawned, "but don't count on it."

Chapter 3

Snow Job

Thanksgiving and Christmas came and went. Due to several technicalities Earl walked on the bank job *and* the motel murder, or I should say, he hobbled on them, since the brain injury caused lack of full muscle function on his left side. Jamie and I got involved in another case (concerning a housemaid who was found murdered in her employers' mansion a week before Christmas Eve). After we'd solved that one, things settled down for a while.

Then one Sunday night in late January we had dinner at O'Neal's, a cozy Italian joint on Bayview Street, with the lead detective on that case, Brad Bailey, and his wife, Lissa.

Lissa was originally from Utah and said she thought I looked like an actor in a TV series that was shot near her hometown, but which supposedly took place in Colorado.

"I think I know the guy you mean," I said, breaking a breadstick. "He's incredibly handsome and he has a beard?"

Jamie hit me with the back of her hand.

"I wouldn't say 'incredibly' handsome," said Lissa. "But , he *is* kinda good-looking."

Bailey said, "He plays a doctor who moves from New York to Colorado, kinda like you moved to Maine. We don't watch it on Monday nights, though. We TiVo it and watch it on Tuesday."

Lissa added, "We don't even answer the phone on Monday nights. That's our family-home evening with our kids."

"Really?" said Jamie. "That's really cool." When she was growing up her father, who was a famous neurosurgeon, was rarely home, which was similar to the back story of the TV show. She said, "We should do that when *we* have kids, Jack."

The next night Jamie decided we *had* to watch that show to see the handsome actor Lissa Bailey had been talking about.

As we were sitting together on the big leather sofa, eating popcorn, there was a brief scene in a high school hallway, where two of the teenage characters are having a conversation, and another kid, a Eurasian girl, comes up and has a brief interaction about a homecoming dance or something, and I was suddenly interested in the show for the first time.

I had seen that girl somewhere before. She was tall and slender, and had that long-limbed yet ample roundness you can't get at the gym. And although she wasn't a very good actress she *was* very pretty; she had a petite nose, black almond-shaped eyes, and tight, shimmering black hair, cut short. Then one of the other characters said something that angered her and, as she got upset (or was "acting" upset), hard lines unprettied her face.

That's when I knew who she was.

"It's her," I said. "Damn! I wish we had TiVo."

"What do you mean it's her?" Jamie asked. "Who her?"

Frankie and Hooch looked up from their spot by the hearth to see what we were so excited about.

"That girl! In the high school corridor! That's Cady Clark! Or Janet Slemboski! Whatever her name is."

"Are you sure?"

"Of course not. Why do you think I wish we had TiVo?"

"But she's in her twenties; she's not a teenager."

"Hah! You'd be surprised how old some of the 'teenagers' in these TV shows really are." I picked up the phone and tried to call Detective Bailey but he didn't answer.

Jamie put down her popcorn bowl. "He's having his family night with his kids, Jack. Remember? And what if you're wrong about her?"

"Well, if I'm wrong," I said, dialing the phone again, "what's it gonna hurt this actress out in Utah?"

"What do you mean?"

"So, some dog trainer in Maine calls up, mistaking her for a multiple-murder suspect back east. It's all just publicity, right? And in show business, there's no such—"

"—thing as bad publicity." She shook her head. "Okay, make the call."

We contacted the state police, the FBI, and the authorities in Utah, state and local, and gave them all the information. They all indifferently said they'd look into it.

The next morning I contacted Bailey and he let me come over to see the show again, using his TiVo. We played that one scene—the one Janet Slemboski was in—several times, in slow motion, and I was convinced that it was her.

She'd had her nose done—it was smaller and more pert—and maybe her eyes, too—they were now almond-shaped, though that can be done with theatrical tape, hidden by loose bangs or hair that hangs close to the face.

We watched the credits to see if we could find the name of the actress, and there it was: *Girl in Hall—Amanda Hitchcock*.

"I don't believe it," I said.

"Maybe this Hitchcock girl is the one you're really after," Bailey said.

"Maybe," I said, unconvinced. "But I don't think so."

I contacted the TV series' production company, they gave me the name of Amanda Hitchcock's agent—the Lucy McCarthy Agency in Salt Lake City—and I spoke to someone there, hoping to get her address and phone number, which they refused to give over the phone.

I contacted the Salt Lake City Police and they sent someone over to get the info, but all they had was a PO box in nearby Heber City, which is where they sent the checks, and a prepaid cell phone number, which is where they called when they had auditions for her.

The Salt Lake cops didn't pursue it. It seemed like no one but me was interested in following up on the case. Their feeling was that Cady Clark, AKA Janet Slemboski, had died in a murder/suicide several months earlier, somewhere in Maine, so who's this idiot dog trainer to tell us to override the local DA's decision in that case?

So that's how Jamie and I came to be driving a rented QX4 up I-84 in the Wasatch Mountains, in a snowstorm, the night of the awards banquet at the Sundance Film Festival.

"Jack," she said, turning down my Townes Van Zandt tape, "what is it about this music you like so much?"

"You mean other than the fact that he's possibly the best writer of folk-type songs who ever lived?"

"You're forgetting Bob Dylan and Joni Mitchell and—"

"—Greg Brown, I know. But Townes is still the best."

"But he can't *sing*! And you also love Tierney Sutton, who is a truly *phenomenal* singer. I just don't get it."

"Well, she's the best jazz singer there is right now, bar none. The thing is, they both do what they do with absolute honesty and simplicity. What could be better?"

"If Van Zandt had a nicer voice, it would be better."

"Maybe, maybe not. What do *you* want to listen to?"

"I don't know. We're in Utah. Don't you have a Beach Boys tape?"

I said I had tons of them and put one in the player, though I wasn't sure what the Beach Boys had to do with being in Utah.

Before taking the drive up to Park City, we'd had a pleasant conversation with Amanda Hithcock's agent, Lucy McCarthy. She told us that the last time she'd spoken to Amanda, the girl had mentioned getting an invitation to the film festival's awards banquet.

"That's all she thinks about," McCarthy had said, "Sundance. It's her dream to win an award there some day."

We pulled up to the event tent just as the snowstorm went on hiatus, and as the last stragglers, dressed in ski clothes and talking on cell phones, their breath making important, decision-making clouds in the cold mountain air, made their way toward the entrance. The tent was set up in what appeared to be a high school parking lot.

As I got out, feeling overdressed in my rented tuxedo, I told Jamie to try to keep the car ready.

"Okay. But can't I come inside?" she said. "I'm all dressed up. Plus, I want to see Matt Damon and Ben Affleck."

"Maybe we'll rub elbows with them at an after-party."

"Okay," she griped. "But how come you get to have all the fun?"

"In this case, it's because I'm the only one of us who's qualified to recognize the suspect even though she has radically changed her appearance. And because one of us has to keep the car ready in case there's trouble."

"Oh, sure," she said, "use logic."

I kissed her through the open window and went around to the back entrance, showed my NYPD identification card to a bouncer who looked like he could probably play the second goon from the left in any Hollywood action film. I was very careful to put my thumb across the word "retired" on my ID before I showed it to him.

"What's it about?" he grunted.

"I have reason to believe that a murder suspect who's wanted back east may be inside the tent."

I stepped into the back of the tent, past The Second Goon From The Left, and hoped Lucy McCarthy had been right, that Amanda Hitchcock (or Janet Slemboski) was at the banquet inside.

I came into the main part of the tent behind and to the left of the platform, where someone who looked semi-familiar (isn't there an actress named Posey Parker?) was at the podium reading off the list of nominees for best actress in a supporting role.

I trained my eyes on the audience, ignoring the famous faces; I was scanning the crowd for a tall, slender girl, about twenty-two, with three or four murders under her belt.

As I came around the side of the podium I spotted her at a table, about seven or eight rows back.

Oddly enough, there was a black toy poodle in her lap. Maybe Paris Hilton's Chihuahua had made small dogs a popular fashion accessory.

Posey, who was wearing casual ski clothes, had finished reading the nominees and was about to open the envelope when I came around front and headed toward Janet Slemboski, who I now saw was also wearing a casual but hip ski outfit.

I got to about the first row of tables when she looked up at me. She tried to look past me, as if she didn't know me, but she couldn't ignore the recognition in my eyes or the determination in my step. The dog started barking and from the sound of his voice and the look in his eye, I knew it was Charley, with an ebony dye-job.

Slemboski stood up suddenly and screamed.

I rushed toward her.

She jumped over her companion's legs, threw Charley at me (I caught him neatly), and ran toward the exit, screaming, "Stop him! Stop that man! He's a killer! He wants to kill me!" This was designed to give her time and room to get away, to get the crowd between us, but I was smarter than she was.

"I'm a cop!" I shouted. "Stand back! Make a path!"

She ran past one of the buffet tables at the back of the tent, swooped up a carving knife, and kept running.

I held my wallet up with the hand not holding Charley, as though showing a badge. "Police business! Coming through!"

I was gaining on her until someone who looked like Steven Seagal, but probably wasn't, got in my way. I don't know if his interference was intentional or not; I didn't ask. I slammed an elbow in his face, jarring my funny bone, and went on my way, that arm tingling, then had to jump a leg that tried to trip me; another face got smashed. Charley was barking the whole way, having a helluva time.

Cady, meanwhile, made her way screaming through the door that led to the street. When I got there I had to smear a bouncer's face. My tuxedo shirt was now a welter of other people's blood: bouncers, action stars, well-meaning fools.

I ran outside where my face, hot with adrenaline, was stunned by the sudden shock of cold, dry mountain air.

I saw Cady, brandishing her knife at the open door of a black Mercedes. She pulled the driver—a frail old woman—out, then got in.

I looked around for Jamie, or a ready vehicle to follow in, but Jamie and our rented Infinity were nowhere to be seen.

A guy in a calf-length shearling coat, smoking a slim cigar, and who reminded me a little of James Coburn, but wasn't, casually caught my eye and tossed me a set of keys.

"The red Ferrari," he said. "I hope you're insured."

"Not really."

"Ah, what the hell. But I get the film rights!"

"Fine with me," I said.

He pointed to his car, I ran to it, clicked the door open with his key-chain, tossed Charley gently into the passenger seat, dove inside, found the keyhole, started her engine roaring, and took off after the black Mercedes, swerving and fishtailing through the lower gears.

My mind ranged in all necessary directions: clutch, gas, brake, gearshift, receding taillights, Ferrari—god-this-is-fun, I wonder where Jamie is, clutch, gas, brake, curve, how's Charley doing? Ferrari—god-this-is-fun, gearshift, receding taillights, curve, clutch, gas, hang in there Charley. . . .

The snowstorm was still on hiatus, though a few lingering flakes fell here and there as I followed the Mercedes out of town, where it ignored the on-ramp to the Interstate, and swerved onto a small canyon road, traveling beside a rushing creek.

She had a good lead initially, but Ferrari is to Mercedes as rock, paper, scissors, is to, well, sawed-off shotgun. I was on her ass in the space of two mountain curves.

I won't lie. I love it when my movements, the thrust of my intentions, is exact, ordered, precisely aimed at a specific target or result. But then came the storm again. Deep snow, blanketing, hard, and full, and where the hell is the lever, the button, the dingus that makes the windshield wipers work? The Mercedes took a hard right across a wooden bridge, over the rushing creek, toward a rustic cabin, hidden in the pines—a perfect Mike Delgado hideout.

I went after her but my wheels skidded, swerved, lost purchase, spinning me sideways toward the bridge. Damn! I needed that windshield wiper lever. How could I see without it?

Then my borrowed, beautiful red Italian racing

machine flew across the icy bridge, spun out of control, glided in a dozen slow-motion circles, and sailed easily and neatly into a power pole. *Bam!* The unbelievably quick explosion of the air bags was followed by more snow falling softly and slowly from the wires above me. Then, when all was still, I heard another car come over the bridge and then around mine.

I looked out and saw a gray panel van come to a stop. A dark figure got out and came lurching forward, his movements not exact, not precise, barely on the edge of specific or ordered, and yet somehow more purposeful than mine.

God! It's Earl! How'd he get here? How'd he get to her? What's that in his hand? A gun?

The door of the Mercedes, which was parked next to the cabin, flew open.

I threw open mine.

Cady sprang out of her car, a bright flash of steel—the knife in her hand.

I stumbled out of the Ferrari, Charley leapt over the driver's seat and past me, barking his way onto the snowy gravel drive, then ran over to Earl and grabbed his pants leg.

Earl was shouting something at Cady, asking, pleading for an answer to some impossible desire.

Her mouth was an angry gash. She spat words and brandished the knife as she came quickly toward him, her arms wanting terribly to stab him.

He stepped toward her with Charley at his ankle.

I shouted something, a pathetic attempt to stop the inevitable.

Earl pulled a gun. Cady lunged at him with the

knife. The gun went off and both figures stumbled backward in the snow.

From behind me I heard another car pull up to the bridge. A door opened and faint Beach Boys music wafted through the air. I ran toward Cady and Earl. Charley was jumping around, barking. I heard Jamie on her cell phone, "I need an ambulance, now!" A pause. "I don't know. Just off I-84, about a mile west of Park City, I think. I'm on a side road by a wooden bridge and a stone cabin."

I got to where Earl and Cady were lying in the snow. I took Earl's gun with no resistance. He was holding on to the knife with his other hand. It was still stuck in his gut.

"How did you find her?" I asked.

He smiled at me. "I just followed *you*, you jackass. You ain't as smart and I ain't as dumb as you think."

Jamie came running to us and landed on her knees next to Earl.

She shouted, "Don't touch the knife!"

"What?" asked Earl.

"The knife! Don't pull it out! It's keeping you alive!"

"This?" he said, looking down at the bloody hole in his grimy, dark blue parka.

"Yes. It's probably holding back the internal bleeding."

He lifted his head and looked over at Cady, who wasn't moving, then smiled at Jamie, a sad smile, a tragic, inevitable smile, and said, "So?"

He took the hilt deliberately in his hands and pulled it out, gasping, grimacing as he did. Jamie made to stop him, but knew any pressure *she* put on the knife would only do more internal damage. There was a soft sound like suction then the black, bloody flow of life followed after the blade as it left his body, and he gasped again, once, twice, and was gone.

Jamie cried, "Earl, you fool!" but by this point there was nothing that could be done. He was no longer living.

Then we heard Cady moaning in the snow. We went to her.

"Is he dead?" were her first words to us.

"Yeah," I said, bitterly. "You killed him."

"You saw," she said to me. "It was self-defense."

"*This* killing was, maybe. But you're going away for all the other murders, Janet."

"Don't call me that."

She'd been shot in the abdomen; blood was oozing out of her side. Jamie unwrapped a scarf from around her neck and used it to staunch the bleeding.

With a smug smile, Cady said, "I'll never go to prison."

"This isn't just about Earl, Janet—"

"—don't call me that."

"It's about the real Cady Clark, it's about Dr. Atkinson, and Joe Bruno, and the real Amanda Hitchcock, and an attempt or two you made on my life."

"You can't prove any of that."

"Yes we can. You killed them. And the thing is, except for Cady Clark; you killed them all in Maine."

"So? They all got in my way."

"That's not the point. You're in Utah now, Janet. They love the death penalty here; it's practically biblical for them. So, you're not only going to prison, you're going to die here in Utah for killing Earl Brown."

"No. You *saw*; you can't lie. It was self-defense."

"It doesn't matter. It's part of an ongoing felony; that's felony murder, and that means the death penalty."

I looked at Jamie. She gave a quick shake of the head; the girl wasn't going to make it to the hospital, let alone prison.

"What about Mike Delgado?" I said. "Where is he?"

"That creep?" Cady said, her eyes fluttering.

"Where's Delgado?"

"They'll find him," she said with a weak laugh.

"What does that mean?" I said, and wanted to also ask why she'd done what she'd done, why she'd been bent on destroying so many lives, but I already knew the answer to that.

"Easy, easy," Jamie said, holding her scarf to the wound.

"Tell us where to find Delgado," I said.

She shook her head, still smiling. "You'll find him in the spring," she said. "He got in the way too."

"Got in the way?"

"Of my dreams," she said, then closed her eyes and was gone.

After that it was just the two of us, me and Jamie, the only two left living, except for loud, wonderful

Charley, who stopped barking suddenly, lifted his nose into the air, and raced toward the cabin.

I got up and followed him and found him digging at a bullet hole in a canvas tarp, next to the snow-covered firewood stacked up by the back door. I pulled back the canvas and found Mike Delgado's blue, icy body lying there, with a black, bloodless bullet hole right between his staring black eyes.

"Good boy," I said, feeling my arms and shoulders tremble with waves of relief that it was all finally over. There was also a little grief for Delgado's sad end and Dr. Atkinson's sorry fate mixed in. Then I heard the sound of sirens in the distance and said, "You're a good dog, Charley."

He looked up at me and wiggled his butt, his round, dark eyes bright with happiness.

Jamie came over, looked at the body closely, and said, "She's really something, this girl."

"I know."

"Do you? Look at the bullet hole. There's no blood around it and bits of canvas inside it." My mind was too numb to think clearly; I asked what it meant. She said, "She put a bullet into him, through the tarp, after she'd already killed him."

I shook my head. "God, she really is evil."

She put a hand on my shoulder. "*Was*, Jack. *Was*."

Delgado had kept a diary. We found it in the cabin and the story it told was pretty much the way I'd outlined it for Jamie that night after I'd gone jogging with Frankie. I'd gotten only one thing wrong:

Mike Delgado hadn't been in love with Janet Slemboski; he was her father.

"God and family first," I told Jamie when we read that.

"Yeah, it makes a nice motto for a tattoo I guess, but in this case . . ."

Slemboski's mother had gotten pregnant just before Delgado shipped out for duty overseas. While he was gone she had the baby and gave it up for adoption. One day, about nineteen years later, Delgado saw Cady Clark at the shopping center in Belfast and was dumbstruck: she looked exactly like her mother.

He followed her, found out who she was, checked into her background, found out about the real Cady Clark, the missing girl from New Jersey, contacted that girl's parents, but eventually decided not to tell them about her. He'd been keeping tabs on Cady on his own ever since.

He pulled her over on the highway one night, told her who he was, and that he wanted to help her cover up the murder of the real Cady Clark (her body was finally found in a creek bed in New Jersey, thanks to info from the diary). He'd been helping her evade the consequences of her actions ever since, right up to the day she killed him (the autopsy showed he'd died of arsenic poisoning), then laid him out under the tarp and shot him between the eyes, just for the fun of it.

Nice family.

We never found out the real identity of the woman who'd been burned in the car explosion.

Like I'd told Jamie, some cases you just can't solve.

Charley spent the plane ride back to Maine happily chewing a bone in a carry-on crate stashed under my seat.

Once we were airborne, Jamie sipped her Bloody Mary and said, "You know, I think I'd rather work on a case with an outright serial killer than on another one like this."

"No you wouldn't," I said. "Trust me. A serial killer will get under your skin far more than this girl ever could."

"Why?"

"Because," I sipped my scotch, "since a girl like this one has no empathy for the rest of the world, it's easy not to have any for her. But a serial killer has a wounded psyche; and you're a doctor and you'll feel a grain of compassion for him no matter how much you hate what he's done. And he'll play on that, if you happen to get close enough to let him. Trust me, a case like that will screw with your emotions for a long, long time. You may never get over it. But by the time we get back to Maine we'll have forgotten all about what's-her-name who died in the snow back there in Utah."

"Now that you mention it," Jamie said, stirring her cocktail with a celery stalk, "what the hell *is* her name?"

Over our soft, convivial laughter you could just make out the sound of Charley happily chewing his bone.

The Case of the London Cabbie

J. A. Jance

Getting up from the table, Maddy Watkins found her two red-dog golden retrievers, Aggie and Daphne, watching her avidly. After a lifetime's worth of reading mysteries, it was only natural that she would name her dogs after two of her favorite writers—Agatha Christie and Daphne DuMaurier.

"Not yet, girls," Maddy said, avoiding saying the magic word "walk," which would have sent the two dogs into spasms of anticipation. Instead, she gave them their after breakfast treat. Disappointed, the dogs followed her into the living room. With resigned sighs they settled down on a nearby rug while Maddy deposited her coffee cup on the table next to her easy chair and picked up her newspaper. With pen in hand, she was about to embark on that morning's *New York Times* crossword puzzle when the phone rang.

"Aunt Maddy?" a woman's voice asked. "It's me—Shannon."

The second part of the introduction was not only grammatically incorrect, it was also totally unnecessary. Shannon Lester, Maddy's only niece, had been taught grammar by a generation of teachers who had evidently never grasped the difference between the subjective or objective case, and who wouldn't have known the difference between a transitive or intransitive verb if one had walked up and smacked them in the face.

"Good morning," Maddy said. Suppressing a small sigh, she put down her pen and pulled the coffee cup closer. Once Shannon got on a telephone, she was often incredibly long-winded. Talking to her niece made Maddy wonder why it was some people never worried about *long*-distance charges. "How are you today?"

"It's Mother," Shannon said, sounding very near tears. "I just don't know what to do."

Shannon's mother, Genevieve Gaylord, was Maddy's sister and only sibling. As far as blood relatives were concerned, Genevieve sometimes made Maddy wish blood *wasn't* thicker than water. Maddy had been told time and again over the years that, at age three, she was far too young to remember the day her mother had come home with her "adorable" baby sister. Yet in that regard, Maddy remembered all too well—and Genevieve, with some notable exceptions, had been a pain in Maddy's neck ever since. Still, when Maddy's husband, Bud, had taken sick and died, no one had been more supportive than her sister Gennie. That had to count for something.

"What now?" Maddy asked.

"Mother's in love," Shannon said, deteriorating into real tears now. "You've got to help me, Aunt Maddy. She's really gone off the deep end this time."

Genevieve's falling in love was hardly news from the front, either, and her taste in men was usually, to put it charitably, unfortunate. Gennie had fallen off the rails the first time at the tender age of fourteen when she had lied about her age and eloped with a sailor from the Bremerton Naval Station. That marriage had ended in an amicable divorce prior to Genevieve's eighteenth birthday.

Childless for years, Gennie had been astonished to find herself pregnant with Shannon, a "change of life" baby. Maddy could never remember from which marriage Shannon had come, number three or four. The father had disappeared into the ethers when Shannon was five, and there had been several more short-term marriages to several eminently forgettable men. Genevieve's lifetime's worth of often juvenile behavior was part of the reason Maddy had gone to great lengths to maintain a cordial and supportive relationship with her niece. Poor Shannon deserved to have some adults in her life who actually behaved like adults.

"That's hardly surprising," Maddy said briskly. "It was bound to happen sooner or later. Joe—that was the last one's name, wasn't it? He's been gone a good year and a half now."

Joe Gaylord had been more than a little rough around the edges, but in many ways the retired naval chief had been the best one of the lot. He hadn't made bundles of money over the years, but he had been tight as could be with what he did have. When he succumbed to a massive and completely unexpected heart attack, he had left his widow in far better financial shape than she could ever have imagined.

"I married him for love," a bereaved Gennie had declared to her sister shortly after the attorney had revealed not only the contents of Joe's will but also the extent of his considerable assets, all of which now belonged to his widow. "I had no idea Joe had that kind of money."

So much the better, Maddy remembered thinking at the time. If Genevieve had known there was money, there would probably be a whole lot less of it by now.

"This one's nothing like Joe!" Shannon said heatedly. "Nothing at all. You've got to do something about it, Aunt Maddy. You've got to put a stop to it."

Despite having very strong opinions about the dubious propriety of Gennie's general behavior, Maddy nevertheless found herself bristling. Yes, Genevieve had made some bad decisions over the years, but so had Shannon. The idea of Shannon suddenly calling the shots where her mother's life was concerned definitely rubbed Maddy the wrong way. As far as she was concerned, adult children suddenly taking it upon themselves to boss their parents around was an idea whose time had not yet come. And for good reason—namely Maddy's own son, Rex, and his fashion plate of a wife, Gina.

Rex, a middle-aged Seattle real estate developer, was not only very bossy—having inherited a healthy dose of bossiness from his mother's side of the family—he also had a very high opinion of his own opinions. With his father dead, Rex seemed to think his mother was supposed to look to him for all kinds of counsel and advice.

When Maddy acquired a pair of puppies after her old dog Sarah had to be put down, Rex was dead set against it. (Fortunately for Aggie and Daphne, she had ignored him.) On the other hand, he had been all for the idea of Maddy's moving out of her modest waterfront home on Whidbey Island's Race Lagoon, two hours west of Seattle, so it could be redeveloped into what Rex liked to call a "real waterfront property." As if the house Bud and Maddy had built together—the house Rex had been raised in—hadn't been good enough to suit him.

Fortunately for Maddy's personal financial situation, she had disregarded Rex's expert advice on that score, too. In the aftermath of the terrible and deliberately set arson fire that had burned Maddy's home to the ground, she decided to make her own arrangements rather than accept her son's "sweetheart" deal. The idea that she had bypassed him on the issue left Rex's nose permanently out of joint. In fact, he barely spoke to his mother anymore, which, from Maddy's point of view, wasn't as bad as one might think. She found Rex to be far less annoying when he wasn't speaking to her than he was when he was.

Upon hearing Shannon's tale of woe, Maddy's first thought was that her niece was barking up the wrong tree and should get a grip. People Gennie's age ought to be allowed to make their own mistakes, which meant that their children should mind their own business. That was what Maddy thought, but she was far too polite to come right out and say so.

"What's the matter with your mother's new beau?" Maddy asked, envisioning some nice retired civil engineer or maybe another navy guy, an officer this time, who, after being widowed, might have moved into the adult community—Lakeside Senior Living on Lake Union—where Genevieve and Joe had moved shortly before Joe's death.

"For starters," Shannon said, "he's twenty-nine years old."

That took Maddy's breath away. "Did you say twenty-nine?"

"Yes."

"But Gennie's forty years older than that!"

"Exactly," Shannon replied.

"What does he do for a living?" Maddy asked.

"He's from Saudi Arabia," Shannon returned. "He claims he's a computer engineer but that he can't find work right now, so he's driving a cab for that new London Cabbie Company, the one that uses those funny-looking black cars that look like they're from the thirties. That's how he met her. He drove Mom from her hair appointment downtown back to Lakeside."

"A computer engineer who can't find work in

Seattle? Impossible!" Maddy exclaimed. "What's his name?"

"Jamil bin Mahmoud, which, as far as I can tell, means 'Handsome son of Mahmoud.'"

"Handsome is as handsome does," Maddy muttered.

"Yes," Shannon agreed. "Mom is just ga-ga over him. The problem is, he has a wife and a little boy with another baby on the way."

"You mean he's not even divorced?" Maddy asked in dismay.

"Divorced? Are you kidding. Mom told me that he's Muslim and he said, according to Sharia, Islamic law, he's allowed to have *four* wives."

"Not if one of the four happens to be my sister!" Maddy vowed, doing an immediate one-eighty on her initial determination to not let Shannon dictate the conditions of her mother's life. This was different. "Do you think he's a terrorist?" Maddy added.

"A terrorist?" Shannon responded. "Of course not. Being a Muslim doesn't automatically make him a terrorist. I just think the guy's a jerk. All he's after is Mom's money."

Maybe, Maddy thought. *Then again, maybe not.*

"Can you help me on this?" Shannon continued. "If you talk to Mom, maybe you can get her to come to her senses."

Coming to her senses wasn't something that was in Genevieve Gaylord's makeup or in her repertoire, so Maddy didn't hold out much hope on that score. After a strict Lutheran upbringing, Maddy and Gennie had both left home in search of forbidden fruit. Fortunately for eighteen-year-old Maddy, Bud Watkins had been there when she was ready to take her first bite. Unfortunately for Genevieve, she either had never encountered that same kind of good raw material or else, with the singular exception of Joe Gaylord, she hadn't had brains enough to hang on to it when she did.

"Let me think about this," Maddy said. "I'll take my girls for a walk. That's when I do my best thinking. Once I decide what, if anything, I can do, I'll let you know."

Aggie managed to pluck the word "walk" out of context. Her ears pricked up and she came to attention. Daphne, following her sister's lead, leaped up as well.

"Thanks, Aunt Maddy," Shannon said. "I knew I could count on you."

Maddy wasn't so sure about that. Pushing aside both her cold coffee and the unworked crossword puzzle, she got to her feet.

"You're right, girls," she said. "We need to go for a walk. Go find the leashes. Bring them to Mommy."

The dogs needed no further urging. They raced off to find the leather leashes that Maddy kept in a basket near the front door. She had taught them to bring the leashes as an add-on to the "Find it!" command they had learned during their thirty-day obedience training boot camp at the Academy for Canine Behavior. Their ability to bring their own leashes had been a necessity back during the time Maddy had been struggling to recover from hip replacement surgery. Now having the dogs bring their own leashes was more a convenience than anything else—and a trick they enjoyed performing.

"Okay," Maddy said, once the leashes were in place. "Go find the purse. Bring it to Mommy."

And so the dogs raced off and brought that, too.

"Good dogs," she said, slipping the strap over her shoulder. "All right, now. Off we go."

And off they went. The three-year-old goldens walked demurely at Maddy's side while she held the leashes slack in her hand. Their Academy-fostered canine manners made them obedience standouts with the other dogs they met on their treks through Oak Harbor. Rex had been appalled when he found out how much she had paid for that single round of obedience training.

"It was an investment in my future," she had replied. "You wouldn't want them pulling me down an embankment and rebreaking that expensive bionic hip of mine, now would you?"

Thankfully, that one comment had been enough to shut him up. That was how you had to operate with someone like Rex, Maddy had learned. One had to be firm—calm but firm—and utterly uncompromising. It worked the same way with the dogs—although Aggie and Daph were far less trouble, and infinitely less demanding, than Rex Alan Watkins.

Wearing a light jacket as a barrier against the cool March winds and even cooler possible showers, Maddy and the dogs set off at a brisk pace from her cozy cottage on Oak Harbor's Fidalgo Street for the short walk to Hester Block's waterfront property on Bayside.

Maddy had been astonished by the amount of money that was offered when she looked into the possibility of subdividing and redeveloping the Race Lagoon waterfront acreage she and Bud had bought for a song back in the 1950s when they were newlyweds. But even with all that money at stake, Maddy had been close to turning the deal down based solely on the fact that Ag and Daph would no longer have private beach access. That was when her childhood chum, Hester Conrad Block, had come to the rescue.

"You can bring your dogs down to my place whenever you like," Hester had offered. "I'll give you a key to the gate. You and your precious puppies can come and go as you please."

Which is exactly what they were doing right now. Maddy's comfortable new house a few blocks back from the beach had been purchased at a fraction of the price of waterfront property, but she still had all the benefits. What could be better? Beach access and none of the accompanying headaches.

Once through the gate Maddy let the girls off their leashes. They raced ahead of her down the bank while she followed at a far slower pace, thinking all the time of Gennie. Poor Gennie. She had always been the cute one—petite and good-looking. She took after their mother, which included being somewhat on the dim side.

Maddy took after their Scandinavian father—big-boned, big-framed, and smart. All through their school years lots of people doubted the two of them were truly sisters. And the fact that Gennie's schoolwork had compared so poorly to that of her brainy older sister's hadn't helped the situation, either.

But Gennie's real problem, her fatal flaw, was that she had always been incredibly kind-hearted. That fact alone accounted for all the broken human flotsam and jetsam she had taken in over the years, married, and then tried to rehabilitate. Her taking up with an impoverished and underemployed computer scientist was simply a new verse in a very old song.

Settled on a huge chunk of driftwood, Maddy spent the next half hour throwing sticks for Aggie and Daph to swim out and bring back. And while Maddy was exercising her pitching arm, she was also considering her best course of action. How did you find out whether or not someone was a terrorist? She remembered reading something about a "terrorist watch list." Wasn't that what that lady customs agent in Blaine had used when she caught the guy coming down from Canada intent on blowing up the Space Needle? Or was it the L.A. airport?

By the time the dogs finally tired of the game, Maddy had made up her mind. "Come on, girls," she told the wet dogs. "Let's go home and dry you off. Then it's time I went looking for some professional help."

As it turned out, the professional help Maddy Watkins sought was none too helpful.

When she walked into the Island County Sheriff's Office substation a half hour later, the officer in charge, Lieutenant Sonja Knutson-Evers, happened to be someone who had started school in one of

Maddy's kindergarten classes. It was difficult to look at this poised young woman, sitting behind a desk in her very businesslike uniform, without remembering Sonja as a bright little student with long blond braids and glasses.

"Well hello, Mrs. Watkins," Sonja said cordially. "How good to see you again. What can we do for you today?"

"I came to see the watch list," Maddy announced.

"The what?"

"You know," Maddy said impatiently. "The terrorist watch list. I hear about it on the news all the time. Now I want to watch it."

Sonja's welcoming smile faded. "Do you think you may have encountered a terrorist?" she asked.

"No, but I could," Maddy returned. "And I want to be prepared. If I do see one, I certainly want to be able to recognize him."

"I'm sorry," Sonja said. "Our BOLFs come from the FBI and Homeland Security . . ."

"What's a BOLF?" Maddy asked.

"Be On the Lookout For," Sonja answered. "They come through on a regular basis, and they're part of our daily duty briefings, but they're not for public consumption. We don't put them out to ordinary civilians."

You probably should, Maddy thought, but she didn't say it aloud.

"What about Amber Alerts?" she asked. "You use ordinary citizens for those."

Sonja sighed. "Mrs. Watkins, we're all aware that a year ago you had an extremely difficult encounter with a killer, but—"

"I'll say it was difficult," Maddy interrupted, annoyed by Sonja's patronizing tone. "The man burned my house to the ground, all because no one in this office was prepared to address my concerns."

"I'm sure everyone here did the best he or she could," Sonja said. "And we're all terribly sorry about your losing your home, Mrs. Watkins, but the suspicions you brought to us initially simply weren't solid enough to warrant our taking action—"

"Until it was too late," Maddy finished. "And you're doing the same thing now."

"As I started to say before, just because you've had one encounter with a killer, doesn't mean you're going to run into another one. The fact that your dogs found that murdered woman's purse was a complete fluke."

"I see," Maddy said, rising to her feet. "And all of us ordinary people are just supposed to sit on our hands and let the professionals mess things up." She walked as far as the office door where she stopped and turned back. "Do you remember the story of 'The Little Red Hen'?" she asked. "I'm sure I read it to your class. It was one of my favorites. I read it to all my classes."

Sonja nodded.

"Well," Maddy said. "I guess I'll have to do the same thing 'Little Red Hen' did—do whatever needs doing all by myself!"

"Mrs. Watkins, please—" Sonja began, but Maddy didn't wait to hear what she had to say.

"Not solid enough indeed!" She fumed as she made her way back to the car. "I returned that poor woman's purse and nobody even bothered to send so much as a thank-you note. Of course she was dead. It was as plain as the nose on your face. What more than that did the cops need?"

As Maddy started the car and drove home, the entire unlikely chain of events played itself back in her mind as vividly as if it had occurred only yesterday.

The whole thing had started on a flawless fall morning in early September when she and the dogs had set out for their usual morning ramble down to the beach from her old house. After tiring of chasing sticks into the water, Aggie and Daphne had come back to Maddy dragging an expensive woman's purse, working like a little team of horses to carry the dripping, seaweed encrusted thing between them. Back at the house, Maddy went through the purse's many contents finding, among other things, a large amount of soggy cash as well as a passport.

Maddy did her good-citizen duty. She dried out the cash—all eight-thousand-dollars worth—and the passport, and cleaned up the purse as best she could. Using identification she gleaned from the purse, Maddy tried to track down the purse's owner, Laurel Riggins, but there she ran into a brick wall. Told that Laurel was out of town, Maddy, instead, turned it over to the woman's husband, Hadley Riggins.

That should have been that. Maddy's encounter with Hadley Riggins left her feeling that she had done a good deed, so she sat back and waited for some form of acknowledgment from his wife. Considering the time and effort Maddy had gone through to return the lost property, flowers would have been appropriate along with a handwritten note. At the very least, there should have been a personal phone call. When none of those were forthcoming, Maddy's suspicions were aroused. She took her concerns to the very same sheriff's substation she had just left, where she attempted to file a missing person report. When the officer on duty put her off and refused to do anything about it, Maddy investigated on her own.

It turned out that Maddy's suspicions had been well founded. Laurel Riggins hadn't sent a thank-you note for the simple reason that she was dead—murdered—having been pushed off a Washington State Ferry by her estranged husband. Once the guilty husband learned about Maddy's single-handed investigation, he came to Race Lagoon intent on silencing her once and for all. He torched Maddy's house, believing she and the dogs would be trapped inside. But Maddy's timely and courageous decision to take her dogs and escape to the beach had saved their lives. Later Hadley Riggins was found dead, the victim of a self-inflicted gunshot wound. Along with his body, the authorities had found a handwritten note in which Riggins admitted to having murdered his wife.

In the aftermath of those profoundly disturbing events, Maddy had her fifteen minutes of Oak Harbor fame. Local reporters dubbed her the "Thank-you Note Vigilante." Some people referred to her as a Gray Crime Fighter as opposed to a Gray Panther. And she assumed that eventually her life would return to normal, but the encounter continued to disrupt her staid existence in ways she never could have imagined.

Losing her house that way allowed Maddy to see the sense of redeveloping her property and making herself a small fortune. Naturally Rex wanted to step in and handle it for her, but she told him that she was more than capable of handling her own affairs, thank you very much. Knowing Maddy had fended for herself against a dangerous killer gave her reputation a cachet that somehow carried over into her real estate dealings, and she had money in the bank to prove it was true. She no longer had to sell Avon door-to-door in order to supplement her meager retirement income, either.

Once settled in her new place in Oak Harbor proper, everyone, including Maddy herself, had assumed she would return to living exactly the way she had before. But she hadn't. That day, huddled on a cold dark beach with her dogs, Maddy had watched helplessly as her house burned to the ground, because she'd had no way to protect herself. All that changed. In the months since, she had taken and passed a course in firearms safety. Maddy Watkins now held a state-issued license-to-carry. She kept her cute little Glock 17 in her purse right along with her cell phone.

Another big change in her life was her television-viewing habits. She gave up on situation comedies in favor of crime-time TV. She watched and re-watched countless episodes of *American Justice*, *Cops*, and *Cold Case Files*. And she made sure she was home every single Saturday night when that nice man John Walsh came on her local Fox channel with *America's Most Wanted*. She would watch every single moment of each program, taking detailed notes as she went along because you could never be sure when one of those dangerous criminals might cross your path, even in Oak Harbor. You'd be able to provide the missing clue that would, as Mr. Walsh said, "Put this bad guy away."

Back at the house after her futile visit to the sheriff's office, she was met by Aggie and Daphne greeting her with utter enthusiasm. As far as they were concerned, Maddy could have been gone for days not only for little over an hour—This was one of the things she liked most about dogs. They were constant and loving—*and* very forgiving.

The coffee from morning was cold and bitter, so she splurged on a brand-new pot and then sat down to think some more. What she needed was information—the kind of detailed information her niece had failed to supply. There was only one source for that. Picking up her telephone, Maddy dialed Genevieve's number.

"How are you doing?" Maddy asked when her sister answered.

"Shannon called you, didn't she!" Gennie said accusingly. "I was afraid she would. She's really selfish that way. She just doesn't want me to have any happiness at all. Or fun. As far as she's concerned, people our age have no business falling in love."

"Are you in love?" Maddy asked, deflecting Gennie's finger-pointing.

"Well, yes," Gennie admitted. "As a matter of fact, I am."

"Tell me about him," Maddy commanded. "I'm all ears."

That wasn't entirely true. Her hand was at work as well. Maddy sat with her head bent, using one shoulder to hold the receiver to her ear while she busily scribbled notes.

"Jamil's amazing!" Gennie babbled excitedly. "I just wish you could meet him, Maddy. I've never met anyone like him. He's fascinating, and such a gentleman, too."

As Gennie raved on, extolling the young man's good looks, intelligence, and general wonderfulness to the high heavens, Maddy kept remembering what Shannon had said earlier. She had claimed that her mother was "ga-ga" over the guy. That was hardly an exaggeration.

"What does he do and how did you meet him?" Maddy asked. She had heard Shannon's version, but she wanted to hear the story from Gennie's point of view as well.

"Right now he's driving a cab," Gennie chirped happily. "The first time I met him, he took me from here to my hair appointment downtown. When the appointment was over, there he was, parked at the curb outside, waiting for me almost like he was my personal chauffeur or something. And the next week, when it was time for me to go back to the beauty shop, here he was again. I didn't even have to call. He said he'd put me on a standing appointment basis. Isn't that sweet?"

Sweet doesn't have anything to do with it! Maddy thought.

"But driving a cab is just a temporary measure,"

Gennie continued. "Jamil and his brothers are interested in starting their own business. They've invited me to invest in it as well. That way I'll be able to be in on the ground floor. I'll be able to turn that little nest egg Joe left me into a real fortune," Gennie added. "The same way you did with that redevelopment project of yours."

Maddy shook her head and almost dropped the phone in the process. Here she and Genevieve were—one of them over seventy and the other one within spitting distance of it—and the sibling rivalry that had plagued their relationship as children was still very much in play, and Gennie was willing to put her dead husband's nest egg at risk in hopes of outdoing Maddy's own modest monetary success.

"That sounds very interesting," Maddy managed, hoping she wouldn't be struck dead for lying. "What kind of business?"

"Something to do with the Internet, I think," Genevieve answered. "You know how I am about all these newfangled things. But Jamil tells me it's a terrific opportunity. He's promised to bring me a business plan so I can study up on it, but it occurred to me I should probably have someone more knowledgeable than I am take a look at it. Should I show it to Rex? Shannon's husband is a complete doofus when it comes to having any business sense."

Dragging her son Rex into the mix was the last thing Maddy wanted. He already had his own preconceived notions about how advancing age was affecting what he considered to be his mother's feeble mental capacities. Maddy had no intention of allowing Rex's Aunt Gennie to add any additional fuel to that particular fire.

"I suppose I could take a look at it," Maddy said tentatively. She made the offer more or less expecting that her sister would turn her down cold. Instead, Gennie surprised her.

"Would you?" Gennie asked eagerly. "I'd like that. You're a lot more with it about these things than I am. I mean, you even use e-mail."

That was true. Maddy had bought herself a used computer and had taught herself to use it about the same time the little twit from the animal shelter had told Maddy she was too old to adopt a puppy. She had found her two purebred red-dog golden retriever puppies and her computer at almost the same time. That original computer had been burned up in the fire, of course. The insurance settlement allowed her to replace the old one with a brand-new Apple laptop, which she could now operate like nobody's business.

"When do you think Jamil will have the business plan ready?" Maddy asked.

"Sometime later this week," Gennie replied. "Today's Monday. I'm guessing it'll be ready by Thursday or Friday."

"Good," Maddy said. "Once you have it, let me know. I'll come into town. The two of us will have lunch and go over it together."

"Maybe the three of us could have lunch," Gennie suggested. "Jamil is really charming. You're going to love him."

We'll see about that, Maddy thought. "Sure," she said. "I'm looking forward to it."

After hanging up the phone, Maddy sat and stared at it for a long time. Thursday or Friday didn't give her much time. She had only three or four days to find out what she needed to know and make her move. A few minutes later she logged onto the Internet herself and went looking for hotel accommodations in downtown Seattle, a good two hours from her home on Whidbey Island. If Jamil Mahmoud was out trolling for what he thought were rich but helpless little old ladies, Maddy Watkins intended to give him a run for his money.

In the end she decided on booking a room at the Fairmont Olympic. Rex had once insisted on taking Bud and Maddy there for dinner in the Georgian Room on the occasion of their fiftieth anniversary, but that wasn't why Maddy chose it. By the time their fiftieth had rolled around, Bud's health was already failing, and Maddy hadn't felt much like celebrating. But between having a fancy but reasonably private dinner or being forced to endure a big public party, Maddy had opted for the former, which had seemed like the lesser of two evils.

The dinner had been fine—expensive and rich, but fine. The one thing that stuck in Maddy's head about that evening had nothing at all to do with the meal. As they were leaving the hotel after dinner, they had encountered a woman walking through the lobby. She had been holding the leashes of two snooty poodles—dogs who looked as though they were accustomed to walking through shiny hotel lobbies every day of their lives. The woman and her dogs were trailed by a hardworking bellman pushing a cart stacked head-high with a mountain of luggage—including two airline dog crates.

Knowing those two poodles had stayed at the Fairmont made Maddy suspect that Aggie and Daphne could do the same.

"How many in your party?" the reservations clerk asked.

"Three," Maddy answered. "Me and my two goldens, Aggie and Daphne."

"Will the dogs have any special dietary requirements?" the clerk asked without a moment's hesitation.

"Oh, no," Maddy replied. "I'll bring their own food along."

An hour later she set off for Seattle with a single small suitcase, a laptop-loaded briefcase for her, food and leashes for the dogs, and the dogs themselves, all of them packed in to her Honda CRV. (Rex had wanted her to buy a Buick, but Maddy had opted for the Honda SUV since so many old people wearing their heavy-duty, post-cataract-surgery sunglasses seemed to be driving sedate Buick sedans these days!)

Even with thickening afternoon traffic, it was only slightly past four when she pulled up to the hotel's fully staffed driveway entrance, where a flock of bellmen surrounded the CRV to help her unload.

The ride from the Fairmont's front entrance up to the lobby level was Aggie and Daph's first elevator ride. They greeted the experience with wide-eyed dismay. On the way through the lobby to the registration desk Maddy remembered those two poodles and wished that the luggage now stacked on her own bellman's cart was somewhat more impressive.

At the desk, the dogs maintained a civilized sit-and-stay while Maddy checked in under Bud's mother's maiden name—Margaret Anderson. She had been smart enough to make that arrangement in advance and had told the reservations office that the credit card billing would be in the name of Madison Watkins. After all, if Jamil was a talkative sort of fellow, Maddy couldn't risk using her own name in the unlikely event that he happened to mention Maddy to Gennie.

Once the luggage was on its way to the room, Maddy and her dogs paid a visit to the concierge's desk. "I have a very busy day tomorrow," she told the young woman standing there. Her name badge said she was Sally, but she didn't strike Maddy as a Sally.

"Lots of errands to run and so forth," Maddy continued. "I need to go around town and check on some of my late husband's projects and investments. I'd like to make arrangements for a cab, and I'd like to keep it all day."

"Madame, are you sure you'd like a cab?" the concierge asked. "We have any number of suitable car services available . . ."

Maddy was adamant. "I understand there's a new cab company in town, she said. "I'm told they drive those old-fashioned-looking cabs, the same ones they have in London. The British Cab Company, maybe? The English Cab Company?"

"You mean the London Cabbie Company?" Sally asked.

"Yes," Maddy said, brightening. "That's it. The last trip my husband and I took before he died was to London. For several days we rented one of those, driver and all. It was a wonderful vacation. I'd like to do it again."

This was all a total fabrication, of course. The only time Bud had been near England was when he was on a ship waiting for the D-Day invasion. That could hardly be called a vacation. Maddy herself had never been to London in her life. Everything she knew about London cabs came from the movies or else from those mystery programs on PBS, but it sounded plausible enough—in a sort of flighty, not-too-bright way.

"Really," Sally began, "I do think a car service would be more suitable—"

"No," Maddy insisted. "My mind's made up. I had a friend who used this company when she was visiting Seattle a few months ago. She had a wonderful driver. What was his name again? Let me see. She never mentioned a last name, just a first. Was it James? No, that's not it. Joaquin? No, but it was foreign-sounding like that. I mean you knew he came from some other country. Ah, yes, Jamil. That's it. She said he was terrific, and oh so helpful. When you call them, let them know he's the driver I want. I'll be paying for a full day's work. I'd like to have him here no later than nine A.M."

"Very well, madame," Sally said, making a note of the needed arrangement in her large notebook. "I'll be sure to tell them. If for any reason that's not agreeable, I'll give you a call. In the meantime, will you be needing a dinner reservation?"

Maddy glanced at her watch. It would soon be time for *American Justice*, and she adored Bill Kurtis. "Oh, no," she said. "I think we'll just order from room service."

"Certainly, madame."

"And about walking the dogs," Maddy added. "As you can see, they're very well behaved, but I'm a little leery about walking them myself at night on the city streets."

"One of the bellmen will be happy to assist you with that," Sally said. "Just call down to the bell captain whenever they're ready."

With the dogs still on their leashes, Maddy made her way up to her fifth-floor room. The next elevator ride didn't startle the dogs quite as much as the first one. Once in the room, Maddy let the dogs off leash and they raced around the room, playing tag and leaping on and off the bed as though the hotel experience had been designed for their own personal enjoyment. And that wasn't far from wrong. In the spacious bathroom, Maddy found a paper doggie-motif mat on the floor with both a filled water dish and two matching bone-decorated food dishes. On the dresser she found a fruit basket for her and a pair of individually wrapped milk bones for the dogs.

"Yes, puppies," she said, handing the eager dogs their treats. "I think this will do very nicely."

Undressing, Maddy put on the luxurious robe she found hanging in the closet, then she settled in to do her homework. When she called Rex's office, she hit the jackpot. According to his secretary, not only was Rex not in right then, he was at an out-of-town conference and wasn't due back until late the next evening. Nothing could have suited Maddy better. Using the pretext of a birthday gift, she cagily played the mother card. By the time she got off the phone, Maddy was in possession of the names and addresses of all of Rex's current projects. Then she logged onto the Internet and located each of them on Mapquest.

Pleased with herself, Maddy then settled down to watch *American Justice.* She ordered a room service dinner, which was delivered during *Cold Case Files.* She and the dogs ate their evening meals with crime solving going on in the background. At eight o'clock she called the bell captain and requested assistance with Aggie and Daphne's evening walk.

When a somewhat wary bellman arrived at her door, she handed over the leashes, a sizeable tip, and a list of the necessary instructions—sit, stay, no pull, leave it, and get busy. When Rex was little, his baby-sitters always required much more coaching and a lot more money. Dogs really were easier than children.

Once the dogs came back from their evening constitutional, Maddy, too, was ready to go to bed.

The next morning she was up and out early. She called for her CRV and took the dogs for a brisk walk in Myrtle Edwards Park, then she returned to the hotel, had her breakfast, and dressed carefully for her morning's outing.

Appearances, of course, were everything, and a sufficient amount of feigned dottiness was also es-

sential. To that effect, Maddy wore a little-used outfit her daughter-in-law had insisted on giving her
for her last birthday, in the aftermath of Maddy's
losing all her old clothing in the fire.

It wasn't that she disliked the bright red St. John
knit jacket and skirt Gina had chosen, but they had
been so astonishingly expensive and so amazingly
bright that Maddy had been reluctant to wear them.
The color was far too vivid for Maddy to feel comfortable wearing it to church, where it would have
caused everyone's eyes to pop out of their heads, but
the bright red blazer with its shiny gold buttons was
exactly the right look for today. To compliment the
outfit, Maddy wore a pair of very serviceable tennis
shoes. Along with her purse she carried the battered briefcase as well as one of Bud's old hard hats.

Yes, she thought, perching the hard hat jauntily
on top of her head and examining the ridiculously
incongruous effect in the full-length mirror on the
back of the bathroom door. *This should do very nicely.*

Aggie and Daph were disappointed when
Maddy left without them, but she knew they'd sur-
vive. She stopped by the bell captain's desk and
made arrangements for several scheduled dog
walks during the course of the day, then she settled
down in the lobby to wait.

Jamil Mahmoud appeared a few minutes later.
Living up to both his name and his advance billing,
the young man boasted movie-star good looks—
olive-tanned skin, sparkling eyes, white teeth, a se-
lection of gold necklaces visible beneath an
open-necked shirt, and a very engaging smile.
"Mrs. Anderson?" he asked.

For a moment, Maddy was so startled by his use of her pseudonym that she almost failed to respond. "Oh, yes," she said, after a pause. "You must be my driver."

"Yes," he agreed. "Yes, I am. May I help you with that?" he asked as Maddy reached for her briefcase.

"That would be very nice, thank you," she said. "It contains a list of all the addresses we'll be visiting today."

Jamil held her arm solicitously as they made their way down the escalator. "You're here from out of town?" he asked.

Maddy nodded. "We used to live here, but I live in Olympia now," she explained. "My husband died not too long ago. I needed to come check on some of the projects that were in progress when he died."

Jamil's cab was waiting just outside. When Maddy settled into the boxy but roomy interior, she found it was far more comfortable than she expected—and much cleaner.

"I'm so sorry to hear about your husband," Jamil said, putting the vehicle in gear. His English was slightly accented but grammatically perfect, far better than Shannon's as a matter of fact. "His death must have been sudden."

"Yes," Maddy said with a nod. "It was sudden. A heart attack with no advance warning at all. And here I am left to tie up all the loose ends. It's a terrible responsibility."

"Yes," Jamil said, glancing at her in the rearview mirror. "I'm sure it is. Where shall we go first?"

She gave him the address of a mixed-use development going up just off 45th in the University District.

"Your husband was a builder?" Jamil asked, observing Maddy's reflection in the rearview mirror as he maneuvered the cab through traffic and onto northbound I-5.

"Not a builder so much as a developer," she said. "He would obtain the property and the financing and then do the build-out as well."

"It sounds complicated," Jamil said.

"Jonathan loved making deals," she returned with a sigh, all the while congratulating herself on using Bud's parents' real names—Margaret and Jonathan. It made it much easier to keep her stories straight. "I miss him so much," she added, dabbing at the corner of her eye with a lacy handkerchief.

She still did miss Bud. That much, at least, wasn't playacting.

"He must have been a very smart man," Jamil added.

Maddy nodded. Bud had been smart. He could have had a basketball scholarship to the University of Washington, but all that changed when he went away to World War II, and everything else changed after that. When the war ended, he could have used the GI Bill and gone to college but by then he didn't want to. Instead, he had used his natural gift for mechanics and his joy at tinkering to open and run the machine shop that, along with Maddy's teaching, had kept them in good stead all those years, although in the last few years, he had been losing ground in a world run by computer chips. In that way, Maddy supposed, his death had been a blessing. At least Bud had died before being rendered obsolete.

Jamil pulled the cab up in front of a fenced-off construction zone. "Would you like me to come in with you?" he asked.

Maddy didn't like the way he kept looking at her in the mirror. She worried about whether or not he could tell she was lying. She had always known when her kindergartners were telling whoppers. Hopefully she was older and wiser and a little more tricky than that.

"Oh, no," she said smoothly, donning the hard hat. "I'm sure I'll be fine."

Taking both her purse and briefcase, she dodged around the chain link barriers. Just inside the Tyvek-wrapped building, a construction worker waved Maddy down.

"Hey, lady," he said. "You can't come in here."

"Yes, I can," Maddy replied determinedly, consulting her list, the one with all the information she had wangled from Rex's secretary. "I'm here to see Mr. Hammond. I believe he's the site superintendent."

Sighing and rolling his eyes, the worker reluctantly led Maddy out behind the building to a battered construction trailer. "Hammond's in there," the guy said, pointing.

Straightening her shoulders, Maddy stepped up into a grubby trailer that reeked of cigar smoke and rancid coffee. Inside she found a barrel-chested man seated behind a desk that was covered with mounds of blueprints.

"Who are you?" he demanded rudely, not bothering to rise to his feet. "What do you want?"

"I'm Mrs. Watkins," she said primly. "Rex's mother. And a show of manners might be nice."

Caught off guard, Hammond swallowed his bluster. "Sorry, Mrs. Watkins," he said.

Belatedly he stood up and offered her a chair after first using his shirt sleeve to brush away some of the gray plaster dust that seemed to coat every flat surface in the room. Then he rolled up the blue prints with one meaty paw and brushed away some of the remaining plaster dust there as well.

"It hasn't been a good morning around here," he added. "We're running way behind schedule. What can I do for you?"

"My son's fiftieth birthday is coming up soon," Maddy said. That was conveniently true. In actual fact Rex's big 5-0 was less than a week away. "I'm putting together a little surprise for him," she added, opening the briefcase and removing a brand-new Ziploc bag that she had brought along for this exact purpose. "I'm going around to all his current projects and collecting little pieces of . . . well . . . stuff. A bit of this and that. I'm planning on making a collage from whatever I gather. I'm going to have it framed so I can give it to him for his birthday."

"What kind of stuff?" Bill Hammond asked.

"I don't know. Whatever you're working with right now. A little piece of that insulation I saw stacked outside would be nice. Or a piece of copper tubing. Whatever you're working with at the moment. And it doesn't have to be much. Just enough to fit in this bag. I'd like you to tag whatever you give me with your name, the date, the project, and a description of what it is. That way, years from now, Rex will be able to look at the collage and know just where each project was at the time of his birthday."

"Oh," Hammond said. "Sort of like an evidence bag, only different."

"Exactly," Maddy told him with a smile.

"If you'll excuse me," Hammond said, "I'll see what I can do."

Moving his large bulk with surprising alacrity, Hammond got up and left the trailer. Maddy couldn't help but feel a sense of satisfaction. Her little dig about his minding his manners had awakened some long-forgotten trace of polite behavior in the man. It worked the same way with bad grammar. Some people needed occasional nudges now and then to remind them about what was right and what was wrong in order to get them back on track.

Hammond returned a few moments later with a three-inch square of white foam.

"Insulation," he explained unnecessarily, since Maddy knew exactly what it was. "I cut off a chunk that I thought would fit. Do you want me to label it?"

"Please," she said, handing him the plastic bag. "That would be very nice. And date it as well."

He wrote laboriously, frowning with concentration. Obviously, as a child, penmanship hadn't been one of Bill Hammond's strong points. It still wasn't.

"You will remember to keep this a secret, won't you?" she asked, as he handed the bag back to her and she slipped it into her briefcase.

"Absolutely, Mrs. Watkins," he returned. "My lips are sealed. You can count on that."

When Maddy emerged from the building a few minutes later, Jamil had his cab stationed in a no-parking zone right in front of the construction entrance. He hopped out and hurried around the vehicle to open the door and help her into the seat.

"Thank you, Mr. . . . ."

"Mahmoud," he supplied.

"Thank you, Mr. Mahmoud," she finished. "You're very kind."

"Where shall we go from here?" he asked.

Once again Maddy was struck by the perfection of his grammar. It was downright remarkable.

"The next stop is all the way up in Shoreline," she said. "It's a new strip mall at Aurora Avenue and 176th."

"You just sit back and relax," Jamil assured her. "I'll have you there in no time."

Maddy sat back in her seat and pretended to do just that. "Have you been driving cabs long?" she asked. "You certainly seem to know your way around Seattle."

"For two years now," Jamil said, "although not always for this same company. I was trained as a computer engineer, but when my wife became ill, I needed a job that was more flexible. Software engineers must put in very long hours."

"Your wife is ill, then?" Maddy asked.

Jamil nodded sadly. "She was ill. I brought her

here so she could be treated for cancer at the University of Washington. Unfortunately, it was too late."

"You mean she died?" Maddy asked.

He sighed. "Yes," he said. "And I just haven't had the heart to go looking for a different job. That's why I'm still here."

So, Maddy thought, *I've caught Mr. Mahmoud in his first lie! What about his expectant wife and his little boy?*

"I'm so sorry for your loss," Maddy said. "I know how much that hurts."

"Yes," he agreed. Looking back at her in the mirror, his dark eyes brimmed with emotion. "It is very sad."

As they drove north through the city, Maddy sat back and tried to decode what Jamil's comment really meant. Shannon had said Gennie's boy wonder had a wife and child and was expecting another. That, at least, was what he had told Gennie. The question was did he still have a wife or had he ever had a wife at all?

"How old was your wife when she died?"

Maddy hated asking this particular question. It always sounded as though there were some magic moment in life, a Rubicon of years, before which it was bad to die and after which it was fine. And since Bud had been seventy-three when he died, she should have just straightened up and gotten used to the idea. Moved on, as people liked to say.

But she asked the question anyway, just to keep the conversation going.

"She was thirty-six," he said.

"Any children?"

"None," he said. "None at all."

Maddy found the ease with which Jamil Mahmoud told his lies utterly chilling. At least she had to struggle to keep her stories straight. He seemed to have no such compunction, and he didn't seem to mind changing the story to suit the audience. Listening to him, Maddy had to give her niece a lot of credit. It sounded as though Shannon had been right as rain in thinking Jamil meant trouble.

At the strip mall site, the superintendent was nowhere to be found, but Maddy did manage to track down a pair of electricians. After first swearing them to secrecy, she talked them out of a small collection of wire nuts.

Once again, when she returned to the cab, Jamil hurried to assist her. "People seem to be going to lunch," she observed. "Since I had a very early breakfast, how about our taking a lunch break as well?"

"Where would you like to go?" he asked.

"Fisherman's Terminal," she said at once. "My husband and I didn't go there often, but it was one of Jonathan's favorites. He loved their clam strips, and so do I."

"I'll be happy to drop you off and wait," Jamil said.

"Absolutely not," Maddy insisted. "I have no intention of eating alone. Please come in with me. I'd enjoy having the company."

The restaurant at Fisherman's Terminal had, indeed, been one of Bud's favorites right along with the clam strips, but he and Maddy hadn't gone there often enough to be considered regulars, and there was little danger of running into anyone who knew her.

And no one did. It was early enough that the slender hostess led Maddy and Jamil to a window-side table. Barely glancing in Maddy's direction, the young woman's focus was entirely on Jamil. He was good enough to return the favor with a tooth-some grin that was only one step under a leer.

What are people thinking about us? Maddy wondered as she threaded her way through the noontime diners. *They probably think I'm his grandmother.*

A good deal of the city's fishing fleet had already left for the season. What remained was docked outside. It was a charming scene with the boats bobbing up and down in the foreground while in the background white clouds scudded in a bright blue sky over the equally blue water.

It was almost this time of year, Maddy remembered, when she and Bud had come here for the last time, although neither of them had known at the time that they wouldn't be back, at least not together. It had been a clear day in early March, much like this one. She and Bud had gone outside after their lunch and stood in front of the memorial to lost fishermen, where Bud pointed out the names of the ones he had known personally.

It was almost as though he knew he was going to join them soon, she thought.

The waitress came with a red plastic mesh basket lined with a napkin and containing Chinook's trademark cannery bread. Under ordinary circumstances, Maddy would have instantly collected two pieces of the tasty stuff and stowed them in her purse for Aggie and Daphne. Today she resisted that temptation.

"Something to drink?" the waitress asked.

"Coffee," Maddy said. "No cream."

Jamil ordered iced tea. When the waitress left, Maddy noticed Jamil was smiling at her. "You were far away," he said.

"I was thinking about my husband," she said.

He nodded. "I thought so," he returned. "He must have been a very good man in addition to being a very good businessman. But what will you do with all these properties he has left you? Will you keep them or sell them?"

Yes, Maddy thought. *We haven't even ordered lunch, but he's ready to cut to the chase.*

"I haven't decided yet," she said. "Handling so much property is a big burden to someone my age."

"You're not so old," he said at once. "You can't be over fifty. I've heard that's the new forty."

A couple of decades short of the mark, Maddy thought. *But very smooth.*

"You're too kind," she said. "Much too kind."

The waitress returned just then, bringing their drinks and ready to take their food order. In honor of Bud's memory, Maddy ordered the clam strips just the way he would have—with extra tartar sauce.

"If you decide you wish to sell some of them," Jamil offered, "I have an uncle who is looking to make some investments here in Seattle. I'm sure he'd give you a good price. A fair price."

What happened to the brothers who were so interested in the Internet start-up? Maddy wondered. *This guy really is a piece of work!*

His grammar may have been impeccable, but all the while he was lying through his teeth.

"You don't think he'd try to cheat a helpless old widow?" Maddy asked.

Jamil beamed at her. "As I said before, you are not old," he said. "And I doubt very much that you are helpless. But my uncle is an honorable man. He would not try to cheat you."

"There are lots of people who would," Maddy told him.

"You must not think such a thing," Jamil returned. "There are many very good people in the world as well. I learned that when Fatima got sick. People were so kind to both of us, and they were kind to me after she died. You must have found that, too."

Maddy sighed, because what he said was true. Most people were good, and they were kind as well.

"Yes," she said. "I suppose I did."

"But you are still very sad."

"Does it show?" she asked.

"Maybe not to someone who has not been there," he said kindly. "But for one who has, it is obvious. Maybe that is why Allah brought us together—so we could comfort one another in our sorrow."

"Perhaps," Maddy allowed. "Perhaps he did."

Throughout the remainder of lunch and their afternoon excursions, Maddy had to stay at the top of her form in order to keep up the pretense. It was hard to remember to call Bud Jonathan. Once or twice she almost stumbled, but each time she managed to pull back from the edge. Finally, at three o'clock and with her briefcase rattling with a grow-ing collection of copper tubing and light sockets and switch cover-plates, she was more than ready to go back to the hotel.

In the driveway, when she handed Jamil his money, he tried to return some of it. "Our agree-ment was for a full day's work," he objected. "This is too much."

"No," she said. "Please take it. Consider the extra a tip."

"Thank you," he said. "Thank you very much."

"Does that mean you're done for the day, then?"

Jamil glanced at his watch. Maddy had never seen a Rolex, but she wondered if she wasn't seeing one now.

"I have a few more hours before I need to drop my cab off at the base down in Columbia City," he answered. "Enough time for another fare to the air-port and back."

"And if I changed my mind and stayed over an-other night," Maddy said. "Would you be available to help me do some shopping tomorrow?"

"But of course," he said. "It would be my plea-sure."

"Same time, then," Maddy said. "Or perhaps you'd like to come a half hour earlier and join me for breakfast. I do hate eating alone."

Once inside the hotel, Maddy hurried up to her room, where she found everything in good order. Aggie and Daphne were overjoyed to see her. After greeting the dogs, Maddy went straight to the com-puter and logged on. A few minutes later, dressed in a jogging suit, she called for her car. Then, with the dogs along for company and with the street address of the London Cabbie Company and driving directions firmly in hand, she hurried back down to the hotel's drive-up entrance.

A few minutes later she was parked across the street from the London Cabbie Company's headquarters on S. Graham Street just north of Boeing Field. Usually she left the CRV's back windows open so Ag and Daph could stick their noses out. This time she left them shut. Reaching under the driver's seat, she pulled out the wide-brimmed Tilley hat she kept there for those rare occasions when the sun came out and nearly blinded her. Now she mashed it onto her head, hoping that it would help render her unrecognizable in case Jamil glanced in her direction when he arrived to turn in his cab at the close of his shift.

As the night-shift drivers began arriving, Maddy was surprised at how closely they resembled one another. The same held true for the day-shift drivers who drove into the company's parking lot at about the same time in order to drop off their cabs and switch to their private vehicles. Caught up in watching the drivers come and go, she almost missed Jamil when he sauntered out through the front office and headed for a fiery red Pontiac Grand Am parked a few cars in front of her.

Maddy kept her face averted as he crossed the street, opened the car door, and got in. She waited until he was a good two blocks in front of her before she pulled out to follow.

"Well, puppies," Maddy said aloud, as she followed the Grand Am toward I-5. "If this doesn't turn me into a latter-day Miss Marple, I don't know what will."

At first Maddy worried that Jamil would drive onto I-5 and she'd lose him in rush-hour traffic. Instead, he went up and over the freeway and then continued on until he turned left on Beacon Avenue. Maddy knew that she was venturing into the Rainier Valley, a part of Seattle that wasn't familiar to her but one where she suspected little old white widow ladies might not be entirely safe. She pulled her Glock-bearing purse close to her side and kept it there.

"Where do you think he's going, Ag?" she asked.

By this time Aggie had assumed her accustomed position in the vehicle and was standing in the backseat on the driver's far side, where she could pant in Maddy's ear and watch on-coming traffic at the same time.

"And what are we going to do when we get there?" Maddy added.

Aggie, of course, said nothing.

As the sun went down, Maddy reached to turn on her headlights. When she looked back up, she noticed that a vehicle had come up behind her with its lights on bright. Under most circumstances, she would have pulled over to let the driver pass, but if she did that, she was afraid she'd lose track of the Grand Am, which, by now, seemed to be slowing. A blue-and-white road sign appeared outside her window, announcing a place called Jefferson Park.

Just then the Grand Am's right turn signal came on. As Jamil slowed to make his turn, Maddy made as if to go past him, but suddenly the car behind her pulled into the left lane beside her then turned in front of her, cutting her off. Her only choice was to turn into the parking lot behind the Grand Am, which had already come to a complete stop. Cornered, she had no choice but to slam on her brakes and stop inches from Jamil's rear bumper. When the CRV came to rest, it was next to a concrete Jersey barrier, and trapped by the other two vehicles. Beyond the barrier, a tree- and grass-lined cliff fell away from the parking lot.

"What are you, crazy?" she yelled at no one in particular, but by then Jamil was already out of his vehicle and approaching the driver's side of her CRV with what looked like a tire iron clutched in one hand.

Maddy reached frantically for her purse, but her sudden-braking turn had sent it flying off the edge of the seat. It now rested on the floorboard, far out of reach next to the passenger-side door.

"Open the door," Jamil commanded menacingly, brandishing the tire iron. His face was distorted by an angry scowl, and Maddy noted there was no longer anything remotely handsome about him. "Open it," he ordered again, "before I smash this window to pieces."

Hearing the obvious threat in his voice, Aggie and Daphne went nuts, growling and barking. But if he carried through on his intention of smashing the window, there would be glass all over. Maddy knew she would be cut to pieces; so would the dogs.

"If I open the door, the dogs might hurt you," she

said, taking a deep breath and rolling her window down a crack instead. "What do you want?"

Jamil looked at Aggie. Her teeth were still bared. The low growl coming from her throat was anything but friendly. He took a cautious step back from the car door and seemed to reconsider his threat of breaking the window.

"I want to know who you are!" he demanded. "What do you want? I've checked you out. There's nobody named Margaret or Jonathan Anderson living in Olympia. And all those places we went to today belong to someone named Rex Watkins. So who are you, and what do you think you're doing? What are you, a cop? A private detective?"

Gray Panthers aside, Maddy knew full well she was too old to be a cop.

"A private detective," she said.

"Who are you working for?"

"I'm not going to tell you," she answered. "Client privilege." Claiming client privilege was totally bogus, of course, but then so was Jamil Mahmoud.

In her rearview mirror, Maddy caught sight of a passing car, but it didn't hesitate at the sight of three vehicles, headlights ablaze, sitting just inside the edge of the parking lot.

"Get out," Jamil ordered. "Leave the dogs inside and get out."

Seeing the implacable look on Jamil's face, Maddy knew if she did what he ordered she was as good as dead. Jamil and his friend had no intention of allowing her to walk away from this confrontation. And, since there was no one else there to save her, Maddy needed to save herself.

"All right," Maddy agreed shakily, and that was no pretense. "Just let me get my purse."

Loosening her seat belt, Maddy bent over to retrieve her fallen purse. With trembling fingers she extracted her Glock and came up firing. Her hands shook so badly that there was no hope of aiming, but Jamil was close enough to the door of the CRV that taking aim really wasn't necessary. A look of utter astonishment passed across his face as a barrage of bullets crashed through the window. A shower of glass fragments and at least one bullet slammed into him, knocking him to the ground. He screamed as he fell. By the time Maddy turned her aim on Jamil's compatriot, the man from the second car was already running for his life. He leaped into his vehicle, slammed it into reverse, and took off.

In the fading light, Maddy saw it was a dark-colored sedan, but it was impossible for her to tell if it was blue or green or black. She noticed the Toyota insignia and a part of the Washington license plate, SLU, but that was all. When she looked back to check on Jamil, he was crawling toward the tire iron that had fallen from his hand and rolled away from where he had landed.

"Don't move, and don't you touch that thing," Maddy ordered through her shattered window. "If you don't think I'll shoot you again, try me."

Jamil took her at her word and lay still. Holding the Glock in her right hand, Maddy used her left one to wrestle her cell phone out of her purse. It wasn't easy to dial 9-1-1 with her left hand, but she managed.

"Seattle PD," a voice responded. "What are you reporting?"

"I've just shot someone," Maddy said. "He and an accomplice were trying to carjack my CRV. I shot one of them. He's still here. The other one took off."

"Does the victim need an ambulance?"

"Looks like it to me, but I'm sure not going to get out of my car to check on him."

"What is your location? You're reporting this on a cell phone?"

"I don't know where I am," Maddy answered. "Not exactly. Somewhere in south Seattle near a park—Jackson, I think. Off Beacon Avenue South. And what happened to that advanced 9-1-1 thing taxpayers paid for? I thought you could locate cell phones."

"We have located you, ma'am," the emergency dispatcher replied. "I have officers and an ambulance on the way. Just stay in your vehicle until they arrive. Are you hurt?"

"No. I'm fine and so are my dogs, but my car window has bullet holes in it."

Maddy knew this wasn't a good thing. The insurance company had been gracious enough about paying the claim for her house fire, but they might put up a fuss about her having a shoot-out from inside her own vehicle.

Jamil was wiggling again, edging closer to the tire iron. "I said don't move!" she ordered.

"Is he armed?" the dispatcher asked. "Are you in danger?"

"Not as long as he doesn't touch that tire iron. If he does, believe me, I'll shoot him again."

By then, though, she could hear the distant wailing of sirens. Officers really were on their way. Minutes later two squad cars with uniformed officers arrived, followed shortly thereafter by an ambulance. While cops and EMTs clustered around Jamil, Maddy ended the 9-1-1 call and slipped the phone into the pocket of her jogging suit. Then she put the dogs on leashes and led them to the edge of the parking lot to relieve themselves. Aggie and Daphne were still circling on the steep hillside when an officer hurried over and pointed a flashlight directly into Maddy's eyes.

"Are you the one who shot him?" he demanded, and not very nicely, either. "Where's the weapon?"

"I left it on the car seat," she told him, "along with my concealed-weapon permit and my driver's license."

The officer's name tag said his name was Wyatt. A. Wyatt.

"The victim says he drove you around all day," Officer Wyatt returned. "He claims that after he dropped you off at your hotel, you tracked him to his workplace, followed him when he left for home, and then shot him for no reason."

"No reason!" Maddy exclaimed. "He and his friend had me hemmed in. Mr. Mahmoud was threatening me with a tire iron."

"There was no one else here when we arrived," Officer Wyatt countered. "And you do admit that you know Mr. Mahmoud. He says you were following him too close and that he felt threatened. Were you following him?"

Maddy heard the question and realized that she was going downhill fast in a process that somehow was transforming her from victim to suspect. "Are you going to arrest me, young man?" she demanded.

Years of bringing recalcitrant kindergarten students to order had given Maddy Watkins a peculiar tone of voice, one that brooked no nonsense and usually commanded respect. This time was no different. The young officer backed off slightly.

"No, ma'am," Officer Wyatt said. "You're not under arrest, but we will need to take you in for questioning and to check out your weapon as well as your concealed-weapon permit."

"What about my dogs?"

Another man stepped out of the darkness. Unlike Officer Wyatt, this one wore civilian clothing. "We could always call Animal Control," he said. "They could look after your animals until we finish interviewing you."

"My animals, as you call them," Maddy returned, breathing fire, "are *not* going to the pound. I'll drop them off at the hotel until we finish up with this nonsense. If I have to, I'll call my niece to come stay with them."

As the new arrival stepped closer, Maddy saw that he was holding her driver's license. It would have been better for Maddy Watkins if the man hadn't borne such a strong resemblance to her son Rex. He was about the same size, age, and build.

"What hotel would that be, Ms. Watkins?" he asked.

"Mrs. Watkins," she corrected shortly. "Women's lib is one of those things that passed me by, so don't you go calling me Ms. I'll have you know I was a very happily married woman right up until my husband died. As for my hotel? My dogs and I are staying at the Fairmont. Who are you?"

"Detective Caudill," he answered.

"Well, Detective Caudill," Maddy said, "it might be nice if some of you people stopped standing around asking me questions and started looking for the man who was here helping Mr. Mahmoud, the one who got away."

"And he is?"

"I'm not sure," Maddy replied. "Probably another driver from that London Cabbie place. The guy who left is the one who actually forced me off the road. They used that barrier there and their two vehicles to trap me so I couldn't drive away."

"And this other vehicle would be . . . ?" Detective Caudill asked.

"A Toyota sedan of some kind," Maddy replied. "I saw that funny little Toyota insignia on the back of it. And part of the plate. SLU something. I do know it was from Washington, but I couldn't see any of the other numbers. He was driving much too fast. Besides, I was busy keeping an eye on the guy on the ground."

"The one you shot," Caudill said.

Maddy took a deep breath. "I think maybe I'm ready to have an attorney now," she said. "And somebody better be checking that tire iron for fingerprints. I don't see any flat tires around here, do you? And isn't someone supposed to be reading me my rights?"

"We're not reading you your rights because you're not under arrest," Caudill replied. "At this point we're simply trying to get to the bottom of this incident. Now, if you would tell us why you were following Mr. Mahmoud—"

"Detective Caudill," one of the other officers called. "The ambulance is about to leave. Do you want to talk to them?"

As soon as Officer Wyatt and Detective Caudill turned away, Maddy reached into her pocket and retrieved her phone. For the first time ever, she was glad she had her son's home phone number on a single-number dial. Expecting to talk to Gina, Maddy was gratified when Rex himself, already back in town, answered the phone, not that she really wanted to talk to him, either. Once Rex heard what was going on, Maddy was sure she'd never hear the end of it.

"Oh, Rex," she said. "I'm so glad you're there. Do you know any defense attorneys?"

"Defense attorneys?" he asked. "You mean as in criminal defense? What's going on, Mother? You're not under arrest, are you?"

"Not yet, but I probably will be," she told him. "As soon as the ambulance leaves, that rude detective from Seattle PD will probably be taking me in for questioning. And I'll most likely need you to come get Aggie and Daph. I'm not sure the Fairmont will let them stay there if I'm in jail instead of in my room."

"In jail!" Rex exploded. "Mother, what the hell is going on?"

"Just find me an attorney," Maddy said hurriedly. "Have him call me back on this number as soon as he can." Just then the ambulance's siren growled to life. "I have to hang up now," she added and ended the call.

Detective Caudill sauntered back over to her. "All right now, *Mrs.* Watkins," he said, verbally underscoring the Mrs. part. "Maybe you'd like to tell us what this is about. And, since it's chilly out here, why don't we do this down at police headquarters? My car's right over there."

"I'm perfectly capable of driving myself," Maddy said. "The driver's window may be blown out, but at least it's not raining."

"You don't understand," Caudill returned. "Your vehicle is going to have to stay right where it is until we finish the crime-scene investigation. When that's over, we'll have it towed to our impound lot."

"Crime scene?" Maddy repeated.

"Yes, crime scene. Assault at least, maybe even assault with intent to commit murder," the detective answered, speaking slowly and at such a high volume, that it sounded as though he was convinced Maddy was both stupid and hard of hearing.

"Officer Wyatt," he added. "Would you please come take charge of these dogs? As for you, Mrs. Watkins, if you'll just step over here and place both hands on the trunk. I'm going to need to search you."

"Search me," Maddy echoed. "Whatever for? You already have my purse and my Glock. What more do you want?"

With her face flushing scarlet in the darkness, Maddy relinquished the dog leashes to Officer Wyatt and then assumed the required but extremely undignified and uncomfortable position demanded of her by Detective Caudill.

"You don't have any needles on your person, do you?" he asked.

"Needles? Of course not," she sniffed, regaining a bit of her gumption. "I've never done drugs. I don't even crochet."

Caudill had barely removed Maddy's cell phone from her pocket, when it rang. He answered it and then handed it to Maddy. "I believe it's for you," he said.

Maddy took the phone, fearing that the caller would be Rex and that he would have disregarded her desperate request for help. "Madison Watkins?" a strange male voice asked.

"Yes," she answered uncertainly.

"My name is Ralph Ames. I'm an attorney. Your son Rex suggested I call. Are you about to be detained by officers from Seattle PD?"

"That's my understanding," she said, breathing a sigh of relief.

"All right, then. I'm advising you to say nothing at all until I arrive and can assess the situation. Now put whoever's in charge back on the phone."

Maddy returned the phone to Detective Caudill who stood listening in silence for the better part of a minute. She could tell from the way his jaw clenched that he wasn't the least bit happy about it.

"All right," he muttered at last. "We're at the bottom end of Jackson Park, just off Beacon Avenue South. Send the car here. Once the dogs have been picked up, we'll meet you down at Seattle PD. If you get there before we do, have them escort you up to an interview room."

Detective Caudill ended the call and then turned to Maddy. "Your attorney is sending a car service to pick up the dogs and take them to your son's place. Then Mr. Ames will meet us downtown."

"Thank you," Maddy murmured.

For the first time in her life, she was supremely grateful that Rex, in a time of crisis, was exactly who and what he was—a chip off the old block— his mother's son.

Detective Caudill's pat-down search uncovered nothing beyond the cell phone and Maddy's single lace-edged handkerchief. When the humiliating process was over, Maddy went over to the dogs and held them close, drawing courage and strength from their sturdy warmth. She wondered how Aggie and Daphne would fare with Gina's all-white furniture and carpeting, but it had been very thoughtful of Rex to provide for someone to come get them.

To Maddy's surprise, the car service arrived within a matter of minutes. As the driver came to collect the dogs, Maddy suddenly realized that it was well past their dinner time and there would be no suitable food for them at Rex and Gina's high-rise condo.

"Please," she said, to Detective Caudill, "if I

could just write a note to the hotel, perhaps this nice man could stop by my room and pick up the dogs' food and their dishes."

Shaking his head, Caudill pulled a notebook and a pen out of his pocket. "All right," he said. "Write away, but I'm going to want to read it."

Maddy had to think a moment before she wrote: "Manager, Fairmont Hotel. I have been unavoidably detained. Please give my driver Aggie and Daphne's food and dishes so they can stay elsewhere. In the meantime, I wish to keep my room. You may put the additional charges on my bill." Signed: "Margaret Anderson."

Caudill took the note from her hands and scanned its contents before handing it over to the driver.

Aggie and Daph were happy to scramble into the backseat of the big Lincoln Town Car. They were not nearly as happy when the door closed behind them without Maddy climbing in as well. As the Lincoln nosed out of the parking lot, hot tears stung Maddy's eyes. The whole time the girls had been with her, she had never once spent a night away from them. This would be a first.

"I thought your name was Madison Watkins," Detective Caudill observed, taking Maddy's arm and leading her toward his own vehicle. "So why are you registered at your fancy, schmancy hotel under an alias?"

"My attorney told me not to answer any questions until he's present," Maddy said tartly. "And I'm not going to."

And she didn't, either. The twenty-minute ride

from south Seattle to the police headquarters building in downtown Seattle was conducted in utter silence. For her part, Maddy was supremely grateful that she hadn't been handcuffed. She worried how her hair, crushed flat by wearing the Tilley, would show up in the photo if they ended up taking a mug shot. In addition, she was busy grappling with what she would say when Detective Caudill finally got around to asking his questions. If she admitted that she had been worried that Jamil bin Mahmoud was after Gennie's money, then Caudill would no doubt assume that Maddy had been following him either to threaten the man or to do him some kind of bodily harm.

When they pulled up in front of the building at 5th and Cherry, a well-dressed man stepped out of a car parked at the curb across the street and hurried toward them. "How's it going, Mort?" he asked, nodding curtly at the detective. "I'd like a moment alone with my client."

Maddy was taken aback to think that her attorney already knew the detective.

"I'm Ralph Ames," he said, holding out his hand to Maddy. "What's going on?"

With Detective Caudill standing nearby but out of earshot, Maddy gave Mr. Ames a quick rundown of events. By the time she finished, Caudill was tapping his foot impatiently.

"So you did shoot him, but you claim it was self-defense," Ames summarized when she finished.

"That's right. Self-defense."

Ames turned back to Caudill. "All right now, Mort. I think we can go up now."

Once in the small interview room, Maddy was relieved when Ralph Ames took the ball. "Has any effort been made to track down the second vehicle?" he asked.

Caudill shook his head. "We don't know that there was a second vehicle," he said. "The victim says there wasn't—that there were just the two vehicles, his Grand Am and Mrs. Watkins' SCRV."

"If I were you, I wouldn't take Mr. Mahmoud's word for it. I'd start looking for that Toyota," Ames said smoothly. "And you did collect the tire iron?"

"Yes, of course," Caudill answered, audibly gritting his teeth. "We do know our business around here, Ralph. We're not all of us amateurs."

Maddy knew that last part of Caudill's statement was aimed directly at her, but she didn't mind. After all, she *was* an amateur. She wasn't even a private detective, but that didn't keep her from wanting to keep Gennie from having a broken heart as well as a broken bank account.

"I still want to know what this is about," Caudill persisted, crossing his arms across his chest.

"My client told me that she believes Mr. Mahmoud was after her money," Ralph Ames said. "Would you please tell Detective Caudill what you told me?"

Maddy looked at Ralph Ames uncertainly. That was part of what she had told him, but it wasn't the whole story.

"When Mr. Mahmoud drove me around this afternoon, I confided in him that my husband had died recently. At first he was very sympathetic. He told me that his wife's name was Fatima and that she had succumbed to some kind of cancer some time ago—within the last few months, I gathered. Then later on, during lunch, he started asking me about my husband's investment properties in a way that made me very uncomfortable. And so, when he dropped me off at the hotel, I decided to try to follow him."

"To what purpose?" Detective Caudill asked.

"To see where he went and to find out if he had told me the truth," Maddy answered. "I wanted to find out whether or not he had a wife."

"Wouldn't it have been more to the point and safer just to ask him?" Caudill asked. Clearly the detective wasn't buying Maddy's story.

"It's easy to ask those kinds of questions if you're a young, healthy male and capable of defending yourself," Maddy pointed out. "I'm none of those things. I'm an old woman and not nearly as spry as I used to be. And if you had seen the murderous look on that horrible man's face when he came after me with his tire iron . . ."

"I wouldn't characterize you as helpless since you were armed to the teeth, but someone else, your son possibly, could have asked him," Caudill pointed out.

"My son is a very busy man," Maddy returned.

"So what happened?"

"I waited for Mr. Mahmoud outside the place where he works—the London Cabbie Company down in Columbia City. When he left, I followed along behind him. Then, all of a sudden, this other car came barreling up behind me and stayed right on my bumper. When Mr. Mahmoud turned off into the parking lot, the second car—the Toyota—pulled out into the other lane and then turned into mine, forcing me off the road behind Mr. Mahmoud's car. When I stopped, he came over to where I was, carrying and brandishing that tire iron. It scared me to death. When he ordered me out of the car—"

"That's enough now, Mrs. Watkins," Ralph Ames interrupted. "I believe Mr. Caudill gets the gist of it. Are Mr. Mahmoud's injuries life threatening?"

"I don't believe so," Detective Caudill answered. "At least the EMTs didn't think so. They said he'd most likely be treated and released."

"Good," Ames said. "I'm relieved to hear it."

"You said Mr. Mahmoud was your driver today," Caudill continued. "You mind telling me how that came about?"

Maddy considered. Should she tell the truth? Sort of, she decided.

"I read about that London Cabbie Company somewhere," she replied. "I thought it would be slick to be driven around in one of those foreign-looking taxis."

"And you hired him for the whole day?"

"That's right. I was collecting materials from my son's various construction projects so I could make a collage for his birthday next week."

"Your son lives here in town?"

"That's correct."

"But you're not staying with him while you're here? You're staying at a hotel?" Caudill asked.

Maddy nodded. "At the Fairmont. It used to be the Four Seasons Olympic."

"Expensive."

"Yes."

"So you do have money?"

"Some," Maddy acknowledged. "I'm comfortable."

"You said that comments Mr. Mahmoud made at lunch made you uncomfortable, comments that made you think he was after your money—or rather, your husband's money. You're in the habit of taking cab drivers to lunch?"

"Not really," Maddy said, rattled. "It's just that we had been busy all morning. I knew I was hungry, and I thought he must be as well."

"Who paid?"

"I did," Maddy admitted. "But there's nothing wrong with that."

"No," Detective Caudill agreed, "but it might make some people think that you were after him rather than the other way around."

"That's outrageous!" Maddy exclaimed. "The man's not even thirty."

"Loneliness does strange things to some people," Detective Caudill observed. "It puts some people right over the edge. Jealousy does the same thing."

Maddy straightened in her chair. "Jealousy?" she demanded. "Are you implying what I think you're implying? Are you under the impression that I followed Mr. Mahmoud because I have some kind of romantic interest in him?"

"Did you?" Detective Caudill asked.

"Certainly not!" Maddy turned to Ralph Ames. "Do I have to sit here and let him insult me like this? I'm tired and ready to go back to the hotel."

"Are you planning on holding her?" Ames asked the detective.

"No," Caudill replied. "Not at this time, but if she plans on leaving the jurisdiction, I'll need to know about it."

"If I go anywhere, it'll be back to my home on Whidbey Island," she said. "Is that considered inside your jurisdiction or do I have to stay here in Seattle?"

"It means don't leave Washington State," Caudill warned. "It would be very bad if we had to come after you or institute extradition proceedings."

The detective's comment made it pretty clear that he still regarded her as the wrong-doer.

"What about my Glock?" Maddy asked. "When do I get that back?"

She could tell by looking at Caudill that he wanted to say, "Never." What he replied instead was, "When we've completed the criminal investigation—and not before. And, if I were you, I wouldn't go out looking for a replacement in the meantime."

"What about the rest of my personal effects?"

Caudill reached down next to his chair and picked up a paper bag. Removing Maddy's handkerchief and cell phone, he slid them across the table to her. "Here they are," he said.

As Maddy gathered her possessions, Ralph Ames rose and reached to help with her chair. "We'll be going then, Mort. Keep in touch."

Maddy waited until they were in the elevator before she cut loose. "What a perfectly dreadful young man," she said. "And the way he treated me like a common criminal. Such arrogance!"

"You're the one who pulled the trigger," Ralph pointed out mildly. "Under most circumstances, the person with the finger on the trigger is the one who's at fault. You can hardly blame Detective Caudill for making that assumption."

"In other words, you're making the same assumption yourself," Maddy said sharply. "I thought you were supposed to be my attorney."

"I am your attorney," Ames replied. "My job is to provide the best possible defense regardless of whether or not you're guilty."

Maddy was steaming as he helped her into his car, one of those new CLS-500 Mercedes, of course. What else could you expect?

"I'm sure this has all been a very disturbing evening for you," Ames said soothingly as he slipped into the driver's seat and turned the key in the ignition. "The best thing to do now is to get some food into you and have a real discussion about everything that went on. I'd like to take some detailed notes before things go much further. Is your hotel all right?"

Maddy nodded. "Do you think it's likely that they'll be charging me?" she asked.

"Not likely," Ames said. "But it's certainly a possibility."

Maddy's phone rang just then. When she went to answer it, she could see it was Gennie calling. She was tempted not to answer, but finally she did anyway.

"Where are you?" Gennie asked.

"Out," Maddy answered.

"Well," Gennie said, sounding wounded. "I tried your home number, but all I got was the machine. Something terrible has happened."

There had been all together too much going on in Maddy's life that evening. The idea of some other disaster occurring at the same time was more than she could bear. "Now what?" she asked.

"It's Jamil," Gennie wailed. "One of his friends just called me. He's been injured, not seriously—in a car accident of some kind. He's at the emergency room right now. He'll probably be released in the next few hours, but that's not the worst of it, though. It's his mother-in-law. She's desperately ill back home in Saudi. He and his wife are going to need to fly back home as soon as they can book a flight."

Maddy bit her lip to keep from blurting out "Jamil bin Mahmoud told me that his wife was dead." Instead, she held her tongue and kept on listening.

"They're hoping to leave tomorrow evening," Gennie continued. "Naturally, flying at the last minute like this is dreadfully expensive. Jamil asked me if he could borrow money for the tickets from me, just until he gets back home and can send me a check. The problem is, he needs it in cash. I can go to the bank tomorrow morning and get it, but I'm just not comfortable riding around Seattle in a cab with that amount of money in my possession. I know it's a terrible imposition, Maddy, but do you suppose you could come to town, take me to the bank, and then give me a ride over to his place so I can drop off the money? I'd ask Shannon, but . . ." Gennie paused. "Well, you know how she is."

Maddy glanced in Ralph Ames's direction. He seemed intent on his driving. "Of course," she said. "What time would you like me to be at your place?"

"Would nine be too early?" Gennie asked. "I know it's a long way, but . . ."

"No," Maddy said. "Don't worry about it. I'll be there right at nine. See you then."

"My sister, Genevieve," Maddy explained to Ralph once she was off the phone.

Maddy sat in silence for a while after that, wondering. This was the time she should probably spill the beans to Mr. Ames. After all, he was her attorney, wasn't he? If he wouldn't help her in a situation like this, who would? But then again, Ames seemed to be on the same page as Detective Caudill in thinking Maddy was the bad guy here. But what could she do to help Gennie, especially if both the cops and her attorney weren't on her side, especially considering they had already confiscated her trusty Glock? Surely she and Gennie merited some kind of protection.

Maddy made her decision. "Gennie has a doctor's appointment in the morning," she explained. "She's worried about what the results may be, and she wants to have someone there with her. I told her I'd pick her up at nine."

"But you don't have a vehicle," Ralph objected. "It's impounded, remember? I can probably get it out for you later in the day tomorrow, but it's going to be difficult to make that happen in time for you to keep a nine A.M. appointment."

Maddy blushed. She was so used to having her own wheels that she had completely forgotten that her CRV was out of reach at the moment. "I'll manage," she said. "Speaking of that. What about my dogs? They're at Rex and Gina's, but they live in First Hill Plaza. I'm not sure that building even allows dogs. I wouldn't want to cause trouble for them with their homeowner's association."

Ralph was about to turn into the Fairmont's driveway entrance, but he paused at the entrance and switched off his turn signal. "Would you like to go get them right now?" he asked. "I'd be more than happy to take you there."

"I'd appreciate that so much," Maddy said. "And I'm sure the dogs will, too."

"We'll go straight there, then," Ralph said. "Dogs first; dinner later."

He was so obliging that Maddy spent the whole trip up First Hill feeling guilty about lying to him. In fact, she was so concerned about that, that she barely had time to worry about what Rex was going to think. Or say.

When they reached the building, Maddy chickened out. Rather than going up to face Gina, she used the security phone and asked Rex if he would be so kind as to bring the dogs and their equipment downstairs. "I have someone waiting for me," she said. "I really shouldn't come up."

Several minutes later, the elevator door opened. Aggie, minus her leash, pranced through the door as happily and as unconcerned as if she'd been riding elevators all her life. Daph, ever Second Dog, followed more sedately. Rex brought up the rear, pushing a grocery cart loaded with the dogs' equipment.

The puppies were ecstatic to see Maddy. Rex, on the other hand, looked mad enough to spit. "What in the world is going on with you, Mother?" he demanded. "Have you gone completely round the bend? And why the hell are you staying at the Fairmont, for Christ's sake? Do you have any idea how much that place costs?"

Just then Rex caught sight of Ralph Ames lingering in the background. He immediately backed off. "Hi there, Ralph," he said more agreeably. "So you were able to keep them from throwing her in the slammer. I really appreciate it. What in the world has she been up to?"

Maddy wasn't about to stand there and be talked about rather than to. Before Ralph could reply, she did. "I found myself being targeted by what I suspect is a smooth-talking fortune hunter," she told him. "All I was doing was protecting myself."

"Did you ever think of calling the police?" Rex asked. "After all, that's one of the services our taxes support. What happened?"

"He came after me with a tire iron," she answered. "So I shot him."

Rex was dumbfounded. "You what?"

"I shot him with my Glock."

"You have a Glock? Since when? I don't believe this."

"I used to have a Glock," Maddy said ruefully. "I got it for protection after that crazy man burned down my house. And don't look at me that way,

Rex. The gun is legal. I have a license for it and everything. But the cops took it away tonight—pending the criminal investigation."

Rex shook his head and covered his face with his hands. "This is beyond belief! I don't know what to say."

Just then Ralph Ames stepped into the breach. "Don't say anything for the moment," he advised. "I think the situation sounds worse than it is. Just let me handle it. That's what you're paying me for. I'll take your mother and her dogs back to her hotel. Then the two of us will sit down and go over the whole thing."

For once in his life, Rex was speechless. "All right," he said finally. "Thanks, Ralph. Do whatever you need to do, and send me the bill."

"I'll pay my own way, thank you," Maddy said. "I'm not a charity case you know."

Rex sent her a dark look. "No," he said. "But you could be."

Maddy stood on her tiptoes and gave him a glancing kiss on the cheek. "Thank you for looking after Aggie and Daph," she said. "And thank you for calling Mr. Ames. He's been a big help."

Rex sighed. "Good night, Mother," he said. "Now I'd better go upstairs and tell Gina about what's been going on before she sees it on the eleven o'clock news."

On the way back down the hill, Maddy considered her next move. Mr. Ames had been so nice to her—going to pick up the dogs, and all—that she really didn't want to tell him any more lies, but she also didn't want him to know what was really going on until after her meeting with Gennie the next morning. Besides, as he had so kindly pointed out, she needed time to make alternate transportation arrangements.

And so, feeling like a complete hypocrite, when they arrived at the hotel's driveway entrance, Maddy Watkins played her most unbeatable card—the one labeled age and infirmity.

"Mr. Ames," she said, doing her best to sound weary beyond words. "I know we need to talk, but I'm just totally bushed right now. I don't think I could hold my head up during dinner much less hold up my end of the conversation. What I really need is to take myself to bed. Could we have this meeting tomorrow? Not before my meeting with Gennie, certainly. That would be much too early, but maybe for lunch. How about if we meet here at the hotel say about one in the afternoon. I'm sure I'll have myself in better order then."

And because Ralph Ames was—as he appeared to be—a gentleman, he agreed at once. "Of course," he said. "That'll give me time to be in touch with Mort Caudill and work on extracting your vehicle from the clutches of the impound lot."

"That would be wonderful, Mr. Ames," Maddy said. "And don't think I'm not grateful. It's just that I'm so tired."

"Not to worry, Mrs. Watkins," he said, handing her a business card. "Here are my numbers. I'll see you tomorrow at one unless you call to tell me otherwise."

"Please," she said. "Call me Maddy."

"Of course," he agreed. "As long as you call me Ralph."

By then the usual cluster of bellmen was grouped around the car. Once outside Ralph's Mercedes, Maddy commandeered a pair of bellman. One of them she sent off with the leashed dogs for their final evening walk and the other up to the room with all the dog accouterments. Intent on renting a car, Maddy then took herself off to the concierge's desk. Much to Maddy's dismay, Sally was back on duty.

"Why, good evening, Mrs. Anderson," Sally said with a smile. "How did that London Cabbie Company work out?"

"Fine," Maddy replied, flustered. "Yes, it was just fine."

"Is there something I can help you with?"

As soon as Sally called her Mrs. Anderson, Maddy realized she couldn't rent a vehicle through the concierge. Her guest name and her driver's-license name wouldn't coincide.

"Sorry," she mumbled. "Whatever it was seems to have slipped my mind."

"Just call down whenever you remember," Sally returned. "We'll be here whenever you need us."

Chagrined, Maddy hurried up to her room and made arrangements for her own damned rental car. Living under an alias was definitely not for sissies.

By then she realized Ralph Ames was right. It was long past dinner time and she was hungry. Once the dogs came back from their walk, she ordered soup from room service—a delicious lobster bisque and a medicinal vodka tonic. For a change she had no urge to turn on the television set in search of crime

TV. She'd had more than enough of the real thing to last her for a very long time.

At nine the next morning, Maddy drove up to the entrance of Lakeside Senior Living. When Gennie appeared, she was wearing a suit with one of those thigh-high skirts that all the lady newscasters seemed to favor these days. As far as Maddy was concerned, skirts that short were iffy even for younger women with good legs. Gennie didn't come close on either count. As for her hair? Someone had failed to mention to Gennie that the days of big hair had come and gone. Her headful of artificially blond hair was teased to within an inch of its life.

Gennie climbed into the front seat and tried to tug the skirt down enough to cover some of her exposed leg. It didn't work. She wasn't especially fond of dogs and usually made no bones about saying so. Maddy fully expected Gennie to start complaining about the presence of the two dogs in the backseat of the rented Taurus. This time, though, perhaps out of gratitude for being given a ride, she simply pushed the dogs' inquiring noses aside and reached for her seat belt. Beggars can't, after all, be choosers.

"Where's your car?" Gennie asked. "I thought you had one of those new CVRs."

"CRV," Maddy corrected. "It's in the shop for its regularly scheduled maintenance," she said. After two days of constant lying, telling fibs was almost second nature. "That's why we're stuck with a rental. Now where to?"

Gennie sighed. "To see the wicked witch of the west," she said.

"I beg your pardon?" Maddy asked.

"That's what I call my trust officer," Gennie sighed. "Her name is Myra Lansing. Joe set up this complicated trust thing before he died. All the bills get sent directly to Myra at the Olympic National Trust Company downtown. She pays the bills automatically and gives me a generous spending allowance for other things as well, but if I want anything beyond that, I have to go in and talk to her. That's the other reason I wanted you along today, Maddy. You're much more experienced with business matters than I am. I thought you could help me with this. You know, talk to Myra; explain to her why I need to do this for Jamil."

Maddy had never been particularly close to Joe Gaylord nor had he struck her as being an intellectual heavyweight, but in that moment she said a small prayer of gratitude for the man's incredible wisdom and foresight. If only Maddy had known there was a sharp-eyed trust officer somewhere standing guard over Gennie's money. Had Maddy been armed with that smidgeon of knowledge, it wouldn't have been necessary for her to worry, to say nothing of putting herself in mortal danger.

"I'll do whatever I can," she told Gennie. "Now give me the address."

The Olympic National Trust building was a low-rise former bank at the far north end of 4th Avenue in Seattle's Denny Regrade neighborhood. The building looked solid but not at all ostentatious. After parking on the street and plugging the meter, Maddy followed her sister inside.

No wonder Joe decided to do business with these people, Maddy thought, looking around the spare but modern office. *They're not into squandering their clients' dollars on interior design.*

A very businesslike receptionist greeted Maddy and Gennie as soon as they entered the lobby. "I'm sorry," she explained. "Ms. Lansing got caught up in a complicated telephone meeting. She asked me to show you into the conference room. Can I get you some coffee while you wait?"

"Sure," Maddy said, following Gennie into a window-lined room to the left of the receptionist's desk. "But first . . . I've had a long drive. Do you have a little girl's room?"

The receptionist smiled. "Right this way," she said. "It's down that hallway."

Maddy went where directed. Once safely ensconced inside the stall, she scrounged a scrap of paper and a pen out of her purse and scribbled a note: "I think this guy is trouble," it said. "Don't give her the money." After signing her name, Maddy folded the paper and stuffed it in her pocket.

On her way back to the conference room, Maddy stopped in front of the receptionist's desk and slid her note surreptitiously onto the shiny desk's otherwise clutter-free surface. "Please see to it that Ms. Lansing reads this before she comes in to speak to my sister," Maddy urged. "It's very important."

The receptionist scanned the note and then nodded. "I'll be sure she gets it."

"Good," Maddy said.

"What was that all about?" Gennie asked when Maddy arrived in the conference room. "I saw you talking to the receptionist."

"The restroom is out of toilet paper," Maddy said seamlessly. "I thought she'd want to know."

Lying was becoming easier and easier.

When Myra Lansing marched into the conference room, Maddy took one look at the tall, uncompromising figure the woman cut and breathed a sigh of relief. Myra was about Maddy's age or maybe a bit older. Her iron gray hair was pulled back in a no-nonsense bun from which no stray hair dared escape. She wore a brown suit with matching lace-up pumps—sensible shoes that went far beyond sensible. Myra Lansing could have been a librarian—straight out of the nineteen fifties. And like librarians from way back then, she didn't look like she allowed much to get past her. The contrast between her staid good looks and Gennie's pathetic striving for a youthful appearance couldn't have been more pronounced.

"Good morning, Mrs. Gaylord," Myra said cordially to Gennie. "To what do I owe the pleasure?"

"This my sister, Maddy Watkins," Gennie said, gesturing vaguely in Maddy's direction. "And this is Myra Lansing."

Myra reached out and took Maddy's hand. "I'm pleased to meet you," she said gravely. "I'm always glad to meet my clients' family members. It makes me feel closer to them. Is that Miss or Mrs. Watkins?"

Good, Maddy thought. *None of that silly Ms. stuff here.*

"Mrs.," she said. "Thank you for asking."

Myra took a seat, gracefully smoothing her wool gaberdine skirt in the process. "Now, Mrs. Gaylord. Is there a problem?"

Gennie gulped like a kid caught doing something wrong at school. "I need some money," she said.

"Of course," Myra agreed pleasantly. "How much? Where? When? For what purpose?"

Gennie took a deep breath. "Twenty thousand dollars," she answered. "In cash. And I need it today."

Myra didn't bat an eyelash. "And the purpose?" she asked.

"Well," Gennie began. "It's for a friend of mine. He's in a difficult situation, and I wanted to help him out. You tell her, Maddy. You're far better at this than I am."

We'll see, Maddy thought. *Did Myra read my note or did she even get it?*

"Gennie's friend, a young man from Saudi Arabia, is in something of a crisis," Maddy began. "It seems his mother-in-law is desperately ill. He needs to fly home immediately with his pregnant wife and child, but due to the fact that they're going at the last minute, the prices are sky high."

"So is it your intention to lend this man . . . ?" Myra paused, picked up one of the yellow pads that had been lying in the middle of the conference table, and retrieved a pen from her pocket. "What did you say his name is again?" she added.

"Jamil," Gennie answered. "Jamil bin Mahmoud."

"So is it your intention to lend Mr. Mahmoud the funds necessary to make his flight arrangements?"

"That's right," Gennie said eagerly. "And they hope to leave this evening. That's why it's so important that we do this in a hurry."

"Haste makes waste," Myra replied with a smile. Maddy wanted to reach across the table and hug her.

"What kind of security is he offering?"

"Security?" Gennie asked.

"If he's going outside the country, he needs to leave you some kind of security, preferably physical property of some kind, so that, in the event of a default, you'll have recourse—some way of getting your money back."

"Default?" Gennie repeated. "Jamil isn't going to default. He promised he'll send me the money as soon as he get to Saudi. That's where his assets are."

"I see," Myra returned. "How old did you say Mr. Mahmoud is?"

"I didn't," Gennie said irritably. "He's twenty-nine."

"And does he own any real estate here in Seattle? If we could put a lien against a home or a condo, I'm sure this wouldn't be all that difficult."

"I don't know," Gennie answered.

One of Myra Lansing's eyebrows rose until it almost touched her hairline. "You don't know?" she asked. "If you're willing to lend him this much money, you must have some idea about his living arrangements. Does Mr. Mahmoud have a job?"

"He drives a cab."

"I see," Myra said.

And Maddy was sure she did see.

"Well?" Gennie urged.

Myra held her pen to her lips. "Well," she said. "Here's the best I can do. He'll have to come in to the office here and sign papers. Since he'll need to put up some kind of property against this loan, he should bring along the title to whatever that is. Once the papers are signed and in order, I'll have to give him a cashier's check. We don't keep that kind of cash here in the office, but if it's made out in his name, he shouldn't have any difficulty cashing it."

"This is outrageous!" Gennie objected. "We'll never be able to get all this done in time for him to leave today."

Myra shrugged. "Then he'll have to make arrangements to leave tomorrow or the next day. I'm a trust officer," she added. "There are certain procedures I'm obliged to follow."

"This isn't fair!" Gennie exclaimed. "After all, it's my money, isn't it?"

Myra nodded. "And we're required by law and by the guidelines set up in your late husband's trust documents to preserve your funds to the best of our ability."

"You won't give it to me?"

"I told you the conditions under which the funds will be made available," Myra said firmly. "If Mr. Mahmoud wants to make this trip as badly as you say, I'm sure he'll be more than happy to comply."

Without another word, Gennie stood up and stalked from the room. Behind her back, Myra gave Maddy a wink and a nod. She'd read Maddy's note, all right. And she'd also understood the message. Wicked witch of the west? Myra Lansing wasn't that, not by a long shot.

Out on the street, Maddy found a furious Gennie pacing back and forth. "What am I going to do?" she demanded when Maddy joined her on the sidewalk.

"I don't have any idea," Maddy answered, and that was the God's truth.

"I'm going to have to go tell Jamil that I don't have the money," Gennie said. "And here, I already as good as promised." Then she turned to Maddy with a sudden hopefulness on her face. "What about you, Maddy? Could you lend him the money? I know for sure he'll pay it back."

"That makes no sense," Maddy said. "I don't even know the man."

That wasn't true, of course. She had a very clear picture of Jamil bin Mahmoud, a none too flattering one of him carrying a tire iron and holding it aloft in a very threatening manner. "If your own trust officer won't give him money that's really your money," Maddy added, "I don't see why I should give him any of mine."

Gennie sighed, giving up. "I suppose you're right," she said. "But I do have to go tell him. I can't just leave him hanging like this. I have to let him know so he can make some other arrangements. Let's go. I'll tell you how to get to his house."

Maddy's heart fell. The last thing she wanted was to be anywhere in close proximity to Jamil bin Mahmoud—especially without her Glock in hand.

While Gennie stood waiting with her hand on

the door handle, Maddy fumbled with the car keys. Suddenly her fingers seemed too stiff to operate the simple entry clicker.

"Which way?" she asked, once she finally managed to unlock the door and get inside the car.

"He and his family live in a small apartment down in the Rainier Valley," Gennie said. "I've never been inside, of course, but I was curious, so I took a cab and drove by once."

"His family" my aching pattootie! Maddy thought. *And I already knew he lived in the Rainier Valley.*

As she followed Gennie's directions, Maddy's heart thumped in her chest. Once Jamil saw her, the jig would be up and no telling what would happen next. Whatever it was, it wouldn't be good.

"There," Gennie said, pointing to an apartment building that sat half a block off Martin Luther King Jr. Way. Only the roof line was visible behind a thriving Seven Eleven and a decrepit abandoned gas station. "It's that one right there."

"I'll tell you what," Maddy said. "I'm sure Jamil has a certain amount of pride. Having to ask you for money must have been terribly humiliating for him. How about if I wait here in the parking lot? That way, when you tell him, you'll both have some privacy."

Gennie's eyes filled with tears of gratitude as she reached out to take her sister's hand. "That's what so wonderful about you, Maddy," she said. "You're the most thoughtful person in the world."

Gennie hurried out of the car and started in the direction of the apartment building, disappearing behind the side of the dead gas station. Maddy, expecting to be struck by lightning at least, remained behind the wheel of the Taurus. Soon she was overcome by something that felt very much like a hot flash, although she hadn't had one of those in at least ten years.

Hoping for relief, Maddy rolled down the windows. No sooner were the windows open than Aggie and Daphne, tongues lolling, stuck their head out. Lost in thought, Maddy paid no attention to the car that pulled in and stopped next to hers–not until someone came up beside her and rapped sharply on the roof of her car.

"What the hell are you doing here?" Detective Mort Caudill demanded.

By the time Maddy turned to look, Aggie and Daphne were greeting the man as though he were a long-lost friend.

"I've got Emergency Response Team guys all over the place. What are you trying to do, screw it up?"

"Emergency Response Team?" Maddy managed. "Why?"

"Early this morning, the latent fingerprint people ran the prints off that tire iron and got a hit. It turns out your friend Jamil is a suspected killer," Caudill answered grimly. "Thought to be armed and dangerous."

"Oh, my!" Maddy exclaimed. The realization that Jamil really might have killed her sent a swarm of gooseflesh shooting down her legs.

"We figure he's not going to give up without a fight," Caudill added. "We've spent the last hour evacuating the other residents from the apartment building, but it turns out there's a glitch in our arrest warrant. We're waiting on that to close down all streets within a three-block radius. Now get the hell out of here and let us do our job."

"But my sister," Maddy objected.

"Your sister? What about your sister?"

"Her name's Gennie, Genevieve Gaylord. I just dropped her off. She came to tell Jamil that she's not going to be able to lend him any money. He's trying to leave the country. He told her he needed help with the plane fare."

"Shit!" Caudill muttered. He turned and sprinted off, disappearing from sight just as Gennie had.

No matter the provocation, Maddy had never uttered that word aloud in her life. She usually protested vigorously when other people dared use it in her presence. This time, however, considering the direness of the situation, the term seemed entirely appropriate.

Naturally Maddy should have stayed where she was, safe and out of danger, but not with Gennie's life hanging in the balance.

"Come on, girls," she said to the dogs, grabbing their leashes. "Let's go."

Desperate to see what Caudill was going to do, Maddy chased after him. Intrigued by this sudden change in circumstances, the dogs darted ahead, dragging Maddy along faster than she could have managed under her own steam. When she rounded the corner of the gas station, she pulled the dogs up short.

Trying to stay out of sight, Maddy stationed herself between a reeking, almost overflowing Dumpster behind the convenience store and the bedraggled laurel hedge that lined the edge of the apartment building's pothole marred parking lot. The building itself was one of those modern complexes where the bottom level is half a flight of stairs down and the second level is half a flight up.

Nowhere was there any sign of life. If Detective Caudill had come this way, it looked as though the earth itself must have opened up and swallowed him.

Just then two people—a man and a woman—emerged from one of the lower-level apartments. The woman wore a very short skirt, and she walked funny. It looked as though the man was holding on to her, hugging her close to him with one arm around her midsection while, at the same time, pushing her forward. Then the sun glinted off something metallic and Maddy realized he was holding a gun to Gennie's head.

"Oh, my God!" Maddy exclaimed. "He's using her as a human shield. What are we going to do?"

She looked around desperately, searching for the sharpshooters Detective Caudill had told her were there, but they were nowhere in sight. There was no sign of them—no sign of anyone. The place seemed completely deserted, and Jamil and Gennie were coming straight across the parking lot toward where Maddy and the dogs stood. That meant Gennie must have told him where the car was.

Needing a weapon, Maddy wondered briefly if there was a tire iron hiding somewhere in the trunk of the Taurus. But these days all those necessary pieces of equipment were usually stowed away in some cute little kit. One of those would take forever to find and open. There wasn't enough time. She looked around desperately for a rock or a brick. Seeing nothing, she turned instead to the stinking Dumpster, grateful that this one wasn't on an early-morning pick-up schedule.

Pulling the dogs with her, she dragged them behind the Dumpster.

"Sit!" she commanded. "Sit and stay!"

Once the dogs did as they were told, Maddy dropped their leashes. It took more effort than she expected to raise the heavy lid and hold it aloft. Inside, however, she found exactly what she needed—an empty gallon jug of Vino Blanco. Fortunately for her the heavy glass bottle was well within reach. Plucking the bottle from the reeking refuse, Maddy decided to worry about germs later.

Not daring to peek out to check on Jamil and Gennie's progress, Maddy took the bottle and tucked in behind the Dumpster along with the dogs. She had absolute faith in the strength of her pitching arm. After all, she threw sticks and balls and Frisbees for the dogs every morning of her life, rain or shine. The question was, what would happen when she nailed Jamil with that bottle? If he was still holding the gun to Gennie's head . . . , what if it went off and struck her anyway? That was probably why the Seattle PD sharpshooters hadn't risked taking a shot either—the very real danger of collateral damage.

Maddy could hear Gennie's voice now. Maddy

couldn't make out any of the individual words, but Gennie was talking a blue streak. Poor Gennie. She'd had not a clue about Jamil's real intentions, so she had to be completely befuddled by what was happening. Their feet crunched in the gravel as they stepped off the parking lot pavement. Now Maddy could hear what was being said.

"Please, don't do this, Jamil," Gennie was pleading. "I don't know what's going on. I'm trying to help you."

"Shut up!" Jamil ordered.

Next to Maddy, a low growl emanated from deep in Aggie's throat. Her hackles stood on end. She may have recognized Jamil's voice from the night before, or she may have simply responded to the naked threat in the way he said the words "shut up." But good to her training, Aggie didn't break the stay.

Maddy held her breath, trying to strategize. She needed to hit Jamil in a way that would cause his arm to go up and make any resulting shot wild enough that he wouldn't injure Gennie or anyone else.

Hit him in the head, she thought. *An upper cut to the chin that's hard enough to knock him over.*

When Gennie's leg appeared around the corner of the Dumpster, Maddy sprang forward. Gennie was twisted to the right, trying to look at Jamil and the gun. Jamil was looking behind him. Neither of them saw Maddy coming. Using both hands to hold it, she smashed the bottle up and into Jamil's chin, pushing him up and back at the same time.

The bottle shattered while gunfire roared in Maddy's ear. She watched, stricken, as Gennie pitched forward and Jamil fell sideways while the gun flew up and away, twirling overhead in a kind of slow motion reality Maddy Watkins had never experienced.

The excitement proved to be too much for the dogs to hold their stay. By the time the gun landed, Aggie had charged forward and had Jamil's right wrist in her growling grip. Meanwhile, Daphne, intrigued by this new game, went off to retrieve the spinning gun, which, according to her particular breeding, must have looked like a some new kind of Frisbee.

And then, appearing as if from nowhere, there were cops everywhere, all of them with weapons drawn, all of them shouting. "Get down! Get down! Don't move!"

As they tackled Jamil, Maddy grabbed Aggie's leash and pulled her away. When Daphne returned, daintily holding the gun by its handle, Maddy ordered her to drop it—which she did. Then, holding both leashes and with her heart aching with dread, Maddy turned to Gennie.

Had the bullet hit her? Was she dead? Dying? Her head seemed to be lying at a weird angle. Maddy's first thought was that her sister's neck was broken. But then, Gennie moaned and moved. When she shook her head, the blonde mane of a wig she'd been wearing fell off into the dirt.

"What happened?" Gennie demanded, rising to her knees. "What's going on? Is Jamil all right? Where is he?"

"Jamil's just fine," Maddy told her. "But it looks to me like he's on his way to jail."

Just then Detective Caudill came careening around the corner. "Are you nuts?" he demanded of Maddy. "He could have killed you! What were you thinking?"

He looked and sounded so much like Rex right then, Maddy almost burst out laughing, except he really was concerned and exasperated with her—and for good reason. She stifled the laughter.

"Somebody needed to do something," she said soberly. "I just happened to be in the right place at the right time."

"But what did Jamil do?" Gennie was demanding. "What's going on? Why are those cops putting handcuffs on him? Somebody please help him."

"I'm sorry to have to tell you this, Mrs. . . ." Stumped, Detective Caudill paused in his explanation and glanced at Maddy for help.

"Mrs. Gaylord," Maddy supplied.

Caudill nodded. "Your friend, Mr. Mahmoud is a suspect in two Atlanta-area homicides. Two years ago, two elderly women, one sixty-eight and another seventy, disappeared after emptying their bank accounts. Their remains were found a year later and only a few feet apart when a developer started clearing an open field for a new subdivision. By then Mr. Mahmoud had skipped town and no one could find him."

The comment was so provoking that Maddy couldn't keep quiet. "I'll have you know, Detective Caudill," she said, turning on the man, "sixty-eight and seventy are a long way from being elderly. But that probably explains why I never heard one word about those two cases on *America's Most Wanted*. The victims were *elderly*. Everyone thought it was high time they turned up their toes and croaked out. I believe I'll have to send that nice Mr. Walsh an e-mail about this. It's out-and-out age discrimination, if you ask me, and absolutely inexcusable."

Detective Caudill sighed. "Yes, ma'am," he agreed. "I'm sure you're right, and I do apologize."

The rest of the morning was very busy. Maddy and Gennie were both questioned in detail about what had happened. By the time that was over, Maddy had to call and cancel her lunch meeting with Ralph Ames. Several of the local TV stations had requested interviews with her and the dogs. Maddy wanted to have her hair done and be properly dressed before one of those short-skirted reporters got anywhere near her. Fortunately, the Fairmont was a full-service hotel with a full-service spa. And once Maddy had been properly coiffed and made up, she looked like dynamite in that bright red St. John outfit.

Maybe she'd have to rethink her daughter-in-law's outrageous taste in clothing.

While Maddy was being beautified, so were the dogs. One of the bellmen had brushed them until their red coats shone.

The telephone rang as Maddy examined herself in the full-length bathroom mirror. The caller turned out to be Sally, the concierge.

"The car is here to take you to your interviews, Mrs. Watkins," Sally announced. The name discrepancy on Maddy's hotel registration form had now been fully explained and corrected. "Will you need any help with your animals?"

"Oh, no. I'm quite capable of handling everything myself," Maddy said airily. "The girls and I will be right down."